A W

Forged in Silence

STAND-ALONE NOVEL

A Western Historical Romance Book

by

Ava Winters

MW01596282

Copyright© 2022 by Ava Winters

All Rights Reserved.

This book may not be reproduced or transmitted in any form without the written permission of the publisher.

In no way is it legal to reproduce, duplicate, or transmit any part of this document in either electronic means or in printed format. Recording of this publication is strictly prohibited and any storage of this document is not allowed unless with written permission from the publisher

Table of Contents

A Western Love Forged in Silence 1

    Table of Contents 3

    Let's connect! 5

    Letter from Ava Winters 6

Prologue 7

Chapter One 12

Chapter Two 19

Chapter Three 31

Chapter Three 34

Chapter Four 48

Chapter Five 54

Chapter Six 59

Chapter Seven 67

Chapter Eight 73

Chapter Nine 77

Chapter Ten 81

Chapter Eleven 85

Chapter Twelve 91

Chapter Thirteen 98

Chapter Fourteen 105

Chapter Fifteen 112

Chapter Sixteen 121

Chapter Seventeen 126

Chapter Eighteen 130

Chapter Nineteen...134

Chapter Twenty 138

Chapter Twenty-One...144

Chapter Twenty-Two...148

Chapter Twenty-Three 153

Chapter Twenty-Four...159

Chapter Twenty-Five..165

Chapter Twenty-Six 174

Chapter Twenty-Seven...180

Chapter Twenty-Eight..188

Chapter Twenty-Nine 196

Chapter Thirty...202

Chapter Thirty-One 208

Chapter Thirty-Two 216

Chapter Thirty-Three 225

Chapter Thirty-Four 231

Chapter Thirty-Five 238

Chapter Thirty-Six..252

Chapter Thirty-Seven...262

Chapter Thirty-Eight 267

Epilogue 275

Also by Ava Winters 285

Let's connect!

Impact my upcoming stories!

My passionate readers influenced the core soul of the book you are holding in your hands! The title, the cover, the essence of the book as a whole was affected by them!

Their support on my publishing journey is paramount! I devote this book to them!

If you are not a member yet, join now! As an added BONUS, you will receive my Novella **"The Cowboys' Wounded Lady"**:

FREE EXCLUSIVE GIFT
(available only to my subscribers)

Go to the link:
https://avawinters.com/novella-amazon

Letter from Ava Winters

"Here is a lifelong bookworm, a devoted teacher and a mother of two boys. I also make mean sandwiches."

If someone wanted to describe me in one sentence, that would be it. There has never been a greater joy in my life than spending time with children and seeing them grow up - all my children, including the 23 little 9-year-olds that I currently teach. And I have not known such bliss than that of reading a good book.

As a Western Historical Romance writer, my passion has always been reading and writing romance novels. The historical part came after my studies as a teacher - I was mesmerized by the stories I heard, so much that I wanted to visit every place I learned about. And so, I did, finding the love of my life along the way as I walked the paths of my characters.

Now, I'm a full-time elementary school teacher, a full-time mother of two wonderful boys and a full-time writer. Wondering how I manage all of them? I did too, at first, but then I realized it's because everything I do I love, and I have the chance to share it with all of you.

And I would love to see you again in this small adventure of mine!

Until next time,

Ava Winters

Prologue

Carson City, Nevada

May 1866

A rooster crowed in the darkness as Sam Colt lay in bed. His body felt weary as he rolled off the mattress, though his mind wasn't much better. He did not sleep well; his racing thoughts had made him toss and turn for hours..

There was always too much on his mind.

Sam put his bare feet on the rough, wooden floorboards, taking a minute to run his hand through his wavy blond hair. The cold floor helped him to wake up. As his eyes adjusted to the darkness, could make out the lone dresser across the room and the nightstand and lamp to his right. Otherwise, the room was bare. Heaving a long sigh, Sam finally stood up and dressed for the day. No use putting off the inevitable.

As soon as he was dressed, he found his worn, brown leather boots where he left them by the doorway. Sam could see the sun starting to rise through the window, the dark sky slowly coming to life with shades of orange, purple, and pink. Though he always felt tired, he still tried to take in the beauty. Each day of life was a gift.

The ranch hands would seek him out shortly, as Sam kept to a schedule, doing the same thing every day. Each morning after he dressed, he made the trek down the stairs and along the long hallway toward the kitchen. There, he started making a fried egg with a piece of crusty bread before he started his work. The smell of the egg cooking and the taste of the butter were a comfort to him. Sam felt like he was making an effort, even though he was alone.

Sam lived in a house that was far too much for one person. It wasn't that he didn't try to keep a nice home, it was just that the horses and ranch upkeep were more important. He had animals to feed and let in and out of pastures, mares to be bred, and other horses to train for ranch work. Things beyond the horses were in far worse shape. Fences and buildings were crumbling, and some of the pens were currently unusable. If those weren't fixed, he wouldn't be able to buy more livestock or plant any crops.

Sam was so preoccupied by the never-ending list of things to do, that he nearly burned his eggs. The acrid smell as they began to crust onto the bottom of the pan snapped him out of his reverie. Sam tried to tell himself that it would all be worth it someday; the ranch was the deal of a lifetime. It possessed potential, and if he worked hard enough, it would shine. Sam hoped that people would come for miles to buy their horses from him..

The house wasn't completely bare. He inherited some things from his parents when they passed away—the frying pan that he coated with grease, just like his mother had shown him, had been his theirs, as well as the chairs adorning his living room. They sat between an old table one of his ranch hands gifted him, with an oil lamp he bought after one too many evenings of squinting at his ledgers in the dying light.

Sam didn't consider himself a great cook, but his life had been about survival for so long it was hard to remember anything different. As he cracked an additional egg into the pan and heard the familiar sizzle, he tried to recall the last time he had eaten something different for breakfast and struggled. The routine had once been survival, but now he wondered if he should try something new. Something more exciting.

The idea of changing now seemed absurd. His monotonous routine was lonely, but it was soothing. He knew exactly where to find his plate and fork as he set his lone spot at the table and cut himself off a hunk of bread before sliding the eggs carefully onto his plate. There was already so much to take care of, he simply did not have time to try new things.

When Sam sat down, he didn't say grace, but he did reflect on the same thought each morning; *a day on the earth is better than a day underneath it.* There was a time that he didn't feel that way, a time when he wished he had died on a fated night many years ago. Yet it seemed that destiny had other plans.

Sam supposed that was progress.

He proceeded to eat his breakfast without tasting it, listening for his foreman Jack or the other ranch hands out in the yard. They behaved like clockwork, congregating outside the animal sheds each morning. Yet a feeling of disquiet gave him pause. He could have sworn he heard a noise. He put down his fork and listened carefully. The sound seemed far away, like the distant cry of a bobcat in the night. Perhaps he was so sleep deprived that he was starting to lose his mind.

Sam attempted to ignore whatever it was. He stood up and took a minute to wash the dish in a basin of water he kept on his counter, letting it dry so that he could use it again when he came in for dinner. He typically took his lunch with Jack and the others out on his porch. It was the little bit of interaction he had with other people each day, yet he enjoyed listening to his ranch hands as they told outlandish tales.

There were horses to let into pastures and stalls that needed mucking before he attempted to work on any of the ranch's much-needed repairs. Sam walked down the bare hallway, making his way to the sitting room that he seldom spent any time in. There were the two sad looking chairs, wooden and weathered, on either side of an oil lamp that were anything but inviting. He did not even hang any curtains by the windows.

The same noise he heard earlier returned, and it sounded even louder than before. As he stopped to listen, Sam could swear it sounded like a cry. Had an animal gotten injured and was wailing in pain somewhere on the property? Sam threw open the door, panicking that something was dying or in need of help when the volume of the cries grew even louder. He took a step, and his boot touched the edge of something soft. His porch had a few rotten planks, but this wasn't normal. Sam's eyes widened as he looked down.

A child, less than a year old if Sam had to guess, lay on the porch, writhing and squalling in an old gray blanket. Its little eyes wrenched shut and its tiny hands balled into fists as miniature tears streamed down the baby's face.

Sam's heart pounded as he took in the sad sight. He couldn't help but feel pity for the defenseless thing. The poor baby seemed dirty and unnaturally small, in addition to looking so scared and upset. *How long had it been there, and who had left it?* He scanned his property for any clues, but all he could see were the dry gasses and shrubs. Further off in the distance he could see craggy mountains pointing skyward in the early morning light. The mountains would never reveal the secret.

The babe continued to cry, its sobs scratching its tiny throat. Not wanting to hear or see it suffer any more than it probably already had, Sam carefully picked up the child up and examined it. Sam felt disorientated as he held the baby out in front of him. Somehow, he was expecting it to weigh more.

How do you get a baby to stop crying?

Sam had no children of his own, and he struggled to recall any child-rearing techniques from his own childhood so long ago. He pushed the thoughts away as he looked at the child and its sad blue eyes. He brought the child closer to his body, holding it tight. It no longer sobbed, but still whined and whimpered.

A child left on his doorstep. Sam's stomach knotted with anxiety, and he felt his body shake with nerves as he tried to comfort the baby.. He had so much to do, the sheer weight of his insurmountable tasks part of the reason he couldn't sleep at night. Sam worried that he wouldn't be able to run the ranch and look after a baby until someone came to claim it. Sam's stomach flipped again when a new thought entered his head, sending a chill coursing through him.

What if no one came to claim the baby?

Glancing down at the child in his arms, its watery blue eyes and angelic face, Sam knew there was no way he could just call someone and have it taken away. That baby's sad little face would haunt him for the rest of his life.

Someone leaving it on his doorstep was confusing and terrible, but Sam vowed that he wouldn't make it worse.

Chapter One

San Antonio, Texas

May 1866

"I can't believe I'm going to be a married woman!"

Nina beamed proudly at her reflection, so pretty and poised. She stood in front of the mirror that sat atop her chest of drawers trying to imagine what her hair would look like when she wore it up and away from her face every day like married women often did. The brown braid and ankle length frock she wore seemed youthful in comparison.

Nina's heart fluttered like a fledging bird preparing for its first flight as she thought of her intended, her childhood best friend, Nathaniel Harper. Even though she was a girl, they bonded during their time in the school yard. Nina wasn't afraid to get dirty and liked to race the other children during recess. She'd beat Nathaniel plenty of times. It was one of her proudest accomplishments beyond finishing her studies.

When they weren't at school and they finished their chores, they explored the banks of the river that cut through the town. They talked about their families and their dreams during their time together. There were no secrets between them. Nina lived for the freshness of the water and the lilt of Nathaniel's youthful laugh.

Now that Nina and Nathaniel were grown, things changed. Gone were the days of wading barefoot in the San Antonio River, the water cold and refreshing. Instead, they spent time together with a chaperone at church functions and other social events. Now, as they stood together, the din of music replaced the tinkling water and birdsong. Their conversations became less candid and more proper, but Nina couldn't complain. She didn't think it was possible to be happier, but every day was a blessing knowing that Nathaniel loved her.

Nina let her long, mahogany brown locks fall down her shoulders and smoothed them back into place. Excitement coursed through her at the prospect of planning a wedding, and she could barely focus on anything else. Her thoughts danced from what she would wear to who she would invite from town, and of course, how she would decorate the farmhouse once it was ready for her.

Sweeping the house and cleaning the kitchen took far longer than they should, and she struggled to find motivation to cook come mealtime. The notion was just too mundane when she spent the day dreaming about moving into a house and starting a family with Nathaniel. That fantasy world was full of happiness and children, something that she'd longed for longer than she wanted to admit.

Today, she completed her chores by lunchtime, and there was plenty of time before her stepparents would return home for supper, so Nina decided she would wander outside for a time. In the woods outside of town stood a hidden spot that Nina adored, filled with soft green grasses protected by a band of trees. It allowed her to feel happy and content without anyone disturbing the peace.

Taking one last look at her reflection and the rose-colored dress she wore, she ventured out of the room, down the stairwell, and out into the open air. As she walked toward the hidden meadow filled with wildflowers and the woods that kept it a secret, she reflected on her fate. Despite the promise of rebirth lingering amidst the spring air, this time of year always felt bittersweet as the anniversary of her parents' death quickly approached.

A wildfire destroyed their home when Nina was two years old. She didn't remember much, just how the heat blazed and tried to blister her skin. The Lord took her parents to heaven, but somehow, she survived. The town doctor once told her that her father was able to get her out; soot covered, but without injury. Her father died of his painful and gruesome burns.

Nina wished she could thank him for saving her, but she also wished that no harm had come to them at all. Life would have been much easier. It was difficult to explain to others that her birth parents were gone. She felt like a piece of her was missing, but because she didn't remember them, it was hard to say why.

Nina was lucky enough to be taken in by a couple who had a daughter close to her age. They favored their biological daughter, but at least she had a home and someone to claim her. On the days they were kinder to her stepsister, Jane, or told Nina she was a nuisance, she tried to be grateful she had a home at all.

Yet she did have Nathaniel, and his love for her would be enough for the rest of her life.

Nina held the hem of her dress up so it wouldn't tear as she navigated through the thicket of trees. As a girl, Nina discovered the meadow and claimed it as her secret hideaway. Any passersby on the road could not see the meadow. Nina found it by accident, on a day that her Jane teased her for not actually being part of the family. That particular day, Nina took a walk so she wouldn't say or do something regrettable. Whenever she spoke her mind about how Jane treated her, Nina was always the one that ended up in trouble. Her stepparents always spun a tale that Nina should know better, as if she were the older child, though the girls were the same age. In her anger and despair, she found herself in the woods. Once she pushed through to the other side, she stumbled into the meadow, the knee-high grass dotted with blue and yellow flowers warm and inviting.

Nina relaxed as she entered the patch of paradise. The grass was so soft, and birds calling to one another created a strange sort of music. She sat down among the flowers before she gently threw herself back onto the grass. The moment was nearly perfect, and only one thing could improve it.

"I wish Nathaniel was here," Nina murmured to herself.

She shut her eyes, trying to imagine what it would be like to have him beside her. Nina often wondered what it would be like to finally kiss him and couldn't wait for their wedding to find out. The event was most likely set to happen in the winter or spring as Nathaniel was in the process of getting his own land and building a farm on it.

She'd only seen it from a distance, but it was far larger than the property her stepparents owned. There were acres of fields to fill with crops and animals. Nina couldn't wait to help him run the house and hopefully fill it with children as soon as they could. She hoped her parents would look down and be proud of her for having a family of her own when the time came.

"I was hoping you'd show up,"

Nina's eyes snapped open when she heard Nathaniel's voice in the distance. *How did he know about this place?* She'd often thought about taking him here, but by the time she discovered it, it would have been improper, even if they were just friends. Nina wondered if he'd saw her walking on the road and followed her.

She sat up and her heart skipped a beat as she sought him amongst the trees around the meadow, but he was nowhere to be found. Perhaps she'd imagined in his voice since she'd been thinking about him. It was easy to get distracted when she daydreamed about his hazel eyes and broad shoulders.

"I'd never miss a meeting with you,"

Nina's stomach flipped when she recognized Jane's voice too. This spot was supposed to be a sanctuary away from her. It was more likely that Jane saw her walking to the meadow and followed her than Nathaniel. Nina looked around again, but couldn't see her either, though she could hear her stepsister's laughter as it bounced and echoed off the trees around the meadow. Feeling like it was taunting her, Nina rose to her feet and started to move in the direction of the voices.

What on earth was Nathaniel doing here with Jane? Did they meet accidentally?

She lingered at the edge of the black hawthorn trees when she saw a flash of a pale blue skirt out of the corner of her eye. It flit like a will-o-wisp, taunting, teasing, and leading Nina astray. She wasn't sure if she wanted her stepsister to know where she was. The girl often had a way of taking Nina's things and claiming them as her own. Growing up, when Nina would go to her stepparents about it, they often shrugged it off, saying that Nina needed to take better care of her belongings. The whole thing had seemed unfair.

Nina didn't want Jane using her special hiding place, it was her haven away from the girl. She hid behind a tree, still trying to figure out what was going on. Nina didn't want to assume the worst, but she found herself confused and upset that they were together without a chaperone. They weren't promised to each other, but it still seemed in poor taste.

"Why do we have to meet like this?" A whine punctuated Jane's voice like she was pouting. "It's dirty and uncivilized."

"I know," Nathaniel replied, and Nina peeked out from behind her hiding spot to see him in a crisp white shirt and gray slacks. Nina wanted to take comfort in seeing him near her hideaway, but she couldn't get rid of the sense of dread that churned in the pit of her stomach. "But talking to you

16

like this, in secret, is more than we could ever do. I have to settle for looking at you from across a room, and while you are more beautiful than a summer sunset, it's just not the same."

Nina gasped as she processed the words. Not sure if she was believing what she was hearing, Nina crept a bit closer to their voices. Her stomach flipped and her blood went cold when she saw Jane with her back against one of the oak trees several yards away. Nathaniel stood close to her, so close that his shirt was brushing against the white buttoned-down blouse.

He leaned in closer than he'd ever stood by Nina, the look on his face was one of adoration. One he often wore for Nina before they parted ways at social functions. Nina choked down a sob so that she didn't give away where she was hiding.

"Do you really love my silly stepsister?" Jane asked, her shrill, nasal voice lilting with petulance. Nina wondered if she somehow knew that she was there listening. It was just the sort of thing she would say to hurt her feelings. "She's so simple and plain."

"I do love Nina, she's a breath of fresh air, not many girls are like her." Nina couldn't believe when he smirked down at Jane and brushed a lock of her blonde hair out of her face. "But I see now that you are the far prettier sister. Every time you smile at me, I fall deeper in love."

"Kiss me, Nate,"

Nate? Nina felt like someone had knocked the wind out of her at Jane's request. That was the name that Nina called him and now Jane was stealing that too. Nina realized that Jane wasn't trying to take what wasn't hers. Nathaniel betrayed her. Somehow, in all her joy about being engaged, she failed to see that he had eyes for Jane all along. She thought of all the times she went out with him while they courted. She had to get away before they discovered her watching them. She didn't want to see Jane's triumphant face when she got what she wanted yet again. Nina knew the longer she waited, the tears that blurred her vision would escape. She wasn't sure if she could control herself once she started crying.

Nina turned and winced when a branch popped under her boot. She all but gave away that she'd been eavesdropping.

"Is someone there?" Nathaniel shouted.

Nina burst into tears, no longer able to hold back. She sprinted through woods to get away before they discovered her.

Chapter Two

San Antonio, Texas

May 1866

Once she returned home from the woods, Nina tried her best to keep herself busy after what she saw and overheard. She pulled vegetables from the garden, yanking them roughly out of the ground and tossing them into her basket. She pulled weed after weed until she thought her fingers might turn raw, trying to throw herself into any task she could. Nina washed the vegetables until they sparkled and once she was inside, she set the table even though it would be hours before they would use it.

Nina stood by the kitchen table, refusing to cry again. Had she missed something? Nina tried to think of stolen glances when Nathaniel was with the family or maybe a flirtatious touch, but she couldn't recall anything. Still, Nina heard Nathaniel said—*every time you smile at me, I fall deeper in love.*

A short while later, the front door opened while she was still working on dishes at the kitchen sink, and Nina knew it was too early for her stepparents, who both had jobs in town, to be home for the day. It must be Jane back from her secret meeting with Nathaniel. Nina felt her stomach flip with anxiety and dread.

Nina knew she should let it go; yet she also knew she had nothing to be ashamed of. She wasn't the one meeting Nathaniel in secret. Shaking her head vehemently, Nina felt like she wouldn't be able to sleep or function if she didn't confront Jane about what she saw. She put down the dish rag she used to dry dishes and walked down the hallway.

Jane began to ascend the stairs leading to their shared bedroom.

"Where have you been?" Nina called to her, trying to sound nonchalant. Jane also had daily chores, but usually less than what Nina was responsible for. Jane was supposed to put the laundry on the line and sweep the front porch, and Nina noticed that she hadn't done either yet.

Jane appeared at the top of the staircase, outside of their bedroom. Her pale blonde hair curled in ringlets around her face, and her blue eyes almost always seemed to glare at Nina. Usually, she regarded Nina with disdain when they talked to one another, but today she looked guarded and nervous, almost like she did not expected Nina to speak to her so directly.

"I was in town, not that it matters to you." Jane finally replied, her voice clipped and cold.

Nina couldn't believe that the lie fell from Jane's lips so easily. Fighting the nerves that threatened to make her shake, Nina pressed as her stepsister tried to get into the bedroom. "What did you do there? Did you meet any of your friends? You still have your chores to do. I'm not doing them for you."

"I'll do them, I'll do them," Jane snapped. "I stopped to look at buttons for a dress I want to make." Jane finally opened the door and busied herself with making her bed.

"Where are they?" Nina asked, pretending to look around the room for them. "Are they for the green fabric Papa got you recently?" Nina thought the fabric looked so lovely and felt jealous that her stepfather hadn't bought anything for her.

Jane turned on her heel and narrowed her gaze at Nina, irritation flashing in her blue eyes. "Will you leave me alone? Why are you in my business? It's not like I'm making the dress for you." Jane's glare became downright rotten when she smirked and added, "Don't you have a wedding to plan? I think your time would be better spent doing that instead of pestering me."

Nina knew she should take the signal and leave her stepsister alone, but she just couldn't. Jane had a lot of nerve bringing up a wedding when it was very clear it wasn't going to happen. Nina felt her blood boiling. Did Jane think she was a fool?

"I saw you in the woods today." Nina snapped, reaching her limit with Jane's condescending words. Jane's narrow, pinched face paled, nearly matching the starched sheet on the bed behind her. Her steely blue eyes broke from Nina's.

Jane just told Nina everything she needed to know.

"What are you talking about?" Jane's voice went soft, like her mind was working on what to do and say next.

"I went for a walk in the woods earlier," Nina continued. "I saw you with Nathaniel." Nina felt as though someone tried to rip her heart from her chest as the images flashed through her mind. "I saw and heard everything."

Nina watched as shock, embarrassment, and fear galloped across her stepsister's face. Yet a smug, triumphant expression soon soured any chagrin in her features. Once again, she took what she wanted from Nina and caused her pain. "Oh, did you?"

"How could you, Jane?" Nina demanded, grabbing onto her wrist. She squeezed so tightly that Jane gasped, fingernail indents tattooing her skin like a brand. "He's my betrothed, you know how much I love him! How could you say those things about me? How could you ask him to kiss you?"

Jane pulled away roughly, the momentum making Nina stumble back a few steps. "Oh, stop it, Nina! The only reason he was going to marry you is because he pities you and your sad life. Everyone, even mother and father, think he would be a better match for me."

Nina's mouth hung open as she stared at her stepsister. That couldn't be true. Nathaniel was such a warm and happy piece of her life. He was there on countless Mother's Day lunches at school when she had no one, offering her comfort when her stepmother only sat with Jane. When they came of age, he was the one to bring up getting married, finally giving her a place where she truly belonged.

Her stepparents favored Jane, but they gave their blessing to Nathaniel when he asked them for Nina's hand in marriage. Why would they do that if they thought Jane a better match for him? The idea that it was all out of pity made her soul shatter into tiny pieces. The fact that he flirted with Jane in the woods had already done that to her heart.

"You're lying," Nina retorted. "You are just doing that thing you always do to me! It isn't fair!"

Jane sat on the edge of her bed, a hint of remorse coloring her cheeks. "Maybe in the beginning. Then I discovered that Nate is a handsome man." Jane heaved a sigh, with a faraway look in her eyes like she was picturing his face. Nathaniel had hazel eyes and dark brown hair with a trimmed beard of the same shade. When he smiled, endearing dimples bloomed on his cheeks. As he grew older, he grew into his strong, broad, and capable shoulders. He could attract the attention of anyone; it should have been no surprise that her sister was smitten with him too.

Nina couldn't believe that she'd been so preoccupied with his looks that she failed to see that his feelings for her weren't real. She believed he was the love of her life, yet he was willing to cheat. The very thought made Nina want to scream with rage.

The cruel, pinched face that Jane often wore returned. "I love him, Nina, and now that I know that there's no way that I'm letting you have him."

Throughout the conversation, Nina tried to keep her composure, but it crumbled with every word. . "How can you say such a thing? We're sisters, I would never do this to you." Despite her best efforts, her anger erupted form her chest.

Jane shrugged and chuckled softly, looking as though the conversation began to bore her. "For one, we're not sisters, my parents were forced to take you in and nothing more. Don't confuse charity with familial bonds. Second, I am being truthful. Nate was going to marry you because he does care for you. He knew you had no real family. That was before he fell in love with me." She glared at Nina across the room, almost like what she was about to say was a challenge. "If you don't believe me, I'm sure you could ask Nate himself."

Nina could feel her heart shattering; her chest ached as though the pieces cut her. Tears blinded her eyes as they threatened to stream down her face, betraying her brokenness. As usual, Jane took something that belonged to her whether they were truly in love or not. Nina should be used to such treatment, but it was different this time.

She saw Nathaniel stand so close to Jane. She heard every tender word he said.

She could be bold and march to Nathaniel's farm, demanding to know the truth. Maybe he could talk her out of the hysteria forming in her mind. Yet as Jane leered at her, Nina worried that maybe he would never be able put her mind at ease again. *What if Jane is right*, Nina's mind raced, *what if, after all this time, Nathaniel just pities me because I am an orphan, and he doesn't really love me? If he hadn't fallen in love with me, would he find comfort with someone else?* Nina couldn't stand the humiliation if that was her future. She couldn't put herself in that position.

Nina strode for the doorway, feeling the weight of the truth suffocating her. She couldn't be in this house with Jane until her stepparents returned from work. The fight would escalate, and she wouldn't be able to control her emotions any longer. She was all but running down the stairs to get away from her.

"Where are you going?" Jane yelled after her.

Nina didn't answer as she groped her way to the front door. Blinded by her tears, she fumbled with the handle, cold and hard, and slammed the door behind her. Normally she would go to her meadow, but after seeing Nathaniel wooing Jane there, she wasn't sure if she could ever return there again. It was tainted by what she witnessed there.

***

Nina walked toward town, not caring that it took nearly an hour. She didn't care if her parents left their jobs and came home, and she wasn't there; she needed to try and clear her head. She couldn't walk by the river—it would remind her of Nathaniel as well—so she settled on visiting an old friend. He always knew what to do or say to cheer her up when she'd fought with Jane in the past. Nina hoped her tears would dry by the time would get to his door.

San Antonio bustled, full of life, as she approached the post office. Horses pulled stagecoaches filled with people down a large dirt road, the clopping hooves and wagon wheels a familiar din as she made her way. The town grew as it became more noteworthy for cattle ranching.

More and more stores and business popped up since Nina and Nathaniel used to play along the river. Nina heard the shrill sound of a train whistle coming from the direction of the station. The railroad certainly helped to bring new people and opportunities to San Antonio. It connected the town to other cities in Texas and destinations beyond.

Hamish Bennett was good friends with her parents before they died—they were once all schoolmates. He was her last connection to them, as nearly everything else was decimated in the fire. He had light blue eyes that sparkled with wonder, and he had tawny hair that started to turn white with age, as well as infectious laughter, which Nina desperately needed right now.

By the time she reached the squat beige building that recently became the post office, Nina's tears ran dry. She sniffled as she thought about how Hamish started off in a smaller place, but it became too small to house everyone's letters and packages properly. Nina felt proud of Hamish's success. She couldn't think of a kinder person who deserved it more. She let out a shaky breath and pulled out a handkerchief to dab at her face, hoping that her puffy eyes wouldn't make it obvious that she was crying before she grabbed the door handle and pulled it open.

A bell jingled on the door as she let herself in. Hamish sat behind his counter, wearing glasses that made his already striking blue eyes appear larger than they were. He sorted mail and used a stamp to post mark a stack of envelopes, and looked up at the noise.

"Is that Miss Nina Mason?" He called, slipping his glasses down his nose so he could see properly. "Why, I swear you look more like your mother each day. She had those same soft eyes."

Nina couldn't help but smile at his words, especially after Jane took her heart and all but smashed it. She didn't remember anything about her parents, so she loved when Hamish told her bits and pieces about them. It made her feel like she had more time with them, and she could fall in love with their personalities and quirks.

"Hello, Hamish," Nina said, her voice tremulous with a soft quiver.

She nearly jumped when Hamish hopped off his stool and quickly came around the corner to see her, a stack of mail in his hand. He narrowed his eyes at her, but not in the malicious way that Jane often did. Instead, it was like he was investigating something, searching her face for a clue that something was amiss.

"You've been crying," Hamish stated simply, still looking her over with appraising, yet empathetic, eyes.

Nina didn't know whether to be impressed or unnerved. Perhaps she wasn't as good about hiding her emotions as she thought. Hamish is always honest with her, so Nina decided to offer him the same courtesy.

"I think you might be the only person who truly cares for me now, Hamish."

Hamish gave her a reassuring pat on the arm before sorting the mail into the dozens of post office boxes on one of the walls. "What about your promised, Mr. Nathaniel Harper? I thought there were going to be wedding bells in the future."

Nina bit her lip, not wanting to cry about the situation again, not that Hamish would judge her for it. "It would seem that his love was not what I presumed it to be." Her tone was weak and lifeless.

Hamish stopped his bustling to meet her gaze, surprised etched upon his face. He knew how long Nina and Nate were friends, and that they were courting for some time. She all but run to the post office to tell him about their engagement months ago.

"Oh dear. I'm so sorry." Hamish put his hands on her shoulders in an attempt to be comforting, his voice sad and disappointed. "I know how close you were."

Nina dropped her eyes to the ground. "I don't know what to do," she despaired as she began to explain the situation. "The entire time I was in the woods, the whole thing didn't seem real. Part of me wants to confront Nathaniel about what I saw. You know Jane, she sometimes does things to upset me because it is fun for her.." She looked up, eyes glassy as she fretted over how Nathaniel could do this to her, even if Jane was being cruel. "I want to know why he lied to me. I deserve an explanation."

Hamish didn't say anything as he listened, instead walking back to his counter, and picking up a letter that was set aside. Nina watched him read it and wondered if he didn't have the heart to tell her that Jane was right. She feared that she didn't know anyone's true intentions anymore. Nina felt the same worry that bubbled up when she argued with Jane starting to return. If Hamish agreed that she was not a fit match for Nathaniel due to her past, she would have no one left on her side. Nina wasn't sure if any piece of her heart remained after Nathaniel broke it, however terrifying the thought.

"Hamish?" Nina asked, reeling at the desperation in her own voice.

"Come here, Nina. I want to show you something." Hamish waved her over to the counter covered with packages and mail to sort, the letter still in hand. "I received a letter this morning. I'm friends with the postmaster in Carson City and he seeks a favor."

Nina cocked an eyebrow at Hamish. Maybe he hoped to distract her from her troubles. "Oh?" She tried to sound interested but felt like she failed miserably.

Hamish passed her the letter. "Read it and let me know what you think." Nina noticed that the sparkle returned to his light blue eyes as she took it from him. Nina's heart skipped a beat when it was clear that Hamish still seemed to care about her well-being.

GOVERNESS NEEDED AS SOON AS POSSIBLE

RANCH OWNER IN NEED OF FULL TIME CHILDCARE AND HOUSEKEEPING. CHILD APPROXIMATELY SIX MONTHS TO A YEAR OLD. LODGING, FOOD, AND SMALL ALLOWANCE PROVIDED. CARSON CITY, NEVADA

A handwritten note appeared below the printed ad, the printing slanted and small. Nina squinted to decipher what it said.

Hamish,

A friend of a friend is in need of some help. I know it's far, but do you know anyone?

Your Friend,

Charles

"A governess?" Nina asked, trying to understand Hamish's intentions. She handed the letter back to him and furrowed her brow.

"Nina, my dear, I don't know exactly what happened with Jane and Nathaniel, but I'd hate to watch them continue to hurt you." Hamish heaved a sigh. "After losing your parents and now this, you deserve better."

"Nevada, Hamish? I've never been out of San Antonio."

Hamish pushed the letter back into her hands. "I can't tell you what to do, but I think it might be a brighter future than staying here."

Nina looked up and stared into Hamish's bright eyes. It seemed that he held her best interests at heart. Nina knew that accepting this position would put an end to him his ability to watch over her. "I would probably never see you again." The thought of leaving Hamish behind made her heart want to break all over again.

"I know, my dear," Hamish replied quietly, but with a sure smile. "But I think it might be just what you need. Why don't you take it and think about it? Get back to me once you make your decision."

Nina clutched the letter to her chest, as if it were precious. "Thank you, Hamish."

She turned from the counter and pushed open the door, the bell signaling her goodbye. She took a few steps in the direction of home before she stopped and unfurled the letter to read it one more time. The sounds of merchants calling out to prospective buyers rang in the distance.

GOVERNESS NEEDED AS SOON AS POSSIBLE

RANCH OWNER IN NEED OF FULL TIME CHILDCARE AND HOUSEKEEPING. CHILD APPROXIMATELY SIX MONTHS TO A YEAR OLD. LODGING, FOOD, AND SMALL ALLOWANCE PROVIDED. CARSON CITY, NEVADA

Nina stopped after the part where it gave the child's age. She remembered her fate, and how tragedy displaced her so young. If no one helped this little baby, would they have a similar fate? The very thought made Nina's chest hurt. She pictured herself, not much older, being led to her stepparents' home. Nina didn't remember it, but she imagined that her stepparents felt a burden by taking her in. Those feelings never went away, and she was never treated the same as Jane. No one else deserved a life like that. If she could go back in time and stop her parents from dying or find some one more apt to take her in, she'd do it in a minute. She turned on her heel and walked back into the post office. Hamish looked surprised to see that she was back so soon.

"Hamish, I'll do it." Nina declared. She couldn't remember the last time she felt so full of purpose.

Chapter Three

Carson City, Nevada

June 1886

On a warm Sunday afternoon, Sam prepared to bring the child into town. Sam wore a suit jacket and his best pants, something he saved for church on Christmas and Easter when he tolerated being with other people for the sake of the holiday. He kept worrying the wrinkled fabric, hoping that it wouldn't be obvious that he hadn't worn them in a while.

The baby boy wore an old white gown, and Sam wondered if it was for a christening. It was the nicest thing he could find that didn't have stains on it amongst the basket of items sent over by one of the farmer's wives. If it hadn't been for Jack making arrangements in town, he'd have nothing for the boy. Sam asked him if anyone knew who might have been the baby's mother and there were no leads.

Sam and the child hadn't left the ranch since Sam had found the baby on his doorstep. Sam tried to keep them both alive while trying to work on his ranch at the same time. Jack had been a huge help, getting the ladies in town to donate baby clothes and other necessities, but Sam felt like he was drowning.

Clean clothes for the both of them were running out, the pantry was bare, and both Sam and the child were exhausted—dark circles ringed their eyes and the baby quick to fuss.

"How about a governess?" Sam remembered Jack suggesting shortly after he found the child.

Sam made a scoffing noise like Jack was proposing insanity. Governesses typically took care of rich children. In his mind Sam pictured sprawling estates and the woman helping older children with their studies. He couldn't afford someone like that.

Even though the boy wasn't his, he couldn't fathom abandoning him or giving him away to an orphanage. Sam felt like there was a reason why the babe had ended up on his doorstep. Maybe God or some other force tried to teach him compassion or get him to open up and ask for help. The situation made him uncomfortable, but something must be done for the child's sake.

Sam carried the child on his hip as he made sure the horses were secured to his wagon. The situation did vaguely remind him of his own. He'd been a lot older when he'd been left to fend for himself. Sam was just fifteen when a horrific tragedy hit his family. In the dead of night, he'd thought he'd heard his horse screaming in distress. A fire started in the barn adjacent to the house. Sam left a lantern out after completing his late-night chores. The side where the horses were kept in their stalls was filled with smoke as the pile of hay and the roof above it were a blazing inferno. It had been over ten years and could still smell the smoke as if he'd just discovered the flames.

Sam couldn't remember what came over him, but he ran to the stalls, letting his father's work horses and his own steed free. He got three cows and a few sheep out before the smoke made his eyes burn and choked his throat. It was then that he thought about his family and how they must hear the blaze roaring like thunder and smell the smoke that stung his eyes. Sometimes, when he shut his eyes, he could still see it. It sent shivers galloping down his spine.

When he finally stumbled out onto the front lawn, he couldn't believe his eyes. Since the house and barn shared a wall, the fire quickly spread. Flames burst out of windows and licked the night sky.

Sam remembered running to the door and when he pulled it open, what he imagined to be the image of Hell greeted him. A gust of skin-blistering heat nearly knocked him over and fire engulfed the path back to his parents and younger sister's rooms. Sam filled with dread as he realized that he couldn't get to them. If he wasn't quick enough, he'd be trapped in the house too.

Sam ran back outside, trying to figure out where to get help or what to do to save his family. As he stood there, he could hear the gruesome screams of his family as the fire overtook them.

Chapter Three

Carson City, Nevada

June 1886

On a warm Sunday afternoon, Sam prepared to bring the child into town. Sam wore a suit jacket and his best pants, something he saved for church on Christmas and Easter when he tolerated being with other people for the sake of the holiday. He kept worrying the wrinkled fabric, hoping that it wouldn't be obvious that he hadn't worn them in a while. The baby boy wore an old white gown, and Sam wondered if it was for a christening.

It was the nicest thing he could find that didn't have stains on it amongst the basket of items sent over by one of the farmer's wives. If it hadn't been for Jack making arrangements in town, he'd have nothing for the boy. Sam asked him if anyone knew who might have been the baby's mother and there were no leads.

Sam and the child hadn't left the ranch since Sam had found the baby on his doorstep. Sam tried to keep them both alive while trying to work on his ranch at the same time. Jack had been a huge help, getting the ladies in town to donate baby clothes and other necessities, but Sam felt like he was drowning. Clean clothes for the both of them were running out, the pantry was bare, and both Sam and the child were exhausted—dark circles ringed their eyes and the baby quick to fuss.

"How about a governess?" Sam remembered Jack suggesting shortly after he found the child.

Sam made a scoffing noise like Jack was proposing insanity. Governesses typically took care of rich children. In his mind Sam pictured sprawling estates and the woman helping older children with their studies. He couldn't afford someone like that. Even though the boy wasn't his, he couldn't fathom abandoning him or giving him away to an orphanage. Sam felt like there was a reason why the babe had ended up on his doorstep. Maybe God or some other force tried to teach him compassion or get him to open up and ask for help. The situation made him uncomfortable, but something must be done for the child's sake.

Sam carried the child on his hip as he made sure the horses were secured to his wagon. The situation did vaguely remind him of his own. He'd been a lot older when he'd been left to fend for himself. Sam was just fifteen when a horrific tragedy hit his family. In the dead of night, he'd thought he'd heard his horse screaming in distress. A fire started in the barn adjacent to the house.

Sam left a lantern out after completing his late-night chores. The side where the horses were kept in their stalls was filled with smoke as the pile of hay and the roof above it were a blazing inferno. It had been over ten years and could still smell the smoke as if he'd just discovered the flames.

Sam couldn't remember what came over him, but he ran to the stalls, letting his father's work horses and his own steed free. He got three cows and a few sheep out before the smoke made his eyes burn and choked his throat. It was then that he thought about his family and how they must hear the blaze roaring like thunder and smell the smoke that stung his eyes. Sometimes, when he shut his eyes, he could still see it. It sent shivers galloping down his spine. When he finally stumbled out onto the front lawn, he couldn't believe his eyes. Since the house and barn shared a wall, the fire quickly spread. Flames burst out of windows and licked the night sky.

Sam remembered running to the door and when he pulled it open, what he imagined to be the image of Hell greeted him.

A gust of skin-blistering heat nearly knocked him over and fire engulfed the path back to his parents and younger sister's rooms. Sam filled with dread as he realized that he couldn't get to them. If he wasn't quick enough, he'd be trapped in the house too.

Sam ran back outside, trying to figure out where to get help or what to do to save his family. As he stood there, he could hear the gruesome screams of his family as the fire overtook them. Despite the fire raging in front of him, it was all he could hear. Sam thought his heart might give out as he imagined what was happening to them.

He tried to shout and yell to drown them out, but nothing came out as tears streamed down his face. No noise came out of his mouth ever again. It was like that part of him died along with his family, or perhaps it was punishment for surviving when his family did not.

By the time the people from the next farm over saw the flames, it was too late. The house was reduced to ashes. Sam stared at the house, unable to move. He was so numb that he felt as though he was rooted to the spot. He knew somewhere in the rubble lay the remains of his mother, father, and sister Jennie. They were dead because of his oversight.

After the tragedy, he bounced from neighbor to neighbor for a while. Everyone tried to get him to talk about what happened or come to terms with what his new reality, but they all gave up on him eventually when they realized he wouldn't speak. It simply became easier to be on his own, and he started working as a ranch hand until he saved up some money. A boom town, Carson City had plenty of land on offer since most who flocked there sought gold in the mines. The rest was history.

The child trying to wiggle down from his grasp brought Sam back to his senses. The baby seemed to be afraid of the horses in all their tack, so Sam took a few steps back and tried to bounce him in attempt to stop him from squalling.

The way he felt lonely and unloved, even now, was the reason why he wanted to help the babe. The loneliness was like a hole that was too deep to climb out of. No matter how hard he tried, he felt trapped, and he didn't want the child to experience the same thing. He was so little and innocent—he deserved a better childhood than Sam had been given. Sam knew deep in his heart what must be done. The boy found his way to Sam whether by fate or chance he could not say, but their lives were irrevocably intertwined. Yet Sam needed the steady influence a governess could provide.

About a week after Sam found the baby, Jack helped him put the ad in at the post office. The postmaster sent it to various towns and cities within a small radius. When no one inquired, they kept pushing the limits of their search. Weeks went by, and just when Sam felt convinced that no one would ever answer the ad, the postmaster got a letter from his friend Hamish Bennett in San Antonio.

Mr. Bennett knew a young lady interested in the position and wanted to know if Sam would like more information about her. Sam felt grateful that someone was willing to help him that he just instructed the governess to come to Carson City immediately. The relief engulfed him like the welcoming waters of a warm bath.

Today was the day that she was set to arrive. He was so nervous; he wasn't sure what to do with himself.

There wasn't much information about the girl. Nina Mason, twenty-one years old, finished her schooling several years ago but had never been a governess before. Yet Sam just tried to be happy with an extra set of hands, even if she didn't necessarily have the experience; the governess-to-be could have been old enough to be the child's grandmother and he would have accepted her with open arms. Sam fidgeted again as he considered Miss Mason's youth. He couldn't remember the last time he'd been around a woman who didn't think he was odd. Sam feared it wouldn't be long until she felt that way too.

She would arrive via the train station, and Sam spent most of the previous night tossing and turning over how he could communicate with her. He had a special sort of language he used with his ranch hands, but they worked together for years. They probably thought it was odd in the beginning, but as long as he paid them their wages, who were they to judge?

He wasn't sure how it would work with the governess living in close quarters every day. Sam feared that it would cause problems. If he couldn't communicate with the governess, she might leave and he'd back in the predicament of raising the baby alone.

The baby babbled happily at Sam, his arms reaching out to grasp Sam's clean-shaven face. The child's large eyes stared at him curiously, as though he wondered what Sam was doing. Sam considered the baby again. *Yes, the child*, he mused, *he is why I'm doing this. Nothing else matters but getting him into capable hands so that I can get back to work.* Sam squeezed the child and gave him an encouraging nod before placing him in a basket in the back of his wagon and climbed atop the seat. Despite his little preparation for fatherhood, Sam couldn't deny that the little boy was adorable. It was hard to not want to make him happy every minute of the day.

Sam's ranch was about a thirty-minute wagon ride from town. It was a sprawling piece of property, nearly two hundred acres. Pride filled his heart as he recalled what he accomplished since he bought it, but there was still so much work to be done. There were parts of the pastures that were as arid and dead as a desert, and there were fences in dire need of repair. He hoped that someday he'd have the time and the resources to make the whole place shine.

About halfway into his journey, Sam slowed his horses to a walk. It was a Sunday, so no one was working, but a large work encampment looming on the horizon nearly made him stop. The railroad continued to expand just like the country. What had once been wild frontier had been blasted and morphed into train tracks, stations, and new towns. Sam shook his head as he looked at the construction site. He could have sworn the last time he went to town it hadn't been this close to his property, but that was before the child came into his life. It had been weeks since he'd gone anywhere.

Maybe now that can change. Sam thought to himself. *There is so much to do.*

More houses and farms dotted the sides of the road, and he knew Carson City wasn't far away. Many people arrived in search of gold in the hills, so the town had every business or place a man could want. There were barber shops and mercantiles, as well as saloons and bordellos off on a few side streets so they were a bit more inconspicuous. The church stood at the end of the street, not far from the sheriff and the post office. He wasn't used to turning the other direction toward the train station.

Black train smoke marred the fierce blue of the sky as a locomotive pulled up to the junction. Based on how high the sun was in the sky, it was nearing two o'clock. Just in time for Miss Mason's arrival.

The train hissed as it came to a full stop, and Sam watched as people began to disembark from the various cars. There were several men in work clothes, and Sam wondered whether they headed for ranches or mines. They did not have much for belongings besides what they could carry on their back. A young woman wearing a sage colored dress with a large, brimmed hat tentatively stepped down from one of the cars furthest from him and onto the platform. Sam's heart beat faster as he recalled how she wrote that she'd be wearing such an outfit when she arrived.

She clutched a decent sized suitcase in one of her hands. Sam noticed that she wore her long brown hair pulled partly away from her face under the hat. Her face turned away from him, and she was taller than he expected, though still quite slight.

The baby cooed, and the young lady turned in Sam's direction. Sam was shocked to see a pair of large hazel eyes take him in with interest and surprise. When a huge smile spread across her face and her eyes bounced from Sam to the child and back to him, his stomach flipped and rolled like it was on open water.

"Are you Mr. Colt?" she asked. Even her voice was soft and delicate, taking Sam's breath away. "I'm Nina Mason."

Sam gave her a nod and a small smile before looking away. He wondered what she would think about him not saying anything back. Would she ever smile at him again? Or would she assume that he was cold and rude?

"Is this the baby?" Nina asked, bending down slightly so she could be on his level. "Hello there, little one." Sam watched as the child beamed back at her, the few teeth he had plain to see. "Does he have a name?"

Sam shrugged in reply, his face growing hot with embarrassment as he failed to answer her. Since she had no idea that he didn't speak, it probably seemed like he hadn't named the child because he didn't care. Nothing was left on the child to help identify him when Sam found him.

He probably could have picked a name but seeing as how he was never going to say it out loud, Sam didn't see the point. Sam then reeled as realized he never said a word to the poor thing; he merely got his point across by picking him up and showing him things.

Nina stared at Sam like she didn't understand what he meant and was confused that he wasn't speaking to her. "You don't know his name?" When Sam shook his head, Nina's brow furrowed more. "Isn't the child yours?" Once more Sam shook his head and Nina's mouth nearly fell open. It was as if she wasn't expecting to walk into such a situation when she signed up for the position. Sam was worried that she was going to run.

I wish I could just tell her what happened to me. It would make things easier.

Filling with shame, Sam was ready to end the awkward encounter by getting them back to his ranch. There he could distract her from his muteness by showing her around and giving her tasks to complete. He stared down at her belongings before he tried to communicate his thoughts to her. Sam pointed at her suitcase before pointing a finger at himself. He then proceeded to point to the babe and gestured handing him to Nina.

"Do you want me to hold him?" Nina asked, still looking utterly confused that he wasn't just talking to her.

When he nodded, Sam could swear that he could see the emotion replaced by sadness. Nina was no doubt misinterpreting his behavior for rudeness. He cringed at the thought of making someone so kind and lovely upset. Sam carefully passed Nina the child and he grabbed her suitcase from the train platform before motioning her along.

Sam was surprised that the suitcase seemed light despite its size, and he wondered what Nina had packed inside. He began to worry that she might not even unpack when she saw the state of the ranch or how undecorated the house was.

He looked over his shoulder once he was off the platform to see Nina not far behind. Sam motioned to his wagon where his team of horses was waiting. He gestured to Nina to come over as he put her suitcase in the back. Sam held his arms out to take back the baby and returned him to his basket before he offered Nina help up into the wagon.

"That's all right, I can manage." Her smile was warm, but it didn't go to her eyes. Nina looked worried and Sam didn't blame her. Sam watched as she climbed aboard the wagon before he took his seat at the front, he snapped the reins gently so that the horses would walk back towards the ranch.

Sam's mind raced over what he could do to remedy not being able to speak to Nina. He wanted to kick himself for not having a better plan before she arrived, but he'd just been so preoccupied with surviving and taking care of the baby. As he drove past the railroad worksite, he had an idea. He couldn't speak, but he could write; he did it with his ranch hands sometimes.

He dropped out of school to get a job and make ends meet, but he remembered enough to be able to read and write. He had an extra ledger for ranch expenses in his bedroom. For the first time since he saw Nina on the platform, he didn't feel completely sorry for himself.

They passed his neighbor's ranch, full of cattle and horses grazing in pastures with an inviting sign hanging over its gate. He wished he could tell her that hoped that his place would be equally as lovely someday. Instead, he tried to tell himself that the wild cacti and yucca gave the place character until it could be spruced up.

Sam pulled off the road and onto the rough dirt path that led to his farmhouse. In the afternoon sun he could see how dry and barren some of the pastures looked. He had a plan to eventually plant things that could survive the heat and make him money, but it was lower on the priority list than building barns and stables and drawing the property line with a sturdy fence.

"Is this all yours?" Nina called.

Sam looked over his shoulder to see Nina taking in the large ranch. He'd expected disgust or disappointment, but her face was neutral, her large eyes might have even been a bit curious. As they passed the lone pasture that currently housed all his cattle, he gave a large nod, beaming at her proudly. Someday all the pastures would be filled if he could just get some good luck.

"It's the largest lot of land I've ever seen," she replied, sounding impressed.

Sam thought that couldn't possibly be true, that someone from San Antonio had to have a bigger and nicer ranch than his, but he appreciated the compliment. He pulled the horses and wagon as close to the house as he could get. One of his ranch hands must have heard them approach and jogged over.

He began to unhitch the team as Sam jumped down and grabbed the suitcase from the back of the wagon. Nina seemed to be on the same page as him; she climbed down to the ground before she picked up the child and followed him toward the house without saying a word. He tried to hold onto the hope that maybe she was already adapting to him not speaking. Sam clutched onto it desperately.

The house had two floors. It had been painted white at one point, but most of it cracked and chipped away before he'd bought it. Some of the shutters rotted, but it was inviting and comfortable, nonetheless. A fresh coat of paint would breathe a little bit of life into it. The front door needed oiling, the squeal of the hinges could probably wake the dead, but just like the pastures and barns, the house had possibilities if he squinted at it hard enough.

Sam opened the door for Nina, gesturing for her to head inside. Once they all gathered in the entrance way, he held up his index finger, gesturing for her to wait a moment. Sam took the stairs two at a time, not wanting to waste another minute. As soon as he was in his room, he grabbed the ledger off his nightstand, as well as a charcoal pencil, before he bounded back down to Nina and the baby.

Nina looked at him curiously, still holding the child tightly. Her large eyes took in the notebook and pencil in his hand. Sam opened to the first blank page and began writing.

Want to see the house and ranch?

Sam knew that things were probably misspelled and blunter than he would like, but he hoped that it would get the point across.

"Yes," she replied, nodding as a look of understanding passed through her eyes. Nina smiled at him cheerfully as she continued, "I'd love for you to show me around."

Sam nodded and off they went. He took her down the hallway to show her the kitchen. Sam showed her the limited supplies and utensils he had in the cupboards before he took his pencil and wrote a new line.

I eat lunch with my men. Breakfast and Dinner are in the house. Baby needs food too.

Nina read and replied, "Would you like for me to cook for you?" When Sam nodded, she added, "I used to make food for my family all the time. That will be no trouble."

Same wondered what Nina's story was as they walked down the hallway and he showed her the living room.

I wonder what caused her to take up the call and work for me.

"I mean no disrespect with what I'm about to say," Nina said as she took in the room with its bare walls and how little furniture it had. Sam watched her eyes look unsure of what she'd walk into. "But your home is very empty."

Sam tried not to be offended, it was the truth after all. He just worried that it might be one more thing to drive her away. He wrote back with a simple explanation.

I live alone.

"I see," Nina replied, pity softening her words. "I'm sorry if I've stepped over the line."

Sam shook his head and continued showing her around. He guided her up the stairs and showed her where her room would be. It wasn't much, a bed and a dresser, but at least Nina would have her own space. After that, he guided her to the nursery where there was a cradle that one of the ranch hands had quickly built as well as the donated items from the families around town.

The child was left on my doorstep. He's not mine. I can't leave him. It's not right.

Nina looked confused as she read his newest words. "He was left? Do you mean that someone abandoned him?" When Sam nodded, Nina looked heartbroken, her brow furrowing like the thought weighed her down. It was an expression he hoped he would never see on her beautiful face again. "How terrible."

***

After looking at all the rooms inside the house, Sam guided her outside to show her where the outhouse was, as well as the water pump, and where he hoped to cultivate a vegetable garden. It was currently a patch of soil full of weeds with a dilapidated fence around it, but maybe now he'd have time to fix it up. He also showed her where he kept the horses when they weren't grazing in the pasture. Sam hoped that Nina could see past the chipped paint and missing roof shingles and notice the ranch's potential.

He took his pad and pencil and wrote her another note.

I hope to get chickens and other livestock someday. It will be cheaper than buying eggs and things from others.

Nina squinted as she deciphered his handwriting, still balancing the baby on her hip.

For someone who never was a governess before, she seems quite comfortable. Sam thought as he took in the sight.

Eventually, she nodded, her eyes growing bright as though excited at the prospect of what the ranch could be. "I'll do my part to make sure you can get your work done." At that moment, the child writhed and fussed. "Well, I suppose that I should go see what he needs." Nina stared up at him with her tender hazel eyes. "Thank you for showing me around. It was nice meeting you, Mr. Colt."

This should have been the part of the conversation where he said that it was nice to meet her too. Sam wanted to say the words out loud, he wanted her to know that even if she did nothing but make sure the baby was happy, it would be a blessing. He felt as though his tongue was made of stone, and he just couldn't do it. Instead, he nodded, trying to give her a polite smile, but he could see the confusion and insecurity on her face, and souring his expression into a dissatisfied grimace.

As Nina turned and walked back toward the house, shame crept into Sam's heart. How could he think about how beautiful Nina was or how wonderful having her around would be? *No one as kind and lovely as Nina would love someone like me*, he fretted.

Such insecurity kept Sam tied to the ranch; he never went out of his way to meet new people. He feared their misunderstanding, and that he would never see or hear from them again. Sam knew he would never be good enough; no one would ever understand why he was so silent, so he just stayed away. The familiar despondent, hopeless feeling returned—his constant companion.

Chapter Four

The sun hadn't risen yet, and the baby still slept, so Nina decided to get some chores done. A creature of habit, she used to get up before the sun in San Antonio too. Nina recalled how her stepparents had to be up and out of the house early, and Jane couldn't cook. Breakfast had to be on the table by the time they came down from getting dressed.

Nina felt her stomach growl and remembered that Mr. Colt wrote something about taking his lunch with his ranch hands—he did not say anything about breakfast. Since she already had to make food for her and the child, what was a little bit more? Nina dressed for the day in a long gray skirt and pale blue blouse and made her way downstairs.

A short while later, Mr. Colt came into the kitchen bleary eyed, though dressed for the day. Nina didn't even think he noticed her until he walked toward the cabinet that housed the few plates he owned. He rubbed his eyes, finally noticing how she assembled a full breakfast over by the stove.

Sam looked surprised to see that she prepared so much at once. Nina fried bacon in one pan, while she used the other to brown some potatoes she planned to turn into hash browns. She also found a sweet potato in the pantry that she thought to mash for the baby since she noticed he didn't have many teeth yet.

"Morning, Mr. Colt", Nina chirped, hoping her light voice and gentle smile would invite Mr. Colt into conversation. Mr. Colt only nodded at her in greeting before he went into the pantry to retrieve a basket of eggs. Nina studied him with a quizzical eye as he pointed to her and then at the basket of eggs.

She didn't understand why he didn't just tell her that he wanted her to make eggs. It seemed much easier than writing down what he wanted from her. She took the basket from him and as soon as her bacon finished cooking, she began to fry the eggs in the same pan. The bacon fat infused itself into the eggs, making them taste so much richer.

"Did you sleep well?" Nina asked cheerfully as she used a spatula to flip the eggs over. When Mr. Colt didn't answer her, she cleared her throat slightly. Maybe he hadn't heard her. "Do you have a lot of work to do today?" She attempted again.

When there was no response for a second time, she turned to check if he was even in the room. Nina saw Mr. Colt sitting at the table, avoiding her gaze. Nina was so confused; the ad Hamish shared with her said nothing about the governess not being allowed to speak to her employer. If it wasn't part of the job description, then maybe she upset him, but she couldn't think of anything she said or did that would cause him not to speak to her.

She put an egg, several pieces of bacon, and a bit of hash browns on two plates and slid one across to Mr. Colt before she sat and began to eat her own. There were so many things that Nina wanted to ask him. Were there any specific things he wanted her to do beyond taking care of the child? What time did he come in for dinner? What time church was on Sunday? Which store in Carson City sold books? Yet she struggled to focus on so many details when all she wanted to do was scream at him, *why won't you speak to me*?

Mr. Colt seemed equally as uncomfortable; his shoulders hunched as he shoveled his food down in what felt like no time at all. He stood up, placing his plate on the counter, holding his finger up for her to wait a moment just as he did yesterday. Nina heard him climbing the stairs, heavy and weary, before he quickly came back down. Just like yesterday, he held his pad and charcoal pencil in his hand when he returned.

He dropped back into the chair and Nina watched mid bite as his pencil scribbled on the paper. She hastily wiped her mouth with a cloth napkin she put out as he slid the ledger over to her.

Watch baby

Do dishes

Make dinner

Anything else is a big help

Nina read the list a few times to figure out what he was trying to say. She noticed yesterday that he wrote well enough to get his points across. It certainly wasn't a conventional means of communicating, but maybe she could learn to get used to it.

"Okay," Nina replied. "Do you have any preferences for dinner? Do you have a favorite dish?"

Mr. Colt shook his head quickly and Nina tried to push away the hurt feeling that crept into her chest. It was as if he tried to end the conversation or brush her off. Nina took Mr. Colt's job to escape the feeling of being unwanted, and now she could feel the self-deprecating thoughts slipping back in.

She stopped dwelling on it momentarily when Mr. Colt seized the ledger again and scrawled a new line. He offered her a tentative smile as he pushed the book back toward her.

Breakfast was good. Nicer than I cook. Thanks.

Nina felt her face flush as a wave of confusion washed over her. She was just wallowing in self-pity over his distant and sometimes rude behavior, yet his thoughtful compliment soothed her anxieties, however, briefly, like a salve over a wound.

She opened her mouth to express her thanks when she heard the baby crying upstairs. The moment broke, and she must try to get through to Mr. Colt a different time. Mr. Colt stood up and grabbed the notebook, tucking it under his arm and pocketing the pencil. He left the room without saying or writing anything else. Not wanting to make the child wait upstairs any longer, she temporarily abandoned her breakfast and went to retrieve him from the nursery.

Determining if Mr. Colt hated her or was just odd would have to wait.

***

"All right, little one," Nina said as she placed the child on a blanket in the center of the kitchen floor. "You've lived here longer than I have. Tell me Mr. Colt's secrets."

Nina knew that there was no way that he could answer in a way that satisfied her. Still, she couldn't help but smile as the baby smiled and babbled at her, looking happy that someone gave him attention.

Nina decided to not just clean the dishes, but to give the whole kitchen a proper cleaning from floorboard to ceiling. It wasn't that it was filthy—in fact, it seemed that Mr. Colt took very good care of the few things he used to cook. Nina could see the meticulous way he kept them cleaned and polished; his belongings were just old. Nina glanced around the cavernous space again. It seemed to her as though parts of the room hadn't been used in a long while. Dust and cobwebs freckled the corners and worn cabinets.

The pantry wasn't bare, but the soft fuzz of mold on a few items caught Nina's eye and inspired her to purge them. Nina considered offering her wage to Mr. Colt to buy different types of nutritious food for the baby. The child looked a bit thin, and Nina wondered what Mr. Colt gave him for milk. Mr. Colt looked young, maybe about five years older than her at most, but it still seemed like it had been a long time since he'd been around children.

Who was the mother of the child and what had caused her to leave him here? Nina couldn't help but worry that something terrible might have happened. Mr. Colt wrote that the child wasn't his, but the whole situation seemed odd. She carried the child outside with one arm, a bucket in her other hand so she could get water to wash the dishes and scrub the floors.

Nina wondered about Mr. Colt's story, his past. Had he had his heart broken and that was why he refused to talk to any woman? Nina supposed that she didn't blame him. She all but ran away when she experienced heartbreak in her life.

When Nina neared the water pump, she saw Mr. Colt and several of his men standing near one of the barns. They stood far enough away that she couldn't hear exactly what they said, but she could see Mr. Colt gesturing wildly with his hands and the others laughing at him. Was he talking to them?

"I really don't understand him," Nina said to the child. He reached out his little hand and placed it on her cheek, the skin soft and smooth against her own. The gesture was so tender that Nina leaned down and pecked his blond head.

"Let's be friends and work together to figure out what he's thinking, okay?"

The baby responded with a gummy grin and Nina decided that even if Mr. Colt was cold and strange, the little boy's smiles made up for it. She hoped that in time the wound on Nina's heart left by Jane and Nathaniel's betrayal would begin to scab over.

Chapter Five

Sam expected Nina to run screaming as soon as she had the chance. It seemed like she wasn't happy most of the time, and she clearly struggled to understand him. Her large eyes were like mirrors, reflecting all her insecurities, but he was happy to see her in the kitchen each morning. It made him hopeful that she might come around and understand that his silence wasn't personal

"I'd like to offer my pay to purchase more food for the house." Nina offered humbly, looking down at the dinner table after his first day back working in fields and barns. "I'd also like to make the house warmer and more inviting if you are open to it. There are no curtains for the windows, and the baby will need blankets when it gets colder."

Sam wasn't sure what to expect when Jack suggested hiring a governess. He assumed she would just take care of the baby and cook his meals and that would be it. When he walked into the kitchen to find it organized and freshly cleaned, he was pleased. That was before he smelled rosemary spiced potatoes and saw Nina pulling a sizzling roast from the oven. He wanted to keep the comforts and improvements coming, so he pulled out his notebook and scribbled down a reply:

We could go to town. You don't have to pay.

Sam watched as joy filled Nina's face as she read what he wrote. "I think that's a great idea. Thank you so much." The sincerity of her voice nearly took Sam's breath away.

They made plans to go to Carson City in a few days. Sam wished he could say more to Nina, to ask her what else she desired or where she came from, but he settled on watching her feed and talk to the baby. They didn't have a chair for him to sit in, so she kept him on her lap.

Warmth flooded Sam's chest as he watched the child coo and babble at Nina. It felt strange to see so much happiness and love after being alone for so long. Nina spoke so sweetly to him. Despite it being her first time as a governess, she seemed to be a natural with the babe. Nina seemed right at home with being a mother. He swallowed as he considered her ease with the boy, and how much lovelier that made her. He imagined her surrounded by a whole family of children, hair wavy and blond like his.

In the days that followed, Sam watched as Nina slowly made his house the nicest it had ever looked. The windows were clearer, and the floors no longer had grime on them, and he could see the specks of dust floating in air when the sun shone in. There were no longer piles of dust or spiderwebs in the corners of the rooms. He noticed a change in the child as well. He didn't cry as much as he used to, and he just seemed genuinely happier. It was as if the little one finally felt safe. Sam was certain that it was because Nina spoke to him and gave him the attention he needed. He tried not to feel bad that he couldn't provide it for him alone.

One night after supper, Nina ventured into his bare living room that he seldom used and read the child stories from the Bible. Sam didn't want to make her uncomfortable watching them, so he stood listening just outside of the room in the hallway. He shut his eyes as he leaned against one of the walls. Listening was oddly soothing; his muscles felt taut after work for the first time in a long while. It reminded him of simpler times, a time when he wasn't filled with pain and regret.

***

"Mr. Colt, can I speak with you about something?" Nina asked over a pleasant, hearty Saturday morning breakfast.

Two weeks passed since Nina's arrival. Nina surpassed Sam's expectations of what she would do around the house, and the place shined like it was brand new. Now, he felt motivated to do his part as well. He intended to weed the patch he hoped to transform into a garden and put some new hinges on the door so that it didn't squeal as much.

Nina sat on the floor of the living room, a deep, midnight blue swath of fabric they purchased when they'd gone to Carson City sprawled out in front of her. The baby sat and giggled as he played with the hem of the panel she sewed. Sam got his notebook ready for whatever she intended to say.

"I'd like to give the baby a name," Nina explained, getting right to the point. "A person needs an identity."

Sam agreed, happiness flooding him that she decided to take charge of the matter. He strode into the room and sat in one of the rocking chairs before he wrote his reply.

Good Idea. What are you thinking?

Nina suddenly looked shy and avoided his gaze. "If it's okay with you, I'd like to name him Henry. That was my birth father's name."

So many thoughts saturated Sam's mind. Did he and Nina have something in common? Had she also suffered loss and that was why she referred to her father in the past tense? It was more than that, though. Sam's heart jumped at the chance to name a child together with Nina; it reminded him of how he pictured her with their own children someday. It seemed so fantastical, but the very idea of being close to Nina made his heart soften.

Sam tried to calm his thoughts. What he and Nina potentially had in common was not important at the moment. She waited patiently for an answer. He took a deep breath and began to write again. He passed her the ledger and waited to see what she would say.

I think Henry is a wonderful name.

Nina squealed with glee, hugging the notebook to her chest. "Then Henry he shall be from this moment forward." She handed Sam back his ledger before she got up from her sewing and came to kneel by the child. "How do you do, Henry? Do you like your name?"

Henry laughed and gave her his usually gaping smile as a reply. Sam noticed the glint of a few new teeth peeking out from the child's mouth. Nina reached her arms out and scooped him into her embrace. Sam caught a faint glimmer in Nina's striking hazel eyes as she held Henry close.

Sam nodded before he let himself out of the room. He opened the door, the squeak reminding him to get oil and the hinges from one of his sheds to make the noise stop once and for all.

Sam tried to think if there was ever a time where he thought he would marry or have a family, but it was hard to imagine life before it became difficult and tragic.

"Oh, Henry," Nina said from the living room, where she must have not realized that Sam could still hear her. Sam froze in the doorway, wondering if he should leave, but desperately wanted to know what she was thinking. "I'm so worried. I feel as if I've done something to upset Mr. Colt. If I did, it was never my intention." When there was nothing but silence, Sam tried to listen even more carefully, praying the door hinges wouldn't squeal and give away that he was eavesdropping on her confession. "I'm worried that he might hate me. You don't think I traveled all this way just to be an annoyance to someone else, do you?"

The situation was so much worse than he thought. Not only did she interpret his silence as rudeness, but he inadvertently dredged up bad memories. What happened to poor Nina Mason that not speaking to her would make her feel that way? Nina seemed so happy and kind that the thought of anyone being annoyed by her seemed incomprehensible. Though the more Sam thought about it, he noticed that sometimes Nina's smile wasn't real—it was too big and felt forced—something she plastered on when situations were uncomfortable.

She wore it like a mask.

They only lived together for a few weeks, and she already eased his burden so much. Without knowing her well, he could tell Nina was a kind and wonderful person. She was so sweet to Henry, and she'd helped make his house a home when she didn't need to. She deserved happiness. Right now, Sam wasn't sure that he could do that for her. Even if he told her the truth, that he was mute and not mean, would it even matter? They would never fully understand each other; there would always be barriers between them. He didn't want Nina to wear her mask for him, but there was no way to tell her that without her knowing he was listening.

Chapter Six

Nina could have lost sleep over Mr. Colt and how he made her feel. She could have retraced everything she did to see if there was something she had done that upset him. When she couldn't think of anything, she worried that maybe it was something more superficial. Maybe he thought Nina was too tall or not experienced enough to be a governess.

If she was a quitter, she would return to San Antonio. Hamish would probably be disappointed to see her back so soon. At the end of the day, Nina knew that he would probably understand. He'd been with her through so many other difficult moments. Whether it was the loneliness of missing her birth parents or a day when Jane had mocked her for having eyes that were too big, Hamish could always cheer her up.

As miserable as she felt sometimes, there was no way she could go home. Not after everything Jane said and insinuated about Nathaniel only loving her because he felt sorry for her. At least here, she had a purpose.

Henry deserved a good life. His helplessness inspired her to take the job in the first place. Nina reminded herself that she was here to be Henry's governess and not friends with Mr. Colt. Yes, they lived under the same roof, but he was her employer and nothing more.

She still made breakfast for Mr. Colt each morning, but she no longer sat and ate with him. Nina decided she wanted to avoid the awkward silence that always lurked between them, silence that made her worry what a person truly thought. Nathaniel seemed perfectly happy with her until she found him in the woods with Jane that day. Nina wondered if she should have paid more attention to what wasn't said, to silence.

Instead, she woke Henry up and got him ready for the day. By the time she brought the child downstairs, Mr. Colt was already out working on the ranch for the day. They would still share supper together at night, but it was less time that she was left guessing what Mr. Colt was really thinking about her. She struggled to convince herself that she didn't need a man to accept her, but it was hard.

"Henry," Nina said in a sing-song voice as gentle as a songbird, as she opened the door to his nursery. "Rise and shine, today is a beautiful new day." It was hard to feel depressed as she looked after the sweet child.

At the sound of her voice, Henry slowly stirred. He then sat up in his cradle, his wispy blond hair disheveled after a night of sleep. Nina loved the way his blue eyes were bright and eager from the moment he was awake until she put him to bed at night.

"We're going to have breakfast," Nina explained as she strode across the room to pick him up and carry him on her hip. "You need a bath today and there is a whole list of chores waiting for me downstairs."

She brought Henry over to the dresser that she'd converted into an area to change his diaper. There were a few cloth pieces that had been donated before she arrived, but when Mr. Colt brought her into town to get fabric for the curtains in the living room, she picked up some extra to make diapers as well.

Changing a soiled diaper was one of the parts of the governess position that she dreaded on her train journey to Carson City, but she found herself surprisingly used to it in no time at all. Nina replaced the wet one with a fresh one and tied it around Henry's waist with a secure knot. Then, she changed him out of his nightgown and into a new outfit for the day. She hoped to make him some new clothes and perhaps knit him things for the colder months, but she did not have the time yet. Up until now, she had been figuring out a daily routine and getting the house in order.

"What would you like for breakfast today, little one?" Nina asked him as she brought him down the stairs. "There's still the sweet potatoes, peas, and applesauce I made you."

Nina boiled and mashed a large pot of each so that she could make use of the food as needed. She smiled to herself as she recalled Mr. Colt's face when he found her stocking the pantry.

Henry couldn't exactly tell her what he wanted, but she started holding up two different items and letting him grab for the one he wanted the most. Nina wasn't sure if he picked his favorites or just grabbing at random, but it was fun to guess what he was going to pick.

One of the ranch hands, Jack, made a highchair out of some scrap wood that had once been fence posts. He did it quickly, but it was sturdy and safe. Now, Henry had his own place at the table instead of sitting on her lap. Nina placed him down in it and retrieved two cans of baby food from the pantry.

"What will it be today? Apple sauce or peas?"

Henry reached for the jar with green mash inside and Nina clapped for him. "Peas are a great choice! You can have apple sauce for your lunch." She placed the jar on the table to use later and opened the jar of peas.

As Nina used a spoon to feed Henry, she noticed Mr. Colt's ledger lying open on the table beside her untouched breakfast dish. She made the eggs scrambled today and cooked a few sausages that they'd bought from the butcher in Carson City. Nina chewed and slid the notebook closer to her. She scanned the writing quickly.

Wash clothes

Make a list of supplies we need

Fix ripped pants

Thank you for breakfast.

Nina wondered what Mr. Colt had done that required mending the pants. She didn't know much about ranch work other than that Mr. Colt raised livestock to be sold at auction. He often came in for supper dirty and tired, so it must be strenuous work.

When Nina wasn't worrying about what Mr. Colt thought of her, her mind would wander back to San Antonio and what Jane and Nate were doing without her. Despite her best efforts to immerse herself in her new routine, they still slipped into her mind if she was idle for too long.

Had they stopped meeting in secret because there was no longer anything holding them back from being in love? Were they going to move to the farm that Nina thought she would live on someday? Those were the days that she'd hug Henry a little tighter, or she'd scrub the floors on the second level of the house until they shone in the sun that came through the hallway window.

Once they ate their breakfast and Nina had cleaned up Henry's face, she started to work on her to-do list. She kept Henry in his highchair, letting him play with a wooden spoon that he cheerfully banged against the chair, while she looked at the pantry and the shelves to assess which supplies were getting low. Nina made her list on the ledger next to Mr. Colt's handwriting to show him later. Many of their daily necessities would be remedied once they had a working garden and chickens that could lay fresh eggs. Nina contemplated bringing up using her wages again so that they could buy chickens and feed.

After writing down eggs, several vegetables, and a sack of flour, Nina took Henry into the living room. Laying him on a blanket, Nina put a rattle and a few other donated toys out for him to play with as she mended Mr. Colt's pants. All the while, she sang songs to Henry, who babbled along with her.

"Maybe Mr. Colt will find a wife someday," Nina said to Henry as he crawled on the blanket closer to her. He soon sat with a huff and looked up at her with those darling blue eyes. "Then you'll have a proper Mama," Nina just hoped that whoever it was showed kindness to the child.

She often watched Henry play, at times gently dropping on the floor to get down to his level. HIs playful inquisitiveness helped bat the thoughts about her past away. With a wistful sight, Nina rose to prepare their midday meal. She served Henry his applesauce with some cow's milk to drink. Nina usually ate something light for this meal, maybe some vegetables or a piece of bread with a bit of cheese.

After that she'd take Henry back up to his nursery and rock him in a chair by his crib. Sometimes she read him the Bible, she really liked the parables that Jesus used to teach about his Kingdom, but often she just hummed until his little body felt heavy in her arms and his eyes shut. Then she'd carefully set him down for his nap.

Nina saved her difficult chores for this time of the day. They were the things that would be hard to do with a baby crawling underfoot. Henry napped for several hours, so she grabbed all the soiled laundry from the bedrooms and brought them out to the porch.

Using a washboard, a huge metal basin, and water from the pump, Nina scrubbed and rinsed the clothes before she carried them over to the wash line to dry. When she'd first arrived, it hadn't been very stable, but one of the ranch hands had taken a moment to reinforce it with some nails. Now she could hang everything without worrying about clothes falling down the minute she went back into the house.

As she hung up one of her dresses, Mr. Colt came out of the barn, guiding a horse by a lead rope toward the pasture where he typically kept the livestock. She found herself blushing as she took in the gentleness of his touch. Her heart skipped a beat as she stared at him across the yard.

There were moments that she could see that Mr. Colt was a good man. He cared deeply for his ranch, and he had been thoughtful enough to ask for help with Henry instead of giving him to someone else or abandoning him. Sometimes, he wrote notes to her that complimented her cooking or praised her for something she'd done around the house.

As Mr. Colt walked by with the russet-colored horse, Nina admired his wavy blond hair under his hat, as well as tall and lean physique. If Nina were honest with herself, she would admit that Mr. Colt was a very handsome man. He didn't smile often, but when he did, there was something special about his face. Nina noticed some dimples that made his face seem boyish and more approachable.

Nina heaved a sigh, shaking her head to clear it. Nina needed to put the thoughts about Mr. Colt out of her mind. Nothing good would come from pining for him. She lost her head once before when she fell for Nathaniel; she considered where that caused her to end up. *It would never work out,* Nina thought as she hung up one of Sam's work shirts freckled with dirt stains wouldn't come out of the tomato-red cotton no matter how hard she scrubbed.

There's always someone prettier. There is always a Jane that will steal their heart. Sometimes, when images of what happened that day in the meadow in San Antonio haunted Nina's thoughts and dreams, she convinced herself that Jane tempted Nathaniel because Nina was too tall, her eyes were too large, and that, in comparison to her stepsister, she was just plain ugly. *Even absurd, untrue things become believable when you say it to yourself long enough*, she mused, wringing out the cotton until the damp threads groaned.

With her basket empty, Nina returned inside to check on Henry. Sure enough, his eyes were open, and he smiled at her when he noticed she had returned. At least with Henry, it was easy to know that he liked her. She was falling in love with the little boy, just when she feared that she might be unable to love again.

The whole cycle began all over again, where she picked up Henry and brought him to the top of the dresser to be changed. After that it was time to start getting ready for dinner and watch Henry play him until Mr. Colt came in for the day. After supper she might try to embroider in the living room. When Henry was tired, he typically crawled over to be picked up.

Sometimes Nina didn't even bother going all the way up to nursery. She'd rock him in the chair by the oil lamp while Mr. Colt wrote his business expenses and dealings in the other one. When Henry finally fell asleep, she'd excuse them both from the room and put him in his cradle.

The part that came after Henry was asleep for the night was always the same too. Nina would head to her room and prepare for bed. She'd braid her hair and lie under the sheets, staring up at her ceiling.

She ran to Carson City to escape the crippling feeling of being not good enough and alone. Now that she was here, she still felt it choking her. Henry was sweet, and she was glad she was making a difference in his life, but it wasn't enough. All she wanted was just one person to talk to. All she needed was just one friend. As she rolled onto her side and tried not to weep, she feared it would never happen. She would always have no one.

Chapter Seven

A few weeks later, Jack stood in front of the barn, worry furrowing his brow. "It's not looking good," he said as the sun had started to rise, and the sky transformed from dark blue to orange, gold, and pink. "I used to not be able to see the tracks and worksite by the property line, but now I can. They've definitely moved forward."

Sam tried to keep his face neutral as he heard his ranch hands talking before they got to work, but he was just as aware of the encroaching worksite as Jack was.

He didn't consider himself against the railroad. It wasn't like he didn't want things prospering around here, but it had left a path of destruction in its wake. The demolition and explosions ruined the land, rubble landing in farms nearby. People who owned ranches for years were forced to sell their land to make room for all the people who moved west because of the railway. Now the Central Pacific Railroad sought to expand even more.

At first it lay just outside of Carson City at the current train station, and it was easy to ignore. Over the past several months, it crept closer and closer to his ranch, and Sam realized he could no longer deny its path—it loomed in the distance like a thundercloud on a hot day.

If Sam rode one of the horses to the edge of his land, he could see Central Pacific's supplies and where the train tracks abruptly stopped. At the moment, it was just visible on the horizon, but Sam knew it was only a matter of time before it was closer. He knew he probably should have prepared better for that possibility, but he could be driven and stubborn if it meant a thriving ranch.

"I heard they've stopped paying people for their land," Another ranch hand named Jim said with a shake of his head. "They're just taking it and they don't care if you are on the property or not when they burn the house down."

"That sounds like a ghost story a kid would be afraid of," Jack replied with a groan.

Sam didn't want to appear afraid, but he couldn't hide the shudder that coursed through him. Last time Sam visited the general store, he overheard the rumors that the Central Pacific liked to be manipulative to get people to give up their land, but this was a new angle. Were the people who ran the company that greedy that would be willing to harm innocent people? Couldn't they just move the tracks slightly out of the way?

Unfortunately, he knew it wasn't that simple. It cost money to build and lay those tracks and the most direct path cost the least. It seemed that Sam had bad luck because that short, direct route ended up going directly through his land. After all his hard work, they would just blow it up so they could lay their tracks and keep moving.

If that wasn't bad enough, it was hard to get business to come out this far because they were concerned that the ranch wasn't going to last. Several other farms succumbed when the railroad first branched out of Carson City, and many people relocated to other parts of town.

"What do you think, Sam?" Jack said, punching him on the arm and bringing him into the conversation. "You think we're doomed here, or do we keep working until they're at our doorstep?"

Sam set his face into a stern mask before he pretended to knock on an invisible door. He mimed holding a gun and then he kicked the door open, showing Jack and the others that he would defend the property or die trying.

The group of men laughed and understood what he was trying to say completely. "We'll be here with you to scare them off," a third ranch hand named Amos assured with conviction.

They had all worked together for several years and quickly fell into an easy understanding. He started off writing lists for Jack with things to delegate, but their relationship blossomed so that the men seemed to understand and look forward to his miming and gesturing.

There were still times that it was easier to write down what he needed. Today, for example, he needed to go into town and check the price of lumber. One of the old sheds was about to cave in and he wanted wood to build a new one. Jack had a small pad of paper he would hand to Sam inconspicuously if he needed a bit more of an explanation. All Sam had to do was tap the man on shoulder and he'd pull it out.

I'm going into town. Be back later.

Sam hitched the horses and took the half an hour ride to Carson City. When he neared the worksite, he tried to ignore the tense stares of the workers as he passed. No one knew him by name, but it was obvious that they felt like he and the other landowners on this side of town prevented them from getting their job done. The tension was palpable, as though if he got too close, they might want to fight. He did not have the heart to tell them that if he had his way they would never finish.

Once he arrived in town, he made his way to the lumber mill. Sam felt pleasantly surprised to find that the boards he needed for his shed were reasonably priced. With all the railroad work, lumber became scarce and drove prices to unbelievable heights. He bought enough to fill the wagon, trying to picture what he could use the new shed for once he built it. He could move some of the tools he currently had in the horse barn and make more stalls if he did that.

The lumber mill wasn't far from the post office, and it had been several days since he stopped by to check on his mail. He also never formally thanked the postmaster for sending the ad for a governess to his friend in San Antonio. Without them, he'd still be struggling with Henry. Sam couldn't say it, but he still hoped to explain himself best he could.

Sam went to the counter and waved to the postmaster. He gestured in the direction of the post office box before he mimed using a key to unlock it. The postmaster named Charlie was slightly used to his silent antics by now and got up to unlock it for him.

"How's the girl?" he asked as she went over to Sam's mailbox and opened it. "She making things easier for you?" Sam made sure to give an enthusiastic nod as well as a deep bow, removing his hat to show his gratitude. The postmaster looked at him warily before he replied, "Glad to hear it." Sam could swear the man almost stopped himself from chuckling before he returned to his counter.

Sam looked the man square in the eye and wouldn't back down before he checked the box. He'd rather have someone tease him than avoid him all together. A single letter lay inside the box. Pulling it out, Sam wondered if maybe it was the payment he expected from a recent sale, yet the Central Pacific Railway emblem stamped on it caught his eye. Sam swallowed hard as he recalled the conversation he had with his ranch hands earlier. Why did the railroad company write to him? He tore open the letter right there in the post office and began to read.

Dear Mr. Colt,

Greetings and salutations! I am writing to introduce myself and provide an explanation of Central Pacific Railway's expansion plans. As project manager, I am tasked with expanding the railway through the Sierra Nevada in hopes of connecting with the already large and prosperous Union Pacific Railway. In doing so, we can provide people a means to travel long distances in a much shorter time. We are truly doing something special.

Unfortunately, to create new rails to new destinations, there are sometimes setbacks and sacrifices. I'm writing to inform you that your land is currently in the path of where the Central Pacific Railway plans to build. I would like to meet with you to discuss the sale of your land so that we may continue with our build without interruption. If you could kindly reply to this letter so that an agreement can be made, it would be greatly appreciated. I look forward to hearing from you.

Sincerely,

Donald Henderson, Railway Project Manager

Sam scowled at the overly chipper tone of the letter and the way Mr. Henderson made it sound so easy to just sell his land and move. He felt his hackles raise at how presumptuous this man seemed. If he could scream in frustration, he would. He didn't know how long it had taken him to save up for it, or how hard he'd worked to get it even somewhat functioning. To turn his back on the ranch seemed so wasteful, and it felt like giving up. Sam refused to move.

He ripped the envelope and letter into bits, causing the postmaster to look up from sorting mail to see what was going on. Sam stalked over to a waste bin, throwing the remnants of the letter away.

If they really wanted to talk to him, they knew where to find him.

Chapter Eight

The smell of juicy, garlic crusted roast chicken and seasoned vegetables filled the kitchen as Nina pulled the roasting pan from the oven.

"Dinner!" she called, hoping that Mr. Colt could hear her from upstairs. He came in from working and had gone up to change.

As she placed the pan on the table to cool, she looked over at Henry who eyed the steaming food with interest. Nina felt like her inexperience with children made this aspect of being a governess difficult. She wondered if she should try giving him little bits of what she made to see if he could eat more solid food as Mr. Colt came in from the hallway.

He nodded at her as he always did before he gave Henry a gentle brush on the cheek with the back of his knuckles. Nina thought the gesture was sweet and wished to see that side of Mr. Colt more often. Once more, she felt her heart beat faster as she thought about him this way. The way Mr. Colt made her feel sometimes excited her and made her nervous at the same time.

Nina cut them both several slices of meat and spooned the peas and carrots onto two plates. She placed one in front of Mr. Colt before she put the other one in front of her. As it cooled, she began to feed Henry spoonfuls of mashed carrots. Then came the next part of her ritual. She tried to make small talk every night even though it bordered on painful.

"How was your day?" Nina asked. "I saw you went into town." When Sam began to write in his ledger, she waited patiently.

Got lumber for a new shed.

"That's lovely." Nina replied. "I know how badly you want to improve the ranch." Nina watched as he smiled softly. The dimples that she thought so endearing the last time she saw them had returned. Nina thought they made his whole face youthful and handsome.

This was typically where she would leave him alone, taking care of Henry and eating before she cleaned up. Today something motivated Nina to keep talking.

"Do you live far away from your family?" Nina asked. "I assumed you wouldn't need me if they were nearby."

Mr. Colt shook his head and avoided Nina's gaze. She noticed that he often did this when whatever they were talking about wasn't an easy yes or no answer. She didn't want to push things too far, but she was desperate to know as much as she could about him.

So much for keeping him as my employer and not caring about getting to know him. Nina wondered if she told him a little about herself if he would be apt to open up.

Maybe I'll finally get him to speak.

"My stepfamily will probably never leave San Antonio. They love the weather and the river that flows through downtown." Nina noticed that Sam wrote again. He pushed the notebook over to her.

Stepfamily?

Nina noticed that he ignored her question completely, but they began talking about something other than household chores, so she decided to keep going.

Progress! I wonder how much farther we can go?

"Yes, or perhaps adopted family is a better explanation. My parents died in a fire when I was two."

Nina jumped out of her skin when Mr. Colt dropped his fork with a clatter. He stared at her with wide, surprised eyes. Nina's heart beat quickly as she could swear she could see compassion and understanding in his piercing, direct gaze.

Mr. Colt opened his mouth, and Nina felt so hopeful that he was finally going to say something to her. Maybe he'd offer her a word of sympathy, or he'd tell her the struggles that he'd been through. The thought of finally breaking that barrier down made her chest fill with warmth. Her body nearly pulsed with excitement as she waited.

She had to bite her lip and busy herself with feeding Henry when Mr. Colt's expression changed completely. Gone were the king, understanding eyes. Instead, she looked into a crimson face, his lips clamped shut. Nina watched with a breaking heart as he reached for his pencil and wrote something instead.

Sorry for your loss.

"Thank you." The words came out like a hiss. Any louder and Nina worried that her voice would crack. From across the table, she watched Mr. Colt's brow furrow like he hadn't meant to make her upset.

After that moment, she let it go. Nina worried that if she continued to press him for information, he would dislike her even more and ask her to leave. The thought of being fired made her swallow back a cry, yet it was the possibility of leaving Henry that hurt like a blow. Nina had grown attached to the boy after no time at all. She decided to focus on feeding the child and then herself, feeling defeated.

It wasn't until later, when she washed dishes and cleaned up, that something dawned on her. Maybe it wasn't that Mr. Colt disliked her. If he truly felt that way, he wouldn't write nice things when they communicated with the ledger. He wouldn't engage with her at all. Was it possible that Mr. Colt *couldn't* talk and that was why he wrote and used gestures instead?

Nina scrubbed and thought about how the entire time she stayed at the ranch she hadn't heard him hum, say a prayer, or grumble to himself once. Yes, she'd seen him with his ranch hands, but had he said something to make them laugh, or had he done it another way?

She remembered a thought she had when she'd first gotten the governess position. Nina wondered if someone had broken Mr. Colt's heart and that caused him to be silent. Now after his tense reaction to learning about her family, she wondered if a different reason forced his silence—something else entirely.

Chapter Nine

Sam's best horse looked like she limped.

The black and white painted mare was sturdy and well-suited for ranch work, and he hoped to sell her to a man across town that focused just on cattle farming. The horse usually could run faster than the rest, but today Sam instantly noticed her sluggish pace and favoring one side. He felt that something was off when he brought her own to the pasture in the morning, but now, observing her several hours later, she still looked as though something was wrong.

Please don't be lame, Sam fretted as he walked over to her. He slid a halter over her nose and clipped a lead line to it, but not before giving her a gentle scratch behind the ears. *I need this sale to go through.* Now that the railroad continued to drive ranch business away, he needed every bit of money he could get.

The horse didn't seem like she felt any pain, so Sam hoped that maybe there was just something wrong with her shoe. He took a minute to stroke the horse's forehead gently before he carefully guided her toward the barn so he could take a more careful look.

Sam didn't consider himself a farrier, but he knew enough about shoeing horses thanks to all his years as a ranch hand. It was a convenient way to save some money since he could solve most problems himself. As he guided the horse into the stable and clipped her to the set of cross ties, he tried to remember how much the last visit cost him.

He was so deep in thought that he didn't notice Nina and Henry standing at one of the stalls until he went to fetch his tools. Nina wore her brown hair braided down her back and she held Henry close, guiding his hand carefully to rest on a gray gelding's head as it peered over the edge of his stall.

"See, Henry," Nina said in such a soothing tone that Sam stopped in his tracks and stared. "Even though this animal is large, it is still friendly." She helped Henry stroke the horse's mane. "Horses are very sweet once you get to know them."

Sam witnessed Nina's sweet and gentle way with the baby countless times since her arrival but seeing her act so kind and attentive toward one of his horses made his heart sing even more. He felt the same way about all his animals on the ranch.

Each one has a unique personality, Sam mused, *and all are good natured if you earn their trust.*

Sam wondered if he just discovered something else that he may have in common with Nina, and he put his tools down and decided to try to make conversation in his own way.

Nina met his eye as he approached, turning so that Henry could no longer touch the horse even though he held his hand out and squirmed.

"Hello, Mr. Colt," Nina said indifferently, like she wasn't expecting him to interact with her. "I thought that was you. I hope we aren't in the way."

Sam waved before he pointed at the horse, making a gesture like he was holding reins. He wanted to know if she rode horses back in San Antonio, but he didn't have his notebook with him.

Nina looked thoroughly confused at first, and Sam could see by the look on her face that she couldn't understand why he wouldn't just tell her what he was trying to say. *Please bear with me.* Sam thought in her direction. *I want to do more than just give you orders and leave.*

Sam thought about what he could do to get her to understand. He held up a finger as he ran back to where he kept his bridles and saddles in a storage room in the corner of the barn. He pulled the closest leather bridle off a hook and dashed back to her. He held it up before he pointed at the horse one more time.

He felt as though he could dance when understanding finally flashed across Nina's face. "Oh, you are asking if I ride," Nina said with a nod, "I do. My stepparents had a team of horses and my best friend growing up had many horses. We rode together often," her voice cracked.

Sam watched as Nina's face fell as she mentioned her friend. She looked sad, almost like she mourned them. Pity moved his heart as he wondered what happened to them. Sam didn't want to see her sad and he thought about what he could do to make the expression disappear from her face. Maybe if Nina could ride the horse, it could make her happy again.

Sam didn't know what caused him to act, but he closed the space between them. He planned to take Henry from her and hand her the bridle to tell her what he meant. Sam reached out and gently put a hand on her elbow to get her attention.

It was as if his hand were a smoldering brand, burning her delicate skin. Nina shrunk away from him, taking a step back so that his hand hung in the air. Her face pale, horror filled her eyes as she clutched little Henry tightly against her chest.

"Please don't," Her voice sounded distant, as if she were in a trance, and she continued to back away from him. "I'm...I'm sorry." Then she turned and ran past the horse still standing in the cross ties and out of the stables.

Sam stared after her, letting the bridle slide from his hand and onto the floor. He had been so excited and hopeful to potentially bond over something, and Nina fled from him.

Had something happened to Nina to cause her to behave this way? Or was merely the same story—his muteness made him a freak, an abnormality, and she couldn't stand to be close to him? She seemed so disgusted she ran away. Sam guessed he should have expected it, but it still hurt just the same.

Chapter Ten

Nina slammed the front door behind her, still holding Henry as she rested her back against it. As she caught her breath, her mind raced over what just unfolded. Mr. Colt touched her, and she ran away. She didn't know if she should laugh or cry at her behavior—behavior that was both confusing and embarrassing.

Was that an overreaction?

When Henry made a frustrated noise and tried to wriggle free from her arms, Nina temporarily returned to the present. She needed to look after Henry; she didn't have time to dwell on what happened in the stable.

"Lunch?" Nina asked as she shook her head, trying to clear it. She carried Henry to the kitchen and placed him in his highchair. "I think we're going to try a bit of real food with your mashed vegetables today."

As Nina went to fetch everything for them to eat, her mind wandered once more to her interaction with Mr. Colt. She wasn't afraid of him; he certainly wasn't the most outgoing, but he wasn't cruel.

She cut herself a few pieces of bread that she topped with butter before she broke part of one into pieces and placed it on Henry's highchair for him to try. Nina took a bite of her own piece of bread as she remembered how she felt on the crowded train to Carson City.

Every time her elbows bumped into another passenger, regardless of whether they were a man or a woman, discomfort writhed beneath her skin. Nina thought that maybe her anxiety stemmed from leaving home and going somewhere unknown, but now she wasn't so sure.

Nina mulled over her brief courtship with Nathaniel. She could see him standing beside her at a town potluck where all the families gathered to eat and socialize. She wrenched her eyes shut as she recalled the way he grasped onto her arm and guided her to where her stepfamily found a table.

At the time Nina thought him eager to say hello to her family, but now she could only see Jane standing there, taking him in with wide, enraptured eyes.

Nina felt her eyes welling with tears as she watched Henry taste the bread because she knew her outburst with Mr. Colt stemmed from more than just Nathaniel guiding her by the arm once. She fled from San Antonio to avoid heartbreak, and over the course of her journey, she came to fear closeness and intimacy. If Nina allowed herself to grow close to someone, she let herself become vulnerable to getting hurt. Maybe she *wanted* Mr. Colt to dislike her—that way, her heart would remain hole when he found true love with someone else.

Yet in her heart, she knew that wasn't true; she would try so hard to talk with him if she hoped he would find love with another.

Oh, what am I to do about Mr. Colt, she fretted to herself. He had every reason to fire her and hire a new governess based on how she just behaved. It wasn't personal, but she was just so surprised by his touch that she didn't know what to do.

Nina fed Henry his mashed sweet potatoes after he finished his bread, and once she cleaned him up and got him ready for nap, her guilt began to eat away at her, twisting her stomach into knots. Mr. Colt deserved an apology.

He went out of his way to say or do something besides telling her what needed to get done around the house. Sure, he didn't say it out loud, but he still tried to communicate with her, and she didn't want him never to do so again. The realization surprised her like someone dumping a bucket of cold water over her head.

As soon as Henry fell asleep, Nina put him down in his crib and forced herself to go find Mr. Colt. She trembled as she searched for him around the ranch. She finally found him building a frame for his new shed. His foreman Jack noticed her approach as he helped Mr. Colt hold two boards together that would become part of the wall.

Jack cleared his throat and motioned over to Nina. "I think Nina might want to talk to you." He gave Nina a soft look that almost looked like he begged for her patience, like he understood her plight. Did Mr. Colt somehow explain what happened between them? She felt embarrassed and almost entertained the idea of running back into the house again. She shifted her weight from side to side as she waited for what would happen next.

Jack left them alone. Nina stood there awkwardly for a moment, trying to figure out what to say. Mr. Colt continued to work while he waited for her to make her move. Eventually, Nina let out a shaky breath and took a few steps closer.

"I wanted to apologize about my behavior in the stable," Nina began in a trembling voice. "It had nothing to do with you. I guess I'm just not used to being touched." She hoped the explanation didn't sound as flimsy as it felt.

Sam nodded as he continued to work, and Nina assumed that it was his silent way of accepting her apology. She searched his face to see if he would betray any hint of his inner thoughts, yet his expression remained inscrutable. He did not look upset, but he didn't look at her with the soft eyes he had for her earlier when she showed the horse to Henry.

His face was blank, and Nina felt surprised to discover that it made her feel disappointed.

I never realized how much I longed for his acceptance and approval.

She wished that she thought to bring out his notebook so that he could write her a reply and she wouldn't have to guess at his thoughts.

Deciding it better to not push the issue, she excused herself and let Mr. Colt and Jack get back to work. Nina tried to feel better about the situation as she walked back toward the house, but as she felt her eyes blinding with tears, she struggled to understand why.

Chapter Eleven

"You got to tell her, Sam."

The workday came to a close, and Amos and Jim already headed home for the day. Jack stood out by the water pump as Sam rinsed his hands. Several days passed since he and Nina experienced their awkward encounter in the stables. Any communication that wasn't clarification of his daily tasks ceased, and even though Sam tried to be at peace with it, his face must have betrayed him. Jack wasn't usually one to talk about personal matters, but concern hardened his normally jovial features.

"She's got the wrong idea about you," Jack said. "I'm sure if she knew the reason why you don't talk, she'd understand."

Jack made it sound so easy. *What should I do, write my feelings and life story in the ledger for her to read like some sad novel*, he mused bitterly. He probably needed a whole notebook just to explain everything that happened and how it made him feel. There was a part of him that he wasn't sure was bitter about or afraid of putting himself in such a vulnerable position. What if he poured his feelings out for her and she still didn't understand? What if she still shied away from him? It was just easier to be closed off; there were less opportunities for pain.

Sam rolled his eyes and shrugged. Of course, he should tell her. Nina was sweet, and she would probably find a way to help him or make things easier around the house, even if she didn't understand completely. He just didn't know how to start the conversation.

Jack handed Sam his tiny memo pad and the stub of a pencil. Clearly, he was not happy with Sam's response. Sam heaved a sigh before he began to write.

I will. I'm not ready yet.

"You're going to make it worse the longer you wait," Jack replied, before he took the pad back and put it in his work shirt pocket. "I'm going home. I'll see you in the morning."

Sam waved and went into the house for dinner. As always, the succulent aroma of supper hit him in the gut when he walked through the door. *You're going to make it worse the longer you wait.* He tried to ignore the guilt that Jack inspired in him as he made his way down the hallway and into the kitchen.

Henry clapped and babbled at the sight of him, temporarily lifting Sam from his stupor. Henry held a tender place in Sam's heart, more than he realized before. Sam just wasn't sure how to look after him. Unfortunately, it didn't take long for him to go right back to feeling sorry for himself.

Nina placed a bowl of stew in front of him and didn't say a word. Typically, she gave a brief explanation of what she made or gave him an overview of her chores from the day. Nina didn't even ask him how his day was. He realized with a sense of dread that the situation was worse than he thought if she refused to speak. If it weren't for Henry taking breaks from cooing and singing to eat, Sam wouldn't even have known she was there. Her silence made the house feel barren and lonely, as if she were a ghost.

Defeated, he ate his fill and excused himself. Normally he sat in the living room while he kept track of any sales made or expenses incurred on the ranch that day, but he took the ledger upstairs with him instead. The stew Nina made tasted great at first, but now it was like a rock in his stomach and as soon as he finished documenting the wages he paid Jack and the others, he laid down to sleep. He tried to shut his eyes, the sun barely touching the horizon.

Several hours later, the faint sounds of Henry's cries woke him. It was pitch black outside his window, so Sam wasn't sure how much time passed since he fell asleep. The poor child sounded absolutely miserable. Sam hadn't heard Henry cry like that since before Nina arrived.

Was Nina still asleep? Sam didn't want to assume the worst, but she was always so good about minding Henry; the continued wails made him worry that something was wrong. He rolled out of bed and trudged into the hallway to find out what was happening.

The nursery stood at the end of the hall, and when Sam opened the door, the cries intensified. Sam expected to see the child sitting in his crib with tears streaming down his face but a sight he wasn't prepared for greeted. In the soft, delicate light of the oil lamp, Nina stood in the middle of the room, barefoot and in her nightgown, as she held Henry and tried to rock him.

Heavy bags tugged at Nina's large eyes, desperation and exhaustion muddying their normally brilliant hazel hue. A thin shawl draped over her shoulders as she bounced and soothed the child. The sight of her, her slight frame wrapped in thin, gauzy fabric, made Sam hyper aware that he wore just his night shirt as well. He felt vulnerable and intimate at the same time. Little Henry clutched onto Nina tightly, his little face screwed up like he was in pain. The sight of the sweet, happy child in such anguish squeezed Sam's heart.

"Sorry if we disturbed you," Nina apologized, looking down at Henry as she shifted her weight from one hip to the other. She looked exhausted, like she tried every method to get the child to quiet yet to no avail. "I think he's cutting a new tooth."

Sam shook his head and gestured dismissively. He tried to show her that it was no trouble as he crossed the room. If he could speak, he would tell Nina that he struggled with sleep even when Henry slept soundly. Instead, he reached out his careworn hands, offering to take Henry for a while. Sam expected Nina to refuse or back away again, but she gladly accepted and passed the child off. Sam tried to hide his disappointment when Henry took a breath and proceeded to scream louder.

He paced the room, patting Henry's back gently. Sam stroked the babe's blond hair behind his ear, a trick he learned before he hired Nina, but Henry tried to pry his hand away. Sam held him tighter, rocking with him in the chair. He began to empathize with Nina's palpable exhaustion. He had been at it for a lot less time and felt equally as hopeless. Out of options, he simply let Henry be on the nursery floor.

"I have an idea," Nina offered. "If it doesn't make you uncomfortable." When Sam held her gaze and gave a shallow nod, she continued. "I could sing."

Since nothing else seemed to work, Sam couldn't see the harm in trying. He gestured for her to begin. He also tried to not look overly eager about hearing her sing. He wanted to learn as much as he could about Nina, and this was his chance. Sam watched as she exhaled and leaned against the window. The moonlight shone in and illuminated her face like an otherworldly spirit. Nina shut her eyes and began to sing.

The day is done,

It's time to rest like the sun

Close your eyes

No more cries

I am here

Have no fear.

I will be here when you wake

Another day together we will make

My love for you will always be

Burning bright and tenderly

Nina sang the song three times, her voice light and sweet, making his chest shake as he fought against a memory. One of his younger sister Jenny sitting beside him at church, her voice lilting toward the rafters. He never realized how much he missed her singing until he heard someone else's voice.

During the third time refrain, Sam felt Henry's little body finally grow heavy and when he peered down at the little boy, his eyes shut at last. It was as if Sam gazed upon a completely different child, one at peace.

When Nina sang the final note of the lullaby, she met Sam's gaze across the room. Nina looked like she could have slumped to the floor with relief. Sam carefully adjusted Henry's sleeping body to give her a soft round of applause.

"I don't know why I didn't think to try it earlier," Nina whispered. "It's a song I remember my mother singing." She looked away, as if lost in a distant, pleasant reverie. "It's the only memory I have of her."

Sam wished he could tell her how he tried to forget what his mother looked like; forgetting made his grief tolerable in times of struggle. He didn't want to dwell on the negative. He felt getting Henry to finally fall asleep was a victory, so he tried to focus on the good.

Nina looked like a nymph in the near darkness, the moonlight casting a radiant glow on her high cheekbones. Even though he never said anything to her, he felt closer to her than ever before. They commiserated over poor Henry's discomfort and she shared more of her past with him through song.

Sam knew he needed to stir, the morning would arrive far too quickly, but he was rooted to his spot in the rocking chair. If he pretended and forgot the circumstances, he could see Nina and Henry as his makeshift family. Sam could imagine working together with Nina to raise Henry. He could see them getting along perfectly if only he could speak. As he sat there, staring at Nina with soft warm eyes, he felt motivated to try for the first time in ages.

Chapter Twelve

The next morning came far too quickly. Nina cocooned herself under the sheet once she finally gotten into bed. The soft, warm sanctuary easily lulled her to sleep. Now the rooster call tried to wake her; the shrill, incessant greeting from reality jarred her spirit, and her body only wanted to keep resting.

Unfortunately, there was too much to do. Mr. Colt's breakfast needed to be made, there would be a to-do list to complete, and all too soon, little Henry would wake and need food. Nina smashed her lips together to beat back the groan that wanted to escape her lips as she forced herself to get out of her blanket bliss and get up for the day.

Still groggy, she rifled through her dresser until she found a slate blue dress to wear. She hastily gazed at her bloodshot eyes in the mirror as she fixed her braid. Nina heard that sleepless nights and babies were often a common thing, but she was not prepared for how much it would affect her. Dark circles hung from her eyes as angry red lines branched and twisted around her hazel irises. She looked as bad as she felt.

Nina hated to see Henry suffer. He was normally an adorable bundle of joy. Sometimes all she had to do was make an excited face and he would squeal with uncontrollable laughter. To see Henry be so inconsolable was heart wrenching, and she knew that being a governess wasn't always going to be cuddles and fun. What were babies but miniature people, and they had emotions just like she did.

It was more than Henry's pain that gave her pause as she fastened her boots. After he fell asleep, his breaths deep like a hibernating animal, she and Mr. Colt sat there in silence, as still as a tomb.

Eventually, Mr. Colt stood up, creeping like a person walking on eggshells over to Henry's cradle. Nina watched, holding her breath to the point that her chest hurt. She feared that one sudden move or noise would wake the child and they must start all over again. Nina wasn't sure if she could hold back the tears that were threatening to spill from her eyes before Mr. Colt came in to help.

Mr. Colt gently placed Henry in his cradle and crept away. When the child rolled onto his stomach, but didn't make a peep, Nina let out the shaky breath she held in. She nearly slumped to the ground with exhaustion.

Nina reeled when instead of leaving, Mr. Colt strode over to her, clapping his hands in silent applause once more. She wasn't sure if he was congratulating her for finally getting Henry to fall asleep or complimenting her song, but her stomach flipped and danced as though the mere gesture made her tumble to the floor in a swoon. The excitement of being so near him sent her pulse galloping, yet crippling fear quickly overtook her elation as she worried that he would put his hands on her.

Her mind flashed to Nathaniel in the woods with Jane. Someone she thought she loved once held all of her trust and faith; if someone she knew so intimately could be so cruel, what could a veritable stranger do?

What once felt like joy soon soured to nausea. Nina knew he wasn't going to hurt her, but when Mr. Colt reached out like he might place his hands over hers, she quickly moved away from the window and toward the door. It was a strange sensation that she did not expect to feel after sharing such an important moment with him.

"It's late," she said hastily, holding her hands out to stop him if he tried to get close to her again. "The sun will rise before we know it. We should sleep." Mr. Colt frowned glumly, as though he didn't understand, and Nina could see his confusion over her behavior etched on his face. What he did not know was that Nina was not entirely sure what transpired herself. "Thank you for your help."

A soft smile quickly transformed Mr. Colt's sulking face, and he offered his customary shallow nod to express his appreciation. Nina feared she would lose her nerve if she lingered any longer, so she quickly made her exit and flung herself onto her bed.

She fell asleep before could lose herself in her thoughts. Now, as she made her way down the stairs and toward the kitchen, she couldn't stop fretting over what happened after they had put Henry to sleep.

Henry was the only person whose touch didn't make her skin crawl. Nina tried to pinpoint the exact moment or event that had caused this change, and she couldn't think of any violent event. She only shared very casual touches with Nathaniel over the years.

Nina breezed into the kitchen, prepared to get out the skillet and start melting a bit of butter in it, when she froze by the kitchen table. There was a neat pile of scrambled eggs with a little bit of cheese melted over top. Beside it was a large hunk of bread with a bit of butter smeared across the soft, pillowy crust. Nina used her index finger to poke the eggs and while they weren't piping hot, they were still warm, like they hadn't been made long ago.

How long have I been asleep?

Mr. Colt's ledger lay open next to the plate. Nina sat down in a rush, nearly losing her balance in the chair, burning to know what he wrote and why he made her breakfast after she shied away from him again.

Seemed like you needed to sleep.

Do what you can today.

As Nina tucked into the eggs and reached for the hunk of bread that Mr. Colt left for her, she felt grateful that he didn't seem to hold a grudge against her. Gratitude washed over her for Mr. Colt's cooking ability as she shut her eyes and savored the taste of the butter and cheese.

It tasted like heaven.

***

"Say 'hello,' Henry,"

A short while later, Nina woke Henry up and prepared his breakfast. Even though Mr. Colt was kind enough to not give her anything specific to work on, Nina knew that she should work on the kitchen. He was kind enough to make her breakfast but left behind all the mess. Dishes were usually her responsibility, and allowed her precious time to think things over, but her mind wasn't ready for more insecurities or soul searching.

Still feeling tired, she took Henry into the living room and sat with him on the floor. She heard some of Henry's babblings sounding very close to real words and she felt determined to get him to say them for real. Nina felt so lonely from the lack of conversation with Mr. Colt that she was compelled to have at least *someone* who could talk to her. The dishes and counters could wait.

"Say 'hello,' Henry," Nina repeated patiently. "Hello."

Henry scrunched his eyes up at her and wrinkled his nose. "'Lo. 'Lo."

Nina sucked the air out of the room at the sound with an exhilarated gasp, her excitement hard to contain. "Good boy Henry! Hello!"

The child giggled and flapped his arms with pride. "'Lo!"

Nina looked around, trying to see what else she could get him to say. She picked up a wooden toy train and a very sad looking doll with yarn for hair and held them in front of him. "Henry, do you want to play with one of these?" She held them just out of reach, so he'd have to pick. "Which one do you want to play with?"

Henry reached out for both toys, grunting with effort since they were just out of his reach. "Want," he repeated, his little face looking at her in confusion, like he didn't understand why she was making him work so hard. "Want!"

Nina squealed as she handed Henry the train, scooping him into her arms for a tight squeeze. Henry resumed giggling, but Nina found herself consumed with emotion at how the little boy mimicked her and communicated his needs.

As she sat there hugging Henry, a thought passed through Nina's mind. In the end, Henry told her what he wanted. He used a few words and he got what he needed in the end. Nina knew the more words he learned, the easier it would be. It suddenly reminded her of Mr. Colt, his notebook, and the way he interacted with her.

Suddenly, her thoughts raced back to the nursery after Henry gave in to exhaustion the night before. Mr. Colt could have whispered to her, but he silently clapped to congratulate her instead. Nina recalled the day he met her at the train station, and how he pointed at things to get his point across. It would have been so much easier to bark an order, but he didn't.

I don't think he's silent by choice.

The thought was a slap of a realization. Now that she lived at the ranch for some time and gotten to know Mr. Colt better, the opportunity for conversation should have come up. Her interactions with Mr. Colt were like holding something out of Henry's reach; eventually, the baby got to the point where he made it clear that he wanted the toys. If Mr. Colt really wanted to tell her something without his notebook, he would have by now.

What could have made that happen? Nina thought as she cleaned up the toys and carried Henry toward the kitchen. *Was he born without the ability to speak or injured when he was younger? Is it possible that I could help?*

Perhaps it was the elation of getting Henry to use words, but Nina wondered if she could encourage Mr. Colt to speak as well. *Maybe I could start off small with basic words or phrases. He'd still need the ledger for his lists or long thoughts, but it could make all our lives easier.*

Nina began to imagine what it might be like to talk to Mr. Colt about her past and her troubles. Beyond Hamish, Jane, and Nathaniel, no one in the world knew the real reason why she left San Antonio. It would probably feel good to talk about it; it might make the aching in her chest finally fade away. Maybe he'd tell her some of the things he kept locked inside as well; they could bond over their struggles, troubles, and triumphs. She placed Henry on the floor and started cleaning the dishes, hoping that by working with Mr. Colt, maybe she wouldn't be nervous around him anymore.

"I do love Nina, she's a breath of fresh air, not many girls are like her."

The cast iron pan in slipped out of Nina's soapy hands and clattered to the floor. Startled, Henry began to wail. Nina knew that she should pick him up and comfort him, but all she could see was Nathaniel standing hauntingly close to Jane, his work shirt brushing against her dress as they met in the woods. She felt as though someone tore a fresh wound into her chest as water dripped off her fingers and onto the dry floorboards.

Nathaniel said those things because I wasn't pretty enough. Mr. Colt would never want to spend more time with me, Nina despaired, *how can I be so foolish?*

Little Henry took a gasping breath as he continued to cry on the floor. Nina shook her head and finally went to him, picking him up and holding him close. As she pecked his blond head, she recalled that being Henry's governess was her top priority. Anything else would just be a waste of time.

Chapter Thirteen

Say something to her. It doesn't have to be much, but just say something.

Sam felt compelled to communicate with Nina as if insects danced across his skin. He wanted to tell her that he appreciated her hard work; he wanted to explain how the flashbacks of seeing his house burn to the ground left him silent and stagnant, but no matter how hard he tried, the words wouldn't come.

He could be in the middle of a job and he'd smell smoke, or wake in the middle of the night hearing his sister's shrieks, and his heart would stop. His trauma and his silence made him frustrated beyond all reason.

Blast this stupid tongue, he thought to himself as he watched out of the corner of his eye while Nina sat beside him, Henry in her lap. *The rest of my body works fine.* That was why Sam was convinced it was a punishment for not saving his family from the fire; the rest of his body and mind were perfectly healthy.

They sat in the living room after supper, Sam writing his business dealings and expenses while Henry played or listened to Nina read—their nightly ritual. Normally, the flickering light of the oil lamp would lull Sam into near trancelike state that he hoped would help him sleep like a baby. Unfortunately, he always resumed his fitful tossing and turning the moment he laid his head on the pillow.

Tonight, his nerves already roiled and writhed before he even felt close to tired. The young woman sitting beside him enamored and intrigued him beyond all explanation. When he struggled to fall asleep at night, Sam often revisited the moment he first set eyes on her when he picked her up from the train station. He could see her large doe-like eyes, staring up at him, trying to figure him out.

Her natural, unconventional beauty captivated him at first, but now all aspects of her utterly entranced him. He wasn't sure when the shift took place, yet now it was all that he could think about.

Sam couldn't believe how well she took care of Henry, her attentiveness beyond the duties of a simple governess. Nina sewed a sort of papoose out of some fabric scraps and wore Henry on her back as she worked. Whether she hung laundry on the line, scoured pots and pans in the kitchen, or swept the hallway floor, she always had the boy with her.

Nina sang sweet songs to him like a songbird or would tell him stories and Sam would watch the child grin and laugh. Sam got the impression that Henry was as much a source of comfort to Nina as she was for him.

Nina and Henry's relationship grew like that of a mother and son, and if Sam thought about it too much or too deeply, he nearly wept tears of joy. Their bond reminded him of his own mother, her tender-hearted care of him and his sister Jenny; it made him homesick.

Something had changed; a quiet companionship bloomed between the three of them. Occasionally, Henry would do something new or sweet, and Sam and Nina would lock eyes. Sam's heart would nearly burst with joy. Sam dared believe that they almost seemed like a family. He couldn't remember the last time he felt so secure and serene.

Nina was graceful as she looked after Henry and made Sam's house a home. It was beyond how she'd cleaned and decorated; the house felt warm and full with her presence. Sam could see the adoration she carried for Henry plainly written on her face when she would sit on the living room floor and play with him or the little one would give into slumber in her arms.

In these moments, Sam yearned above all else to tell her how lovely she was and how much he appreciated her, but no matter how hard he tried, the words would never reach his lips. Even writing them had seemed too much. He worried that his depth of emotion would make Nina uncomfortable or even frighten, and he didn't want to ruin their delicate, fledgling bliss.

"Henry, do you want to hear a story from the Bible?" Nina's soothing and sweet voice brought Sam back to the present. She rose from her seat and picked up the child from the floor.

"Want. Want." Henry replied, nodding vigorously.

Every time Henry said a word, Sam nearly blubbered like a baby with pride. Henry learned and gained so much by having Nina in his life. He said nearly a dozen words now and Sam suspected there would soon be many, many more. If only Sam could discover the secret of being able to form the sounds and syllables like Henry—everything would be much simpler.

Nina brought the child onto the chair with her and reached for the worn leather Bible that lay on the table next to Sam. He kept the careworn book in his room for years, but he seldom looked at it. He was more than happy to bring it down to Nina when she asked for it shortly after she moved in.

"Let's read about how David used the power of God to defeat Goliath," Nina said as she thumbed to the correct book and verse. "Did you know that he was little like you, but he grew into a king? Did you know that Jesus came from his family line?"

All the while, Sam pretended to keep track of how many foals he had and how many would be ready for sale once he weaned them. Instead, he doodled twists and loops on his paper so that she wouldn't realize he took in every word she said like a drought-ridden field in the first spring rain. Sam peered from his notebook to see Henry snuggling into her as she told the story of the shepherd boy who, with his faith, slayed a giant.

"'You come against me with sword and spear and javelin, but I come against you in the name of the Lord Almighty, the God of the armies of Israel, whom you have defied.'" Nina read aloud.

Sam recognized with the story, but Nina read it in such a way that was rich and exciting. Both he and Henry clung to her every word. Sam began to fear that he wasn't merely intrigued by Nina, but completely and utterly in love with her.

When the Hebrews won and the Philistines ran for their lives, Nina closed the Bible and returned it to its spot on the table. Henry wasn't asleep yet, but his eyes grew hooded and heavy like it would not be long until he succumbed to slumber.

"All right, Henry, time for bed," she said softly like the sound would lull him to sleep quicker. "Goodnight, Mr. Colt."

Sam smiled and gave both a friendly wave before he resolved to actually do his work instead of focusing on Nina. Without any distractions, he quickly made his notes for the day. Snapping the notebook shut, he extinguished the lantern and made his way toward the stairwell. He hoped that sleep would come easier tonight, but he his hopes weren't high.

He was about halfway up the staircase when a noise caused him to stop cold in his tracks. Heaving breaths and crying were coming from one of the bedrooms, and Sam feared that Henry struggled to fall asleep again. The pain written on his little face the last time made Sam feel like he'd been stabbed in the heart, and he didn't want to see Nina struggle again either. He all but ran up the stairs and toward the direction of the noise.

Fully prepared to run into the bedroom and do whatever he needed to stop Henry's discomfort, he did not expect the scene that unfolded before his eyes. Sam grasped onto the door frame to stop from making things worse with his dramatic entrance.

Heart slamming against his chest, Sam took in the sight of Henry sitting in his cradle watching Nina. It wasn't his cries that made Sam come running, but hers.

She leaned against the windows, her face buried in her hands. Nina sobbed so hard that she struggled to catch her breath. The sight wrecked Sam, as if he walked into a waking nightmare.

What could have possibly happened to cause this? She just seemed so happy.

Sam wanted to hold her and stop the violent way her body racked, but she flinched and shied away from him even when she wasn't distraught. If touched her while she was vulnerable, he'd probably scare her off for good.

I wouldn't be able to say anything to comfort her anyway.

When Nina first arrived, Sam observed how Nina's smile at times seemed plastered on. He assumed it was his fault, that she didn't understand why he didn't speak. Lately, their interactions improved; the farmhouse began to feel like a home. Perhaps Nina became more skilled at hiding her true feelings, more than he gave her credit for. Sam felt desperate to know what would make her cry as though she would never know happiness again.

Over in his cradle, Henry finally noticed Sam standing in the doorway. His tiny hands reached out to him. Sam shook his head, not wanting to upset Nina if she knew he stared at her, watching her be overcome with emotion like a fool.

"Help. Help. *Help!*" Henry demanded before his little eyes welled up with tears and he too began crying. Sam let out a huffy sigh. So much for not embarrassing himself or Nina.

Things were probably about to go from bad to worse.

Assuming that Henry was calling out to her for attention, Nina pushed off from the windowsill, using her sleeve to wipe at her eyes. It took her a minute to realize that Sam stood just outside the room. She then realized that Sam probably saw more than she wanted, the moonlight just bright enough to make out the crimson of her cheeks. Sam felt like he betrayed her trust, the emotion hitting him in the gut like a blow.

"Mr. Colt," she sniffed, voice still trembling and eyes still shining with tears. "I'm so sorry if I disturbed you."

Sam held up a hand to stop her from apologizing. He would have come to see what was wrong even if he had been trying to sleep. He shook his head sternly so she'd know it wasn't necessary, but he tried to look into her eyes as deeply as he could to make her understand that she didn't have say anything. She owed him no explanation.

"Help. Help." Henry's voice was a sad whine. Sam stepped into the room and scooped the boy into his arms, drawing him close to his body. He could feel Nina's eyes still on him, still trying to figure out how long he'd been standing in the doorway, waiting to see what he would do next.

It's okay, little one. Sam thought as he rocked back and forth on his feet, hoping that he could help Henry feel secure.

When that didn't work, he paced the room, bouncing him gently. *You are safe with me, I promise.*

It wasn't long before Henry's little body felt heavy in his arms. All the worry and self-doubt he felt earlier evaporated at the sign of success. Sam turned to show Nina as he couldn't see the child's face that was resting against his chest. He wanted confirmation to make sure he'd really done it.

"He's asleep," Nina murmured softly.

Pride swelled in Sam's chest. *I comforted Henry. I'm so happy I could do a jig!*

He comforted Henry on his own. There were so many nights where he tried and failed before Nina's arrival, making him feel guilty and unfit to be a caregiver. Sam wondered if this meant that Henry was more comfortable around him, and it nearly made him forget why he came running in the first place.

Nina used her sleeve to wipe her tears away one more time before she stepped closer to the cradle. "He sleeps best on his stomach."

Carefully, as though Henry was a porcelain doll, Sam set him down in his cradle. He was thankful for the advice, especially if it would keep the child from waking up. He and Nina stood there with bated breath, hoping that the boy would stay asleep before they took a collective sigh of relief.

"Thank you," Nina said, suddenly backing toward the doorway. "For helping with him. I..."

Sam waited to see if she would explain why she was so upset. He couldn't say anything to make it better, but maybe just having a set of ears could help her.

I will do anything I can to make you happy again. I promise.

Instead, her brow crumpled like she was fighting back a sob. It was the opposite of what Sam expected to happen. He watched with wide eyes as she turned and ran down the hallway.

The door to her room slammed like it might break off the hinges.

Chapter Fourteen

"Nina Mason, what has gotten into you?"

Nina brushed her hair furiously as she prepared for her day. She tore at the knots like they were the source of her problems, when in reality, it was her unquiet mind that gave her trouble.

"You confronted Jane about her affair with Nathaniel. You made the decision to come here for a fresh start. When did you become so weak?" She demanded of herself.

Nina gritted her teeth when the brush got snagged in a large snarl, a sharp pain tugging and pulling at her scalp. She was so upset after Mr. Colt saw her crying that she didn't braid her hair before sobbing herself to sleep. Now she paid for it.

Nina felt like a failure. Yes, she loved Henry so much, but taking care of him was hard sometimes. There were just so many things he needed and while he was starting to be able to communicate what he wanted, there were still times when Nina struggled. The hours were long and left her body weary, leaving Nina wondering if her duties were more than she could handle.

It was more than struggling with her governess duties. Nina felt so pitifully alone that she felt like the hole that Jane and Nathaniel ripped into her heart continued to reopen, festering instead of healing. It had been over a month since she left San Antonio, and she didn't know a single person other than Mr. Colt and he didn't speak to her, so she felt like it didn't count. Her emotions weighed her down and added to her exhaustion.

"Why can't you just tell him about your insecurities?" Nina asked scolded herself. She raked through her hair in an attempt to secure a new braid. "At least he could write you an explanation for his behavior."

As Nina pulled on a hunter green calico dress and sat on the edge of her bed to tie her shoes, she tried to tell herself that things could be worse. Mr. Colt was generous and had allowed her to take over the decorating of the house. Henry was sweet and seemed to love her. It was more than she would ever have if she had stayed home.

Perhaps I need to force myself to take more chances. Maybe I should ask to go into town or go to church so I can meet other people. She needed to do something to lift her spirits.

It would be nice to know some other women. Nina hadn't been formally introduced to the women who gave Henry the hand-me-downs and she wanted to thank them. Maybe she would have to find a way to change that.

Nina felt heavy as she walked toward Henry's nursery. It was though she dragged a locomotive behind her. She didn't typically drink coffee, but after the restless and emotional night she had, she desperately needed it.

"Good morning, Henry," Nina called as she opened the door. "I hope you slept better than I did."

Nina shut her eyes as she pictured Mr. Colt holding Henry in his arms and the child drifting off to sleep. If she hadn't been embarrassed to know he'd found her crying like a baby, she would have been awestruck by the scene. He was so soft and gentle; the memory of it stirred something warm in her chest, something that filled her with a little bit of hope when she otherwise felt like she had none.

She suddenly wondered how well Mr. Colt slept. Nina feared that he assumed she was upset with him, and she supposed in a way that she was. It wasn't anything he did, exactly, just the stagnant, crippling silence that made her feel so lonely. The idea that he might also feel exhausted from lack of sleep gave her an idea.

Scooping Henry up and dressing him for the day, she quickly bounded down the stairs and into the kitchen. It was later than she normally made breakfast and wondered if Mr. Colt already made something for himself to eat. Sure enough, his plate lay at its usual spot on the counter, a light film of butter crystallizing on its surface. There was no ledger on the table, and no plate of food for her, which made the warmth that Nina felt earlier fade like a snuffed candle.

He must be upset with me, she fretted as she placed Henry in his highchair and figured out what to do next. *I suppose I don't blame him.*

Nina took care of Henry first, taking out one of his mason jars of food and spooning it into his mouth. When he seemed satisfied, she made herself a fried egg paired with a biscuit that she made for dinner a few days earlier. Then she used one of the chairs to climb on so she could rummage through some of the cabinets that weren't easy to reach.

Inside she found a cold stainless-steel coffeepot. She placed it on the stove before she dug through the pantry, taking a moment to smell the fragrant coffee beans when she found the bag. Henry watched with curiosity from his highchair as she ground the beans and began to brew them.

"I'm making a peace offering," Nina attempted to explain to the child. "We're going to pay a visit to Mr. Colt and his ranch hands." She wanted Mr. Colt to know that she wasn't upset with him. Nina also needed to make an effort to not feel so lonely and right now the ranch hands were her only options.

Nina put Henry inside the carrier she had created for him and put him onto her back before she put mugs, the coffee pot, sugar, and a bit of cream on a tray. She carefully carried it down the hall, out the front door, and in the direction of where Mr. Colt and his men worked. It was heavy and she resolved to not drop it.

It was late morning, but it was nearly July, so the sun still beat down on Nina's head as she placed the tray on the porch and went to get the attention of the closest ranch hand. There were three of them besides Mr. Colt, but she didn't know any of their names yet. One came out of one the barns and he looked young, about the same age as Mr. Colt. His brown eyes were soft as he watched her approach, almost sympathetic. A creeping suspicion crept up and down Nina's spine.

How would he know what I'm going through if Mr. Colt doesn't speak to him either?

"Morning, Nina," the ranch hand said cheerfully. "Are you looking for Sam?"

Nina's heart skipped a beat. He knew her name. She racked her brain nervously as she tried to think of how Mr. Colt could have told him about her. Maybe he wrote it down or showed him the letter she'd written when she was set to arrive. She also took pause at someone using Mr. Colt's first name. All this time she had kept things formal because he hadn't told her otherwise.

Sam—she liked it, it was strong and simple. She felt like it suited him. Maybe she would need to make an effort to try using it more often.

Swallowing hard, Nina tried to form her reply. "Not exactly. I brewed a pot of coffee and I wanted to see if you all would like some."

The ranch hand smiled broadly at her. "That's mighty fine of you." He brought his thumb and forefinger to his mouth and let out a shrill whistle that caused Nina to jump in surprise, inspiring a giggle from Henry who sat in the pack on Nina's back. "Fellas, Miss Nina brought out some coffee." He called like it was the best news any of them had heard all day.

It wasn't long at all before all four men stood on the porch, drinking their coffee and chatting—except for Sam. Jack, the foreman, was the one who looked at her with his gentle brown eyes. Jim was very tall and thin but had a bubbling, contagious laugh, and Nina decided right away to find him if she was ever in the mood for a joke. Amos looked strong enough to carry a steer on his back. Nina also noted this in case she needed help moving something. They were a lively group and Nina felt glad she took the chance and made coffee for them.

Mr. Colt—no, *Sam*, Nina chided herself—stood further back. He sipped his coffee and his eyes bounced around to whoever was talking, but Nina could feel them on her the most, despite trying to ignore it. It was as if she stood under the mid-summer sun all day; his gaze made her feel nervous and excited, though she would have preferred he just say something to her instead. Eventually she met his eye, expecting contempt after what she'd done the night before, but instead curiosity shone in them, like he tried to understand her motivations behind the coffee.

Ask me and I'll tell you everything. Nina pleaded with her eyes.

Nina observed him as took his final sip. He abruptly walked to where the tray rested and placed his cup down. Sam gave her his usual nod and half smile before he stepped off the porch and back in the direction of one of his pastures. Nina shouldn't have been surprised, but she felt disappointed all the same.

"This was great," Amos said as he too placed his mug on the tray. He gave Henry's cheek a gentle pinch and Nina a wink as he headed back to work.

"Thank you," Jim added, following Amos off the porch and in the direction of the barns. That just left Jack, who seemed like he was lingering.

"Miss Nina, I just wanted to talk to you for a moment if you don't mind."

Nina kept her face neutral even though her brow wanted to crinkle like a piece of paper. *What would he need to talk to me about?* The thought made her start to sweat. "Sure, what can I help you with?"

Jack looked over his shoulder to make sure that one else was close enough to hear what he wanted to say. "I just wanted to let you know that Sam appreciates that you're here. Things were difficult when the child was first left here, and Sam doesn't always like to heed advice until he comes to the conclusion on his own. To put it bluntly, he's stubborn."

Nina's mouth hung open in shock. "You...you know all that? He talks to you?" She fought the feeling of betrayal that wanted to rear its ugly head. Sam had known him longer; he probably felt more comfortable around Jack.

"He doesn't communicate in the conventional sense, but I assure you, his intentions are pure. If you get to know him long enough, I promise he'll be honest with you too." Jack once again looked at her with sympathetic eyes. "I just ask for you to be patient with him. He doesn't have many friends. His life hasn't been an easy one."

"I see," Nina replied, feeling like Jack gave her even more things to think about. She wasn't sure was a good thing or was going to make sleeping at night even more difficult.

"I just wanted you to know that he doesn't hate you." Jack assured her. "Trust me, he's grateful for everything you do."

Nina wanted to ask him so many questions. *Why won't Sam tell me about his feelings himself? What is the real reason why Jack would talk to me on his behalf?*

Maybe Jack could tell her what caused Sam's silence. None of the options seemed right, so she swatted them away from her thoughts like they were insistent insects. Maybe another time.

"Well, thank you, Jack. I appreciate you sharing this with me."

"Of course," Jack replied. "You and Henry have a good day."

Nina watched as he stacked everything nicely on the tray before he went back to work. Jack had helped her probably more than he realized.

Mr. Colt—no, Sam—doesn't hate me. Maybe things aren't as bad around here as I thought.

It was enough to lift her spirits up off the floor and try to make things work with him again.

Chapter Fifteen

Sam couldn't sleep again.

At least this time he didn't toss and turn over the state of his ranch or the railroad encroaching on his land. Sam felt like there were butterflies in his stomach trying to escape as he lay under his covers. If he put on his boots and ran outside, he probably could have run miles with all his unfounded energy.

He vowed to build a bridge with Nina.

Before the moon fully sank behind the horizon, before the rooster could wake to greet the day, Sam dressed and crept downstairs to not wake anyone else in the house. He wasn't planning on working in the fields or barns today, so he chose a brown work shirt and slacks that weren't worn or ripped.

The ledger that he used to communicate with Nina still lay on the table in the living room where he left it. He took it into the kitchen and wrote his notes for the day before he placed it on the table.

I'll be in town.

Whatever you do is welcome.

Sam made his egg and ate it quickly. There were some days that he would make food for Nina, but there wasn't time today. It was a shame because the act of kindness made him feel proud and satisfied all day long when he did it.

He had a bit of business to attend to on his property before he hitched the team up to go to Carson City. After putting his dish by the wash basin like he typically did, he started to make his way to the front door when something compelled him to stop.

I want to show Nina that I appreciate her. What can I do to help?

He stood by the pantry when he was struck by an idea. He opened it up and pulled out a jar of Henry's food and placed it on the table by his notebook. It wasn't much, but he hoped that Nina would enjoy the gesture.

It was still dark when he finally went out the front door and carefully shut it behind him so it wouldn't slam and wake up Henry or Nina. Sam could still count twinkling stars as he made his way toward his horse barn, though the horizon was starting to turn shades of navy. The rooster finally made his morning call as Sam was giving his horse Sadie a good scratch behind the ears after putting on her bridle and saddle. He wanted to be back from west pasture by the time Jack and the others arrived for the day.

There was a patch of meadow in those particular fields that had fragrant, colorful wildflowers. They remined Sam of jewels among the tall, soft prairie grasses. In the morning sun it looked like something God might have hand painted.

After seeing Nina be so upset several nights ago, he wanted to do something to cheer her up beyond leaving out Henry's food. He led Sadie out of the barn by her reins and hopped on her back, hoping to save time by riding to the spot instead of walking there on foot.

Sam needed to go into town to meet with a potential client. If all went well, he'd lose a good number of his livestock, but he'd have ample money to finally finish a few new barns and even buy a few new stallions for breeding. He also wanted to do something else that would make Nina smile and potentially get her to open up more to him as well.

It's what she deserves. She's been so helpful with Henry, and the house looks the best it ever has looked, Sam thought to himself as the sun finally peeked over the ridge on the eastern side of his property. Shades of pink and gold entwined with the midnight blue sky, and Sam wished he could paint it on canvas so he could remember it always. It was too bad he wasn't much of an artist.

The beauty of that sunrise reminded him of Nina and her heartache. He wasn't sure exactly why, but Sam knew he wanted to fix it. He knew that he couldn't hold back from her anymore. The thought was like a flame; it had been small at first, but the more time he spent around her, the fire grew brighter and brighter.

Sam arrived at the wildflower patch just as the last star disappeared amidst the morning sky. He brought Sadie to a halt, giving her a pat for helping him get here so quickly. Sliding to the ground, he scanned the area for the biggest and most vibrant blooms when something stopped him cold in his tracks.

A week passed since he last ventured into town. The railroad project chugged along, but at the time it seemed like progress was slow going at best. Today it seemed far closer than he remembered. What had once been a dot on a distant hill was a dark, foreboding patch. If Sam squinted hard enough, he could see the men arriving to work for the day.

The scene made Sam's stomach roll like he'd eaten something rotten.

I don't have time to deal with this right now. Sam shook his head to clear it and get himself focused on why he was out here in the first place. *I need to find a flower for Nina.*

Perhaps he felt determined to make Nina smile, perhaps he tried to busy his mind, but Sam picked every flower he could find until his arms were full of them. Grateful that he put his saddlebags on Sadie before venturing to the spot, he carefully arranged what he could fit in the bags and carried the rest back toward the farmhouse in his arms.

She'll certainly be surprised if nothing else, Sam thought hopefully.

Sam gave one more concerned look over his shoulder at the railroad site before he signaled to Sadie that it was time to move on. He must let Jack, Amos, and Jim know about what he saw when he got back to the house. The letter he shredded up several weeks ago at the post office suddenly flashed through his thoughts. Sam wondered if that wasn't going to be the last he'd hear from them, and if the mime fighting he performed for a laugh with his ranch hands may actually come true.

***

Sam brought in the flowers and left them in the kitchen without writing to Nina that they were from him. He could hear her upstairs talking to Henry and Sam wondered if maybe she was changing him for the day. He didn't wait around to find out, assuming Nina would figure out who the flowers were from soon enough. Instead, he went to find Jack, who rolled up rope in one of the sheds. He gestured for his notebook and wrote down his plans once the foreman gave it to him.

I'm going into town.

"Figured as much, based on how you're dressed." Jack replied, giving him a once over. "I assume you'll be skipping lunch?" When Sam nodded, Jack put the notebook back into his pocket. "Enjoy yourself."

Sam gave him a nod as he went to grab his wagon team and hitch them up. Jack was always honest with Sam, sometimes brutally so, and had been part of the reason why he'd decided to show Nina that he was fond of her. Sam made a mental note to tell him what his intentions were later.

"I told her that you don't hate her." Jack had confessed the afternoon after Nina brought out coffee for them. "Honestly, I think it helped. She seemed relieved."

Sam was glad for it, though he wished he could have come to the conclusion that he needed to do this sort of gesture himself sooner. He just hoped that he wasn't too late, and she would never cry with despair again, whether he was the reason or not.

A short while later, Sam passed the railroad worksite with his wagon and realized that it had indeed moved closer to the ranch. The site extended well past the riverbank where they worked the day he picked up Nina from the train station. It was a least half a mile closer, if not more. It could have been the summer heat beating down on him, but the scene made Sam sweat.

The laborers still stopped to glare at him with contempt as he passed and this time, he returned the favor. He did not want them passing through his land; he did not want them disrupting his business. Sam knew that it wasn't these men's fault, that the Central Pacific Railroad stood behind this, but he still felt a bitter taste in his mouth as he passed.

Once in town, he met his business contact at the one of the local saloons over a frothy pint of beer. The bar was too loud, and the smell of cigars burned his nose, but he found that meeting on neutral territory often made these sorts of expensive deals easier. It took the edge off. The man lived on the other side of Carson City, the one the railroad wasn't decimating. He had a thriving ranch and was very interested in three dozen horses. With the price he was willing to pay, Sam was happy to make a deal.

After they shook hands and he left the saloon, Sam walked down the promenade to the general store. He typically had a list of things he often checked prices on when he was in town, such as nails, feed for the animals, and tools. Today he had a specific purpose and didn't browse. In the back of the store was shelf with books on it. Some were Bibles, the leather smooth under his fingers as he ran them over it, the gold embossing sparkling new.

There was a shelf just for children's books. The remaining shelves housed fiction novels, and Sam began to peruse them, furrowing his brow as he tried to determine which ones were the most interesting. He hoped to purchase a few that Nina would like, but he wanted to get a preview of what they were about first. He couldn't tell her what she meant to him, but perhaps he could show his appreciation with a gift.

Nina's voice was sweet like a songbird when she read the Bible aloud before Henry went to bed. Sam wanted to hear her read anything he could get his hands on and ultimately decided to just pick three at random and hope for the best. The gesture would count if nothing else.

I hope she enjoys them even if she can't get me to speak and I'm like this forever. Sam tried to be reasonable that way he wouldn't be disappointed if things with his voice never got better.

Sam paid for the books and went back to his wagon. The anticipation of seeing what Nina thought about the flowers and the books tugged him in the direction of home.

I never thought I'd be so excited about filling my house with flowers and books. It's made it more comfortable somehow.

He regretted taking the wagon and not just traveling on Sadie so he could gallop home, eager to present his gifts to Nina.

What would the railroad workers think of me then?

He was disappointed that he wasn't going to find out.

***

Sam returned to the ranch in the late afternoon. Jack and the ranch hands busied themselves trying to corral the horses that were to stay behind and not be sold. It was easier to keep them separated until the deal concluded. He didn't want to interrupt him and the others, so he crept into the house in search of a bit of lunch. He wanted to leave the books just like he'd left the flowers behind.

He was down the hallway and almost at the kitchen when Nina's voice called out to him from the living room.

"Sam?"

The sound of his name in that sweet, gentle voice made Sam nearly fall to his knees. After the initial shock of hearing the word come from her lips, he wanted to jump for joy or do a dance. Never once had Nina called him by his first name. It was always formal—*Mr. Colt*. He wasn't sure what changed, or if Jack did something else to help him, but he couldn't remember the last time he felt so joyful. Sam wasn't sure when the last time someone other than Jack called him by his first name.

He quickly raced into the kitchen to grab his ledger and noticed that the flowers that he left on the table were now in a clear glass vase. Sam's heart raced even faster as he walked back to the living room, wondering what she would say.

So, she found the flowers, Sam thought, *I hope she's happy.*

Nina sat in the chair, working on what appeared to be needlepoint work. As Sam entered the room, he noticed what looked like a letter *H* and wondered if it was for Henry. The child was notably absent, which now explained why he didn't notice her sitting in the room when he passed. Now as he took her in, she smiled so earnestly that it warmed his insides like a mug of warm milk.

"Henry's napping, if that's who you're looking for," Nina said, staring up at him with curious eyes. Sam could see a bit of pink on the bridge of her nose, as though she blushed, and he felt his pulse gallop harder. "Did you leave those flowers I found in the kitchen?"

Sam never opened his ledger to a clean page faster in his entire life. He wrote quickly, turning the book so she could read.

I picked them for you. I saw how sad you were. I wanted to fix it.

Nina's face went from slightly pink to beet red. She dropped her gaze to her needle work, the thread bobbing quickly through the piece of linen as she sewed with shaking hands. "They're beautiful. Thank you."

Sam wrote down his next thought, hoping that he could make Nina smile or feel even more appreciated. He stepped closer, making sure not to touch her, but flipped his notebook again and held up the books he'd bought at the general store at the same time.

I bought these for you. Could you teach me to read them out loud?

Sam could absolutely read but reciting what was on the page like Nina often did would be a challenge. He watched as her eyes scanned the page, hoping she would be interested in helping him. She let out a shaky breath before she slowly gazed up into his eyes, her smile small, but warm like the sun had been on the way to Carson City earlier.

"You are very thoughtful. I would be happy to teach you. Maybe after dinner we can begin?"

Sam nodded and wrote one last line to Nina.

I would love that. Thank you.

This time when Nina smiled, it went all the way to her eyes.

Chapter Sixteen

"These books are lovely," Nina replied as she looked at each novel that Sam brought her. She opened their heavy covers, scanning the first few pages to get an idea of what they were about. "They will be perfect for reading aloud. Eventually we can take turns reading the pages."

The Scarlet Letter by Nathaniel Hawthorne, *Moby* Dick by Herman Melville, and *Great Expectations* by Charles Dickens were all books that piqued her interest, and she couldn't wait to dig into them by flickering lamp light. Yet, Nina knew that they would be too difficult for Sam to read aloud at the moment; it would be like asking Henry to run when he hadn't even stood up on his own yet. They would there eventually, but they needed to build up to it.

"Perhaps we could go into town together and pick out some more books?" Nina suggested, trying to control the tremble that threatened to shake her entire body. For once it was because of excitement and joy and not something negative. "I know you just went today, but perhaps we could all go. Henry would probably enjoy all the sights and sounds."

Sam started writing in his book. The sound of the charcoal pencil scratching on the paper made her even more antsy with anticipation. Nina had to put her needlework to the side so that she didn't accidentally stab herself with her needle as she waited for him to finish. Sam finally showed her the page and she read his reply.

Maybe tomorrow?

"If I won't be pulling you from you work, then that would be lovely."

Nina nearly jumped out of her skin when Sam made a humming noise and shook his head. It was the first time she had ever heard him make any kind of noise. The sound was deep, like if he had actually spoken, his voice would have been a rich baritone. She suddenly imagined what it would feel like if Sam said her name in that velvety tone. The thought made her stomach flip excitedly.

Nina smiled so proudly at him that she could feel the muscles straining on her face. The last time she might have felt that way, she and Nathaniel were still young and walking along the riverbank back home. She remembered that same nervous feeling that had made her tremble with excitement and was pleased to know that she could feel that way about someone else.

That was my past. It was what I needed then. I think I can move on now. She shut her eyes as she imagined herself cleaning a slate, removing the memories to create something new. She pictured Sam's handsome face. *I think I'm finally ready.*

Sam cleared his throat. Nina opened her eyes to see him holding up his notebook.

I should get back to work.

She'd been so happy and reflective on how Sam was making her feel that she hadn't realized that he'd written to her again. "Oh, of course." Nina was about to let him go when she had one more thought. "Mr. Colt, I mean, Sam," Using his real name would probably still take some getting used to.

"You brought me so many flowers. Tonight, when you're done with work, would you like to help me use them to decorate the house? We probably have enough for multiple vases. We could give the whole place a splash of color."

Sam nodded happily before he waved and excused himself from the room. Nina watched him go and continued to stare at the space he'd just consumed long after he was gone. She found herself letting out a lofty, contented sigh.

He doesn't hate me. Thank God.

She recalled what Jack had told her several days ago over coffee. He had asked her to be patient with Sam and she was going to try her best. Seeing Sam's gestures and reading his responses helped her have that faith. It gave her the resolve to keep trying.

It also confirmed what she'd been starting to assume about Sam and his silence. He wasn't cold or rude; Sam wanted to talk but couldn't. Just now, as they discussed the books, he looked so eager and hopeful, and Nina had a burning desire in her heart to help him succeed.

From the floor above, Nina heard Henry start to cry. He must have been up from his nap. She would have to wait until later to put her plan into motion, but as she walk toward the staircase, she made a vow.

Sam will thrive just as much as Henry does around here if I have anything to do with it.

***

"There," Nina said as she placed the last daisy in one of the new vases Sam retrieved from the attic for her. She'd quicky washed them and now they were crystal clear. "Enough flowers to have a vase in the kitchen, the living room, and my bedroom. Thank you for your help."

After they finished their dinner, Sam, as promised, helped her divvy up the flowers so they could add a bit of color to the house. Henry sat in his highchair happily, the biscuits and gravy Nina made for dinner smeared on his little face. Nina let out an adoring sigh at the scene before she wiped his face with a damp napkin. Henry had an affinity for cuteness regardless of the situation.

Sam gave his usual nod and smirk before he looked like he was going to take the vase into the living room and do his nightly routine of tracking his business expenses. Nina wasn't ready for the moment to end, not yet. They didn't have the easier books yet, but Nina thought of some ideas of ways they could still communicate more while she made dinner.

"Sam, I'd like to learn more about you," she began. "Can I ask you some questions?" When he shrugged his shoulders and hummed something that sounded very close to, *I don't know,* Nina found herself laughing. She wished she hadn't waited so long to try to talk to him like this. Anticipating what he would do next was amusing and fun. "Why don't we start with some easy questions. Why don't you tell me your favorite color?"

Nina had a whole list of questions that she said over and over as she prepared everything she needed for biscuits and gravy. She knew them by heart now and waited to see if he would write his answers. Instead, she watched as he pointed at the green stem on the daisy in vase in front of him.

"Green is a lovely color," Nina said excitedly as she made the connection. "I'm quite partial to blue. I love a cloudless, azure blue sky in the summer." Her heart beat wildly as he peered into her eyes with a look of wonder and understanding. Nina could have gotten lost there if she lingered for too long. She attempted to ask another question. One that would be harder to answer with gestures. "Do you have a favorite song?"

Once more Nina wasn't expecting any noise to come from Sam, but he began to hum a tune. Nina recognized it from church, once more taking in the rich timbre of his voice, nearly shutting her eyes as he made music.

Oh my goodness, we're doing it. We're communicating!

When he was finished, Sam looked equally as surprised that he shared the tune with her. His eyes went wide, and he brought his fingers to his lips like he couldn't' believe what he'd done. Nina swelled with pride.

It was progress. It made her feel like anything was possible.

Chapter Seventeen

Sam was so proud of himself that he couldn't sleep.

I made noises. I didn't know that I could do that. Nina was so happy. It was almost like we were communicating and understanding each other.

He revisited the moments after supper over and over, which probably wasn't helping him sleep either, but he was too happy to stop. Nina's happy face shone like a beacon of light in a storm. Making her smile motivated him even further. He would hum and grunt and do whatever he could if would have her stay close to him.

I can't believe I was reluctant to hire someone to help me.

As Sam lay there with his eyes shut, he knew that Nina meant more to him than a governess. There were moments in his dreams that Nina was his wife and he'd wake up breathless, like he ran to the Carson City on foot. It terrified him and electrified him, but he felt glad to have met her regardless of if the dreams came true or not. It was the closest he'd felt to normal since before his parents and sister burned in the fire.

When it was at least midnight and Sam was just as awake as when the sun shining, he decided to get up and take a walk. Every now and again he'd walk around the ranch by moonlight, absorbing the silence. It was soothing and eased his busy mind.

Sam didn't completely dress for the day but threw a pair of slacks underneath his nightshirt and slipped into his worn leather boots. He inched down the stairs, trying to not wake Nina or Henry and carefully opened the door wide enough so that he could slip through and shut it quietly behind him.

Apparently, he didn't need to creep like a mouse because Nina was awake as well. He discovered her sitting on the edge of the porch working on a lap quilt, her head bent as she focused. Sam noticed that she brought out a candle stick to cast some light on her work as she stitched it all together. He took a minute to gaze at her diligent work; even in the middle of the night she was thinking about others before herself. Sam was still convinced that she wasn't real, but some sort of otherworldly angel sent to save him and Henry. If he was more of a religious person, he'd thank God for her.

"Couldn't sleep?" Nina's called to him, is if they were in a dream. Her voice was soft and soothing, like his subconscious was trying to lull him into a sense of security. Sam pinched himself just to make sure that he wasn't sleepwalking, and the sharp pain reminded that he was indeed awake. Realizing that she awaited his response, he made a noise that was equivalent to a hum and stepped closer to her.

"I couldn't either," Nina admitted meeting his gaze, "I've got a lot on my mind." Something in the way she looked at him made him wonder if it was more than just looking after Henry.

Do you feel the same way I do? Sam wondered with a strange bit of hope. If Nina was as fond of him as he was of her, it could be something beautiful. They would no longer be alone. Henry could have a proper family. Sam stopped himself from letting his thoughts run wild. Nina barely knew him. There was no way that she could possibly feel that way about him, and even if she did, how would he ever let her know that he felt the same way? Taking a deep breath to collect himself, he gestured to the spot beside her, asking in his own way if he could sit down.

Nina slid her sewing things and the candle over to one side to make room. "Please, I'd love if you would join me."

For a few moments, Sam soaked in the moment. He wanted to etch the scene into his mind so that he could come back and recall it later, just like he had felt about the sunrise he'd seen recently. The way the moon was just a sliver of a crescent and how the stars seemed countless were hauntingly beautiful. The sound of Nina's thread weaving through the quilt lulled Sam into a sense of peace.

The candlelight illuminated Nina's defined cheekbones, proving that she was beautiful in any situation. Sam let out a relaxed, contented sigh as he felt like he and Nina were the only people in the world that were awake at that moment. It wasn't true, but it made him feel closer to her anyway.

"I'm making the quilt for Henry," Nina said as she continued to work. "I know it's summer now, but the winter will be here before you know it and he'll need more layers."

As Sam listened to her melodious voice, he noticed a small branch on the ground by his feet. He picked it up, compelled to talk back to her, but he didn't want to run inside to get his notebook. Getting up would end the stillness and closeness of the moment and Sam wasn't ready for it to be over yet.

I could try this instead.

Sam began to scratch his message in the dirt. Nina must have noticed what he was doing, for she abandoned her sewing, and placed the candle stick onto the dirt so that she could read what he had written instead.

You are sweet. Your voice is beautiful.

His heart pounded as she read and reacted to his message. It was the most forward he had been about his feelings since he'd noticed them. Something about her sweet voice and her large eyes drew him in. It made him want to take chances. Even if she rejected him, he had to do it.

Beside him, he could just make out the redness of Nina's face in the candlelight. "You, you are the one who is sweet." Her voice shook like she might have been cold though it was the middle of summer. "Thank you for the compliment."

Not sure what was compelling him to act, Sam crossed out everything he had written except the word beautiful. Maybe the moonlight was possessing him, perhaps he liked how he felt when he'd been able to tell her what he was thinking, but he let his racing heart move him. He began to scratch new words.

You are beautiful.

He might not have said it out loud, but he'd never been so sure of the truth.

Chapter Eighteen

Nina feared her heart would crack her ribs.

He thinks I'm beautiful. Here I thought he hated me, and he just told me I'm beautiful.

Nina was starting to have suspicions that Sam was far fonder of her than she ever realized. A part of her wanted to run as hard as she could until the air burned her lungs. Yet another part wanted shout with excitement. Sam communicated with her, and he revealed more than just his favorite color or what he liked to sing. He shared his intimate feelings with her; the victory made her heart race with curiosity and joy.

Answer him! He just revealed something very important to you. Nina was so wrapped up in her thoughts that she almost forgot that Sam was there at all.

"Thank you, Sam." She smiled up at him, grateful for the near darkness. Her face felt hot as she looked into his eyes. In the dim lighting, they almost look translucent. When it seemed that the gaze lasted slightly longer than appropriate, she dropped her eyes to her lap.

This could change everything. I'm not sure if we've just made things complicated.

Sam nodded before he rose from the edge of the porch, leaving the stick he used to write with behind. It seemed that he reached the limit of what he wanted to say to her.

Suddenly filled with nervous energy, Nina picked up the quilt again, stitching the layers together with tremulous hands. When she accidentally pricked her finger, she hissed and shook it until the pain faded away. Nina looked behind her out of the corner of her eye, wondering if Sam noticed her reaction his compliments.

He found a spot on a one of the old wooden rocking chairs closer to the door. Sam rocked back and forth as he hummed the same tune he shared with her after dinner. The sound of the chair moving and wood on the porch creaking was an oddly calmly as she tried to inconspicuously look at him.

Nina decided when she first met Sam that she thought he was handsome. His boyish face and the dimples that only appeared when he smiled piqued her interest. His light blue eyes shone with honesty, revealing far more than what he could write to her, and his fair hair seemed so soft. Nina often wondered what it would feel like to run her hands through it.

As she watched him rock in his chair, she observed how large his hands were as they grasped onto the arm rests. Taking in the broad set of his shoulders, Nina realized that Sam exuded strength in a way that made her feel secure. It didn't make her want to run to a secret hiding place to daydream about her feelings, like she would in the past. Sam Colt made her want to stick around, and Nina wanted to learn about every bit of him.

When Nina settled herself enough so that she no longer shook, she returned to her work for a while. The hand quilting was coming along, but there was more to be done before it would be ready for Henry's cradle. When the rhythmic rocking of Sam's chair stopped, she looked over her shoulder. Sam slumped to one side, his chin against his chest and his eyes shut. His breathing was just short of snores.

Oh, my goodness, he's fallen asleep.

There was something innocent and disarming about watching him sleep. It was almost like watching Henry. Sam's worries vanished, replaced with a restful, peaceful expression. It made Nina's stomach flip like she was floating off the ground.

Part of her thought about just sitting there and taking in his sleeping form for a while. Her candle burned down to a small stump. It was probably time to go inside for the night, not that Nina could sleep. Even before Sam had joined her, she felt restless reliving how he finally made noise and how they bonded.

I was so proud of myself for taking a chance. Perhaps I motivated Sam to do the same.

The thought made Nina's insides feel warm with pride. She quickly put her sewing things and the candle just inside the front door before she attempted to wake Sam up.

"Sam," Nina whispered softly, trying not to startle him. "Sam, we probably should go in." When he didn't stir, she reached out and gently nudged his shoulder. "Sam, it's late."

It wasn't until she felt the soft cotton fabric of his nightshirt under her fingers that she realized that she touched him. Nina froze in place as her mind attempted to process what she'd done. After the few instances where his touch had made her uncomfortable and caused her to flee, she did not even give it a second thought this time. She was so focused on Sam's progress that she was slow to see how she took an important step towards healing as well. The normalcy of it all made her want to weep tears of joy. The past began to move where it belonged—behind her.

Sam stirred, and instinct told Nina to draw her hand away as though she touched something piping hot, but she forced herself to keep her hand on his shoulder.

You have nothing to be afraid of. Nina told herself as Sam's eyes slowly began to blink open. *He cares for you. Probably more than you even realize.*

The thought that someone cared about her, and that they didn't feel compelled to do so out of pity was better than any gift she could receive. Sam locked eyes with her, the sleep temporarily fading away. The warmth that poured out him as he realized she was touching him confirmed everything that she was feeling. It made her feelings crystal clear.

Nina wasn't afraid anymore.

Chapter Nineteen

In the days that followed, Sam felt like he might burst.

When he wasn't feeling elated—as though he were lighter than a cloud after Nina reached out and touched him—he would cycle through the gamut of emotions, caught in a whirlwind of anxiety, yearning, and joy.

He experienced the pulse quickening hope that he may finally be able to grow closer with Nina now that it seemed like they possessed some sort of understanding of each other. When he finally fell asleep, visions of what his life could be swam behind his eyes. In the light of day, he would imagine his future, one filled with light touches and Nina's gentle voice. Yet doubt soon crept in.

What if I am never able to speak? What if I can only hum or grunt and write notes?

Sam worried that Nina would tire of him, or that eventually Henry would get old enough to not need constant care and Nina would leave. She'd only been with Sam for a short while, and yet she became such a part of his life. The thought of her missing from his existence was too difficult and painful to dwell on.

Sam relied on her just as much as Henry did. Now, he wasn't sure if he could go back to the way things were.

One Saturday afternoon, when he didn't have anything specific to do on the ranch, he paced about, unable to quiet his mind. *I must do something about this nervous energy,* Sam huffed to himself, *I can't sleep and Jack doesn't want to read about my feelings for Nina.*

Maybe he didn't feel comfortable with writing his feelings for Jack to read, but perhaps he could write them for himself.

He had a leatherbound journal that survived the fire. When he first lost his ability to speak, he wrote everything he could to purge his mind. He tried to document every memory from that fated night.

After that, he wrote everything down, and he often wondered what his family would do if they survived. Sam questioned why God would punish him by taking his family and his voice from him. Those entries were especially hard to bear.

Most of the passages were probably illegible due to how distraught he had been, but it poured of him when spoken words could not. As he became busier with work at various farms and eventually his own ranch, he wrote in it less until he had no time to write at all. Sam thought about saving it for communicating with Nina, but he had to do something. He was starting to feel desperate.

Maybe it's time to start writing it again.

Sam kept the notebook in a trunk at the end of the bed, so he got on his knees, sorting through some extra sheets and blankets to find it on the bottom. The cover was worn; he'd had it for almost as long as he'd been alone.

Even though it survived the fire, everything he wrote in it was raw and fresh as he processed his emotions. Sam wondered whether his subconscious would trick him into believing it smelled like smoke or was hot to the touch.

He had several unused charcoal pencils in his nightstand drawer that he could use to put his thoughts to paper.

Sam nearly jumped out of his skin when a scream came from the floor below. When he walked by earlier, Nina and Henry sat in the living room, playing happily. Instinctively, he sprung to his feet, throwing the pencils and notebook on his bed, and tearing down the stairs to see what was going on.

What if there's someone in the house? He worried as he hit the landing and began to sprint down the hallway. He had a revolver tucked in the back of the closet by the front door, but Sam was more concerned about seeing Nina with his own eyes to know that she was okay than grabbing it to potentially defend her.

Skidding into the living room, worried that he'd discover an accident or an intruder. Surprise crashed into him as he found Nina standing in the center of the room, clapping and cheering. Henry gripped tightly onto the rungs of Sam's chair, standing up proudly, his toothy smile the widest Sam had ever seen.

I don't think he's ever done that before. Sam observed as the child stamped his little feet excitedly, as though he danced.

"He just pulled himself up," Nina said, her voice thick with emotion. "I didn't do anything."

Tears welled in Nina's eyes as she stared at Henry with a look of maternal adoration that took Sam's breath away. She loved Henry like he was her own, and that pureness of heart caused a wave of all those excited, anxious thoughts to wash over Sam, making him feel like he tumbled about in the sea. He soon realized that he liked the feeling.

Before Sam could make a gesture to convey how he was proud as well, Nina closed the space between them. She flung herself into him, wrapping her slender arms around his waist. Sam sucked in his breath in a surprised gasp. He never noticed the height difference between them before. The top of her head ended below his chin, and he could smell the fragrant, floral soap that she used woven into the fabric of her soft gray dress.

Well, we've certainly made progress, Sam thought as he tentatively hugged her back. Though returning her embrace may be a lapse in judgment, he resolved to savor the moment anyway, just in case it never happened again.

Sure enough, Nina's eyes widened as realization bloomed across her face. She let out a sharp breath before she carefully unfurled her arms from his body and took several steps away from him.

"Sorry," Nina eyes dropped to the floor, her face burning. "I don't know what came over me. I was just so happy!" Sam tried to gesture and let her know that no harm was done, but Nina shook her head. "It wasn't proper. Again, you have my sincerest apologies."

Nina sat heavily beside Henry on the floor, taking the child into her arms and squeezing him tightly. Sam watched as she kissed Henry's cheek, and something became quite clear to him.

He found Nina beautiful, but he knew now that what he was feeling was more than superficial. He was falling in love with her golden heart, her giving nature and kindness toward him and Henry. If he thought about it too much, it took his breath away.

It had been so long since he felt such strong feelings for someone that he didn't know how to communicate it. Even if he could speak, it would take a lot of soul search to determine his next steps. She was hired help and crossing those boundaries could have potential consequences. Not many people cared about him or what he did, but he didn't want Nina to be gossiped about or considered scandalous.

I must think of her propriety, Sam thought, struggling to hide how disappointed the thought made him feel. His body sagged as he continued to watch Nina and Henry together.

It's all for the best. I doubt that she feels the same way about me anyway.

Chapter Twenty

"Oh, Sam, I'm so embarrassed!" Nina wailed a little while later as she tried to push away the memory of the bold way she touched him from her mind. "First you've seen me cry, and now this."

Nina put Henry down for his afternoon nap. The excitement of standing up for the first time got the better of him, and he fell asleep as she carried him up to nursery. She was temporarily distracted when Henry rested his weary head on her shoulder, but now that he slept soundly in his cradle, the insistent thoughts about her behavior bit at her like fleas on a dog.

Nina felt mortified and fought the urge to fly up the stairs and lock the door to her room behind her. It was hasty but wouldn't solve anything. She would only be trapped in her bedroom and would have to face Sam eventually.

This time, Nina steeled herself—running wouldn't help anything.

Nina found Sam still standing in the living room, as though he waited for her. Nina was ready to beg for his forgiveness so that he wouldn't fire her. Surprise overtook her when he shook his head, his chest looking like it rumbled with laughter. Nina was even more surprised when he gestured for her to sit back in her chair. He all but pushed her backwards without touching her.

Sam held up his finger to tell her to wait like he often did before he quickly exited the room. Nina could hear his footsteps on the staircase and the floor above before they began to return. They moved with purpose.

He must want to tell me something. Nina thought. *Maybe he's getting his notebook.*

Instead of getting his usual business ledger that he wrote to her in, Sam retuned with a journal that looked old and worn. The leather was soft to the touch and was dark like coal. He sat down beside her, passing her the diary. When Nina opened it, she saw that most of it was full of Sam's sloppy handwriting.

"Are you sure?" Nina asked, searching his face for any expression so she'd know his thoughts. "You want me to read your journal?" Doing such a thing seemed so private and intimate, but if he gave it to her, Nina had to believe that he tried to tell her something. When Sam gave her deep nod, she found the first page and began to read, flattered that he thought so highly of her.

Dear Journal,

I'm a sinner. A no good, worthless sinner that shouldn't be alive, but they don't even want me in Hell. How could I be so foolish and forget to extinguish my lantern? I can't believe that I left it in the barn so carelessly. If I had just done my chores when my father had asked me the first time, I wouldn't have needed that light. None of this would have happened.

I wish I could explain what happened to you. In the middle of the night, I awoke from a dead sleep to hear the horses screaming. Why did it wake me and not the rest of my family?

If only I had known what was going to happen, I would have saved my family first. Losing the animals would have been terrible, but we would have figured something out. We could have made a decision as a family. Now I'm alone.

The worst part wasn't the heat or the destruction. It was hearing their screams as the fire burned them. I will never in all my days forget those shrieks. Even now it gives me chills to think about it.

I can't talk. I've tried to cry or scream or say anything and it's like my voice died with my family. Maybe it's my punishment for being so stupid. Perhaps God is trying to teach me something. I have no idea what the lesson is other than that I shouldn't be alive.

I don't know what to do.

Sam

For a moment Nina sat in shocked silence; the words were heart wrenching and awful. She knew if she looked at Sam that she'd cry. No wonder he'd only been surviving on this ranch, not thriving. When she finally calmed down enough to turn to the next entry, she skimmed more pain-filled paragraphs about finding work, moving away from his home, and trying to move on.

Oh my, he was only fifteen years old when this happened.

Nina felt about every emotion there was to feel. She felt despair for Sam and all that he experienced. How did someone move on after witnessing their family die? Nina had only heard stories about what happened to her birth parents, and it sent chills down her spine. She could only imagine that hearing screams as victims burned to death could wreck any person, let alone a member of the family.

As sad a Nina felt, she also felt strangely elated at the thought of Sam and her both having something tragic in common. Fire made them both orphans; maybe God's plan for Sam somehow drew them together. It was a pleasant thought even if it was likely not true.

Biting her lip, she finally risked a glance at Sam as he sat in the chair beside her. He didn't look ashamed or sad. He seemed surprisingly calm despite sharing such a huge part of his life with her.

"I'm so sorry," Nina whispered, looking deep into his blue eyes, "You have been through so much."

Sam nodded, breaking their gaze to look down at his lap. They sat in the silence for a while and Nina experienced a revelation, one that was crystal clear, and she wasn't sure how she missed it before.

All this time she focused on Sam's looks. He was strong and handsome, more of a man than Nathaniel had been. Now, she fell for every part of him, inside and out. Nina loved the tenderness he showed Henry and his animals. She no longer felt afraid to touch him, and the fact that he felt comfortable enough to share his sad past with her proved that he was special. Hopefully, it meant that he was getting comfortable with her too.

She yearned to see him smile again, to help him overcome the sadness in his life so he could communicate and live the life he deserved. Nina flipped to an empty page and carefully pulled it from the book. Then, using a charcoal pencil that he left on the table between them, she numbered it like a test he might have seen in school.

Slyly, she pushed the paper and charcoal pencil over near his elbow on the table. "Let's play a game, what do you say?" Sam raised an eyebrow at her, like he did not expect her to suggest it after she read the entry about the fire. Nina attempted to explain what she was thinking.

"You've expressed interest in learning how to read aloud better, and I saw a few spelling errors in your journal, so how about a spelling test to practice?" Nina questioned, eyes sparkling with amusement. "It can remind you of when you were younger, and things were simpler."

Sam still looked like he wasn't completely convinced, but he smirked as he took the pencil and paper from her, waiting for Nina to begin.

"You first word is 'thankful,'" Nina said, trying to think of the best way to use it in the sentence. "I am *thankful* that you shared this with me. I'm sure it wasn't easy to relive the pain of your past."

Eyes alight with understanding, Sam wrote the word on the paper. He wrote an *I* instead of a *U*, but he was close. When he looked up and readied his pencil for the next word, Nina offered a new word and sentence.

"'Trust' is the second word. I feel blessed that you *trust* me to read your journal."

It wasn't an understatement now that Nina knew his silence wasn't anything personal. Instead, it was some sort of side effect of the trauma of losing his family. Nina wondered if she had been older when her parents died if she'd be mute as well.

She once again watched as Sam wrote the word. This one was nearly correct as well, but he'd used an *O* instead of a *U* for his vowel. Nina had one word left, and she knew it was the most important of all. Sam was gracious enough to share his past with her, and it was only right that she return the favor.

"Your final word is 'sorry.' I'm *sorry* for the loss of your family and I want you to know that I understand what you are going through. I also lost my family in a fire when I was a little girl. I don't remember it, but it has affected my life every day since." Nina smiled at Sam with soft understanding eyes. "Hopefully, now you won't feel so alone."

Nina couldn't exactly explain it. Sam didn't say a word, and yet she could look into Sam's eyes and know exactly what he was feeling. An expression washed over his face; it made his eyes sparkle, like a look of complete adoration. Nina fought the urge to cry happy tears. It had been far too long since someone had looked at her with so much happiness.

It was as if he silently told her, *I haven't felt alone since you've arrived.*

It made Nina's heart soar.

Chapter Twenty-One

She doesn't want me to feel alone. Sam's heart beat so fast he felt lightheaded. *I feel the same way about her. I must let her know somehow.*

He peered down at the spelling test that Nina made for him, a quirky way to get her point across, but it made him so happy that he felt like flying. After reading what he'd gone through all those years ago, he had no doubt that she tried to cheer him up. It was just one more thing that Nina did that made him even more enamored with her.

Everything she did, she did with good intentions.

Sam didn't want the moment to end. He put up his hand to stop her from leaving or taking the paper away. *Please be patient with me,* he pleaded silently, *I have so much to say, if only I could get it out or write it down.*

Something in Sam had changed after he let her read about the darkest moment in his life. She didn't judge him. Instead, she revealed to him that she had a similar thing happen to her; she shared something about herself. He took a risk, yet received an intimate, personal reward. He wanted to find out what would happen if he tried to share more of his feelings with Nina.

With shaking hands, he wrote slowly and deliberately, hoping his script would be neat and easy to read. He prayed that he spelled everything correctly, though the word *heart* looked suspiciously wrong. When he was finished, he carefully handed the paper to her. Sam was proud, terrified, and excited at the same time as he watched her read and waited for how Nina would react as his stomach twisted.

I wanted to tell you because I want to open my heart to you.

Nina clutched the paper to her chest. He was surprised to see tears welling in her eyes. At first, he worried that maybe he pushed it too far, that his feelings overwhelmed to her. When an awestruck expression splashed across her face and the softest of smiles showed, he knew he had nothing to fear.

"I've wanted the same," Nina voice was soft and filled with emotion. "I was so worried that you hated me and would send me away."

The idea that Nina felt that way made Sam want to grovel on his knees and apologize. He reached for his diary and found a blank page, writing his reply.

I would never hate you.

Nina leaned over the side of her chair so she could read. Instead of saying something out loud, she picked up the pencil and started writing back.

Tell me everything.

Sam wished so desperately that he could start at the beginning and tell Nina about how wonderful his life had been before his family had died. He would tell her about his hopes and dreams, and how sometimes she was in them. Yet they would have to settle for writing. While it wouldn't completely get his thoughts out, it was better than before.

I will try. Will you help me?

Nina smiled and leaned even closer, her elbow brushing against his on the table. When he turned to look, he nearly jumped when her brown braid caressed his face, the hair tickling his skin. She wrote her reply quickly before she shoved the notebook back to his side of the end table.

I would be happy to.

She gently put the pencil down and locked eyes with Sam, his mouth falling open slightly as she must have realized the closeness. They were only a few inches apart. All Sam would have to do was lean in, and he'd be able to brush his lips against hers. The thought made him feel intoxicated, as though he had too much to drink, and the room spun madly.

She's Henry's governess. If you go too fast, you might make her have second thoughts.

Sam tried to be rational, but he also said he wanted to give his heart to her, and she replied in kind. Wasn't that almost like an invitation?

He wanted to see her wonderstruck face again, he wanted to know if her lips were as soft as her skin and how he'd react to the feeling of being even closer to her than he was now.

I'm going to do it. I'm going to kiss her. I have nothing to lose.

The table between them made things awkward, but Sam leaned in closer. Nina didn't seem uneasy at all; in fact, she closed her eyes.

It was as if she was ready to open her heart to him even more.

I'm not going to be able to sleep again tonight, Sam thought cheerfully as his lips hovered above her full ones, *but at least this time it will be for something happy.*

A rapping at the front door made Sam and Nina jump apart and onto their feet. Sam found himself panting as he looked about the room, trying to make sense of who or what would have caused the noise. Over by her side of the room, Nina's face shone the color of a bright tomato.

It was Saturday—Jack and the ranch hands were at home with their families. Sam wasn't sure who would be on his doorstep. He didn't often have visitors; lately, it was easier to just meet with any potential business in town.

When the knocking got louder, Sam knew he could no longer ignore it. Giving Nina a nervous look, he strode from the room and down the hallway. All the while, Sam couldn't shake the sense of foreboding filling the pit of his stomach.

He didn't dare risk whoever waited for him on the other side knock a third time.

Chapter Twenty-Two

Nina felt like she was dreaming. She was the heroine in a romance, and Sam's lips hovering over hers were enough to make her tremble with anticipation.

He's going to kiss me, Nina thought to herself as she took in his slow steady breaths and the way his hunter green dress shirt brushed against her arm. *I can't believe this is happening.* All this time, she wanted to get closer to Sam and now she found herself in such an intimate position with him. She was so thrilled she felt like singing.

The sound of aggressive knocking coming from the front door broke the moment. Sam jumped out of his skin and Nina swallowed down a yelp as they broke apart. Nearly knocking over the chair he sat in, Sam stood up and Nina rose to her feet as well.

Perhaps it's divine intervention, Nina thought to herself as her face flushed with embarrassment. *I care for Sam, but if we had kissed it wouldn't have been right. I'm Henry's governess after all. There are expectations placed on me.* The more she thought about it, she could feel her body sag with disappointment.

Sam and Nina shared a confused glance. It was the weekend, and he hadn't written anything about expecting guests. In the entire time she spent on the ranch, no one came to visit even once. She didn't imagine that would change today.

When the knocking grew even louder the second time, Nina feared that the noise might wake Henry if it continued.

"We should probably answer it," Nina stated, trying to ignore the feeling of dread that was fill in the pit of her stomach. It felt heavy as lead.

Sam nodded and strode toward the door. Despite the sense of foreboding, Nina followed at his heels to see who waited on the other side. Maybe someone lost their way and needed help. A small part of Nina wondered if Henry's family had finally come looking for him. The thought of the boy leaving made Nina's breath catch in her chest. Either way, she figured that Sam would probably need help communicating and she was happy to help.

When Sam finally opened the door, they weren't greeted by a young couple or someone looking distressed. Instead, a younger gentleman dressed in fine black clothes stood on the doorstep. His slacks, shirt, and shoes were all the color of coal. He held a black hat in hands, his thinning brown hair looking slightly disheveled as his dark eyes bounced from Sam, to Nina, and back to Sam again.

"Good afternoon, folks!" The man had the audacity to pull the screen door open so he could reach out his hand for Sam to shake. "I'm Donald Henderson of the Central Pacific Railroad."

Nina's stomach flipped with nerves as she watched Sam stiffen as rigid as a board at Donald's name and title. She noticed his reaction to stress whenever Henry fussed, but she'd never seen it in such an extreme way. His shoulders looked so tense, and it made the worry roiling in Nina's stomach sour. She'd never seen Sam react to something in such a way. Even when she didn't know about the cause of his muteness, he hadn't seemed so uncomfortable. He looked as though he might snap.

If Donald Henderson was aware of the affect he had on Sam, he ignored it. "I sent you a letter about our plans for the railroad. Did you receive it? I wanted to meet with you earlier, but I never heard back from you."

Sam clenched his fists down at his sides at the words and Nina wondered if this was something he hadn't shared with her yet. When his knuckles started turning white, Nina worried about what would happen next. Would Sam be able to communicate his anger and frustration if he got to that point? Nina wondered if there was a way to diffuse things.

"Ma'am, why don't you put on a pot of coffee for your husband and I and we can talk about how my railroad needs to be built through this house."

Nina blanched at how Mr. Henderson had called Sam her husband. She supposed that it was an honest mistake; she was old enough to be his bride and they were standing together. The thought of being married to Sam made her feel lighter than air. Every now and again she would daydream of standing before an altar with him. She'd be in her best dress with her hair finally in the bun she once thought she'd wear for Nathaniel. They could be the family that Henry needed.

Unfortunately, Nina couldn't focus on how that made her heart flutter. Instead, her thoughts jumped to Mr. Henderson's assertion that, *my railroad needs to be built through this house.* Her mind became a disjointed mess.

"Excuse me," Nina tried to make sure she was hearing correctly. "Did you say the railway is being built on this land?"

Mr. Henderson's patience quickly seemed to fade. He stamped his foot as he let out a huffy breath. "Are you two simpletons? If you had read the letter, I explained that the path we are building goes through your land. It's nothing personal and I promise I will pay you handsomely for it. The future of the country depends on it!" Bravado punctuated the man's words, like he offered the deal of a lifetime. His speech also raised in volume, and Nina peered over her shoulder toward the stairwell, worried that Henry might be disturbed.

Nina didn't know what to do. She could feel Sam's anger radiating off him like heat off a roof on a hot summer day. Allowing Mr. Henderson into Sam's home would be like a betrayal and might wake Henry if the volume of the conversation continued.

Sam was so proud of his ranch. He did not write too much about it in his notebook, but it was obvious by how early he woke each morning to work on it each day. Even on the weekends, he'd be covered in dirt and grease as he repaired things, but he also wore a smile like badge of honor. Nina imagined it killed him inside to know that all that work might be for nothing. The railroad intended to destroy the ranch as if it were meaningless.

"Is there something wrong with you?" Donald Henderson all but yelled at Sam now. The brim of his hat crumpled in his hand, and the lines on his forehead aged him about ten years as he sneered at Sam. "Didn't your mother teach you manners? If someone asks you a question, the right thing would be to answer them!"

Sam flinched at the words like they were sharp daggers. When the initial spasm of fear from Henderson's yelling passed, Nina felt her heart breaking for Sam. This rude man from the railroad had no idea what Sam had been through; she had no idea until today. Nina took a step closer to the door. She wasn't sure what she was going to say, but she felt like she needed to protect Sam somehow.

"Sir," Nina attempted to get him stop so that Sam could have a moment to think, so that Henry wouldn't be woken up. "Sir, please,"

"Don't you people understand the importance of the railroad! It's going to change the face of this nation!" Mr. Henderson sounded like his throat was scratching with the effort that it took him to speak over her.

Not even a moment later, Nina and Sam could hear Henry's cries coming from the nursery on the floor above. Feeling defeated, she put her forehead in her palm, and shut her eyes, taking a moment to collect herself before she went to soothe Henry.

Sam hit his breaking point and let out a growl so loud and guttural that Nina quickly forgot about being upset. She imagined that the sound reached Henry upstairs and she wondered if it spooked him for a second time. Nina watched Mr. Henderson's eyes go wide with surprise. He shut the screen door and took several steps back.

Nina held her breath as she wondered what the sour interaction would mean for the future.

Chapter Twenty-Three

Sam felt the rage inside of him festering like an open wound as he stared at Donald Henderson through the screen door. His skin crawled as he heard little Henry crying from his nursery. The idea of the child being afraid made Sam even more upset.

If I could scream and yell, the force would knock him into the next county, Sam thought as his whole body shook with anger. He didn't want Nina to see him like this. *I can't allow myself to get that upset. It might make her afraid of me.*

Things had been starting to go so well between them that the thought of ruining all of it made Sam swallow his emotions down and slam the door in Mr. Henderson's face instead. He had to show Nina that he had self-control, that he could be the better man. It was a task that was easier said than done.

"I should go tend to Henry," Nina blurted before she brushed past him and all but fled up the stairs.

As she passed, Sam could see that her face was pale. He wasn't sure if it was from what Mr. Henderson said or how he reacted, but it made Sam angry all over again.

So much for not upsetting her.

Sam thought he had more time. Yes, the worksite loomed closer every day, but it still seemed like it was in the distance, a faraway dream. The more he thought about it, Sam knew he avoided traveling to the property line because he didn't want to know how much the work progressed. He was in denial, just like he was when he received the letter. If he threw it out and pushed it from his mind, the problem didn't exist. Unfortunately, it seemed that the problem and the railway grew larger by the minute.

Too anxious to stay inside, the minute Sam was certain that Donald Henderson was gone, he headed to the barn. He vowed to saddle up Sadie and see for himself how close the Central Pacific Railroad was to ruining everything he worked so hard to build. His body shook as he went to fetch his saddle and bridle.

When he heard the sound of horse hooves coming down the dirt road echoing in the distance, Sam wasn't sure if Donald Henderson was persistent or a fool. What else did he possibly have to say that wasn't an insult? Sam reached for the shovel he used to muck out stalls, prepared to wield it over his head and chase the railroad manager off the property if it came to that. A voice called out to him and temporarily put him at ease, the familiarity like a salve on an open wound. Sam felt like he could breathe again.

"Sam?" Jack's voice called outside the barn. "It's Jack, are you out here?"

Oh, thank the Lord. Sam's shoulders slumped even more as returned his shovel to its resting place.

Sam quickly walked out of the barn to see Jack hopping off the back of his horse. He wore nicer clothes than he typically worked in around the ranch. Instead of worn work pants and his leather chaps, he wore a nicer pair of slacks and a button-down shirt that didn't have any stains. Sam almost felt as though he could chuckle at seeing the weekend version of Jack, so tidy and neat.

"I was in the area," Jack started to explain, "I needed to go to town to get a few things to fix the axel for my wagon." Sam squinted as the afternoon sun beat down on them, waiting for what Jack would say next. "Was that the project manager of the railroad?"

Jack didn't have his notebook with him, and Sam wasn't in the mood to go inside to get the one he shared with Nina. Instead, he nodded a few times, and let his face twist into a caricature of itself. His eyes widened with worry, then he scowled. He wanted to make it clear that the situation troubled him deeply.

Yes, Jack, and I don't know what I'm going to do to stop him.

"Here I thought we would just be joking about fighting the Central Pacific Railroad," Jack said in disbelief. "Seems like me might have actually do it."

Yes, but how can you fight something so much bigger than you? Sam thought, wishing that Jack could hear his thoughts. Maybe he could instill a sense of just how desperate he felt into their interaction. The whole thing just seemed so hopeless.

"Are you all right? Does Nina know?" Jack asked him.

Sam could only shrug, but inside his thoughts bubbled like a pot over an open flame. *I'm not all right. That blasted railroad wants to build where my house is standing. Nina saw everything, including how I behaved. She probably thinks I'm just as uncivilized as that no-good Donald Henderson.*

I'm feeling the lowest I've felt in a long time.

The admission made his head pound.

Jack had known Sam long enough to recognize that there was more to him than just his gestures or even what he wrote when he was able to. Though he couldn't quite crack the inner confines of Sam's mind, he tried to be supportive, nonetheless.

"Me and the fellas, we're with you to the bitter end," Jack gave Sam a pat on the shoulder. He attempted to sound encouraging. "Now, I should get to town before the general store closes."

Sam shook Jack's hand and watched him ride away. He wanted to believe that Jack's words were genuine, but doubt soon burrowed into his thoughts. *I know you say you aren't going anywhere, but work is work.* He worried that if the situation became too precarious with the railroad, Jim, Amos, and even Jack would take off to find greener pastures. Sam tried to tell himself that it wouldn't be personal, it was just how business worked sometimes, but he still felt a stab in his chest, nonetheless.

Eventually, he resumed tacking Sadie up, and once he mounted her, he took off at a brisk trot. A nagging need overwhelmed his heart, pushing him toward the property line. Sam needed to know that he had more time, that Donald Henderson approached him prematurely. Then he could go back to his comfortable denial, just for a while.

As he made his way across his property, he thought of all the fences he fixed and the few pastures he tilled and made usable. Sam could still feel the sweat that made his shirt cling to his back and the dirt beneath his fingernails.

He expected the same sensations when he worked on the other parts of the ranch in the future. Sam wanted every pasture filled with cattle and horses, and enough crops that could establish his ranch as a proper farm. He had so many plans to make it thrive.

He reached the meadow with his special wildflowers, now more precious to him than gems. Just the sight of them soothed him after the drama that unfolded back at the house. He thought about picking a new bouquet to soften the image of the sharp man Nina had witnessed. As he stared at the lovely blooms, he knew that if Donald Henderson had his way, this natural beauty would most likely be destroyed.

Sam's mind was forced to shift focus when not only could he see the railroad worksite in the distance, but he could hear it as well.

It's Saturday. What are they doing working today?

Sam wished that he was dreaming or that perhaps he had his days wrong. There were men working on the site, their pickaxes smashing rocks and their shovels moving dirt. Behind them, more men laid iron tracks, hammers flashing in the sun as they nailed everything in place.

It was a rhythmic, persistent reminder that they inched ever closer.

His blood ran cold as he made out the form of Donald Henderson, dressed all in black, his hat now securely on his head as he stalked about. Sam couldn't hear exactly what he said, but he could hear the frequency of his voice as he barked orders.

Sam's stomach twisted so violently, he feared that he would be sick.

This can't be happening, he despaired, *I have put some much work and effort into this ranch. I can't move. Where will I go? This is the only place that has truly felt like a home since I lost my parents.* A thought crept into Sam's mind like a thief in the night; *what about Henry and Nina?*

Sam felt so ill that he worried he might fall out of the saddle, dizzy and incoherent. All this time, he was so focused on himself and the work he did on his ranch that he failed to consider that he had other people to worry about beyond himself. Up until Henry had been left on his doorstep, the thought never crossed his mind. The company's desire to build on his property not only affected him, but it made Henry and Nina vulnerable as well. He was so headstrong that he did not realize what would happen to them if Henderson decided he didn't want to play nice.

How could I let myself get so wrapped up in falling for a woman? I can't speak to her and now I can't protect her either.

Sam blamed himself for being so foolish and ridiculous, the shame weighing on him like a pile of bricks. If he didn't do something, he wouldn't be able to provide a home for any of them. Without his ranch he had no money—all his business would dry up. He had no family to stay with, and he wasn't sure if Nina was welcome at her former home. She was very guarded about her past.

If the railroad did some of the things that his ranch hands feared, he put Henry and Nina in danger while still turning his back on his problems. Even if he was no longer in denial, Sam wasn't sure if he'd be able to stop what was happening even if he tried.

It's just like the fire, Sam thought to himself, *I'll never be enough. I won't be able to stop the railroad and I won't be able to protect everyone.* He had to turn Sadie away so that he would stop looking at the railroad and the bleak future that was approached him. He could feel the emotions threatening to escape again, the anger and despair. His body shook as he tried to fight it.

I'll never be enough for a woman like Nina.

Chapter Twenty-Four

The tension was so thick that it enshrouded Nina like mist on a frigid autumn morning. It lurked in the knot forming between her shoulder blades when she tried to clean the kitchen. It pounded against her temples from the moment she woke up until she laid her head on the pillow at night. Sam didn't seem much better. He walked around the house with his jaw set and his face taut. Nina caught him sitting on the porch with his head in his hands when he didn't realize she was nearby. The sight of him looking so defeated was enough to make her want to weep.

Several days passed since Donald Henderson paid them a house call. Every moment since, the man's demands whispered in the back of her mind like a ghost.

If you had read the letter, I explained that the path we are building goes through your land. I will pay you handsomely for it. The future of the country depends on it!

Nina felt a little upset that she didn't know about the letter. Something so important that the entire country depended on it seemed like something she should have known. She tried to tell herself that Sam had just started opening up to her and could have received it before she started working for her, but it still hurt. If she had known about it, she might have been able to help with the altercation that had taken place.

Is Donald Henderson serious? Is the railroad really going to build straight through Sam's land? Nina wondered to herself when chores and taking care of Henry couldn't keep her racing thoughts at bay. The idea seemed so wild to her. *Don't they understand that people have lives? Surely Sam's ranch isn't the only one affected?* Nina began to wonder if everyone merely gave in to the tycoon's demands and sold their land.

She also pondered if that meant the railroad was really a cruel as she heard when she went into town with Sam.

When her headache and the tension in her back became unbearable, Nina's mind refused to quiet. She thought of every worst-case scenario possible, and her ruthless mind would attack her heart.

What if Sam sold his ranch? Would she and Henry be on their own? It seemed like such an irrational fear, but it lingered, nonetheless. Even if it did happen, Nina knew she would never give up the child. She knew she didn't have enough money to buy a place to live on her own and she didn't want to go back to San Antonio. Despite the fear and the uncertainty that prickled against her spine, Nina knew that she couldn't go back. She liked her independence now that finally had a taste of it. Now that she was getting to know Sam, the thought of leaving him behind seemed worse than facing Jane or her adopted parents too. The idea of never seeing his smile or standing as close to him as she had before Donald Henderson had interrupted them made her feel despondent.

She was so worried about Sam too. Beyond knowing how hard he worked on the ranch, she feared he would have trouble adjusting somewhere else. People could be cruel. Mr. Henderson was a perfect example that, thinking that Sam was rude when he didn't speak.

As frightening and startling as Sam was when he slammed the door in Mr. Henderson's face, Nina didn't blame him for what he did at all. Henderson all but forced himself into the house and woke Henry up on top of it. He called Sam rude when he behaved exactly that way to her and Sam.

There had to be something they could do. As Nina cooked dinner and Henry sat at the hem of her skirt and played, she tried to think of a solution. Maybe tomorrow she'd find Jack out in the yard and ask if he knew of any places they could go or things they could do to combat the encroaching railroad. Anything had to be better than sitting around and waiting for something to happen.

The screen door slamming alerted Nina of Sam's arrival back at home. When she came down to make breakfast earlier, only the sight of his dirty plate on the counter and a note in his ledger greeted her.

Sorry for skipping breakfast. I have some work to do before Jack and I go on an important errand. I'll be back by supper.

Nina speculated all day what the errand was. She paced the floors as Henry played, wondering if they went into Carson City for something or if perhaps Sam was in the same frame of mind that she was—that he was trying to find a way to fix their issue with the Central Pacific Railroad.

When Sam rounded the corner, the crestfallen look on her face told her everything she needed to know about how his errand had gone. He looked like he was dragging a heavy weight behind him, and he fell into his chair like he could barely keep going. The sight made Nina's heart ache with worry.

"Welcome home," Nina tried to be cheerful, but it was hard to put on a brave face when her body felt like was fighting her. Luckily dinner was ready, and she spooned some beef stew into a bowl for him before she put a smaller serving in one for Henry. It was too hot for him to have yet, so she set it to the side. Nina stared at it as steam rose toward the ceiling. "How was your day?"

Sam heaved a sigh before he pulled the notebook and pencil close to him. Nina continued to focus on the steam rising from the bowl as Sam's pencil scratched against the paper furiously.

When he finally finished, he pushed the ledger away, and Nina sat down at her spot to read what he wrote.

I wish I could tell you that it was a good one. It wasn't and I'm starting to lose faith in this whole situation with the railroad.

"What do you mean?" Nina asked, feigning ignorance. Based on how rigid Sam held his body and how he walked into the room, as if he was being forced to shoot someone, she knew things were bad. She still wanted to hear the words herself instead of making assumptions. She hoped it would put her nervous mind at ease. Maybe there was a chance that she was wrong about her concerns.

While she raced through these thoughts, Sam began to write his reply. Henry's stew was now cool enough for him to eat, so she gave him a few spoonfuls before she read Sam's newest reply.

Jack and I went to the neighboring farm today. I thought that maybe if all of us landowners were a united front, we could make the Central Pacific reroute the line. They sold their ranch and are most likely moving west. They heard the rumors about what the railroad will do to people who don't sell or give in, and they got scared.

As she processed the words, Nina didn't want her shocked face or trembling body to scare Henry, so she tried to keep her face neutral as she continued to feed him his dinner. She also heard these rumors, but she just assumed that they were exaggerated stories that people told children to frighten them. The fact that their neighbors seemed to believing Henderson's stories worried her. If it was bad enough that they were willing to sell their land and move away, it couldn't have been great news for Sam and his ranch.

"I'm so sorry, Sam." Nina finally mustered. "I was hoping for better news too."

Sam had taken the pencil and written a quick line.

I'm alone.

Nina's jaw dropped at the words. How could he think that? The idea that he felt like she wasn't supporting him made her wish that she had talked to her about his fears sooner. It made her want to grab him tightly and never let go. She thought about telling him out loud, but last time he shared something so important with her, she wrote back. It was easier to write out her feelings that saying them out loud anyway, as though she and Sam shared a special secret; it made her feel special. Lately his handwriting and spelling seemed to be improving so maybe writing something back to him could cheer him up as well.

She snatched the book from him and wrote back.

You have me. I'm not sure how I can help, but I'm not going anywhere.

Sam looked up from the notebook to meet her eye, like he studied her to determine whether her words were sincere or not. His earlier worry evaporated, his face returning to the boyish wonder that she found so endearing. She wondered if he would have grown out of that smile if his parents and younger sister hadn't been tragically lost when he was so young, like putting the smile on shelf to only be used very rarely.

He nodded at her firmly, like the thought of them being together in this madness was motivating.

That determination to better himself and everything around him was one of the many things that made her fall for him.

Chapter Twenty-Five

After their confrontation with Donald Henderson, the railroad upped their production to what felt like absurd levels. They began working all seven days of the week, and seemingly around the clock. Maybe Sam was getting paranoid as he struggled to fall asleep, but he swore he could hear pickaxes and dynamite explosions while he lay there with his eyes wide open.

This can't be happening, Sam would groan in his mind as he would try to block out the noise. He even put his pillow over his head to try to sleep. He tossed and turned for what felt like hours. When he would finally fall asleep, locomotives barreling through his horse barns filled his dreams, the sound of the whistle threating to rupture his ear drums. Sam would wake up in cold sweat, his body trembling as he realized that it was only a dream.

Every morning after the dreams and the incessant working, Sam would ride to the property line. As much as he wanted to run and hide, he could no longer deny what was happening. He started a battle the Central Pacific Railroad and now he watched as they strengthen their offensive.

They are getting closer. I would bet they just over a mile from here. Sam stared at the worksite in disbelief. *It's only been a week since Mr. Henderson paid me a visit and they've doubled their distance. What am I going to do?*

On that morning, when he returned Sadie to her stall and prepared to meet with Jack and the others for their daily ranch work, Sam felt his stomach drop down to his boots when he saw Nina standing on the porch, rocking a crying Henry back and forth. He got the feeling that Nina had been waiting for him for a while, though the sun had just barely risen.

Sam had plans to clean all the leather tack he used for his horses and turn a few out in a different pasture than normal so they wouldn't be spooked by all the noise. His heart told him that whatever was going on with Henry needed to take precedence.

He didn't have his notebooks, but he looked at her with concerned eyes and turned up his hands to show that he was confused and surprised to see her waiting for him. The feeling of dread that he felt up at the property line had dulled slightly, but seeing Henry upset made him feel wary again.

"Henry is sick," Nina stated, holding Henry tightly and pressing her cheek against the top of his little blond head. "He is so hot. I think he has a fever."

That means I'll have to call for the doctor. That means I'll have to ride past the worksite and see all those men that hate me. The thought made Sam anxious, like he wasn't sure if he should avoid doing it or if he would fight someone if they mouthed off.

Sam's body spasmed with guilt as he realized that Henry's health was more important than the judgement he'd get from the Central Pacific Railroad or whether it made him feel uncomfortable. He wasn't sure how much more stress he could bear, but Sam knew that he must take care of Henry. He heard stories all the time about people who became sick quickly and by the time the doctor came it was too late. He ushered Nina back inside and wrote his suggestions in the notebook.

I can have Jack or one of the other ranch hands send for the doctor. What about a cold compress? I don't have a lot of medicines or remedies, but we could always go into town for them.

Nina scanned the page quickly before she nodded and took off for one the closets where he stored towels and washcloths. She also had a basin of clean water in her room, and she dampened it before she placed it on Henry's forehead. The child didn't seem to be completely soothed by this, but Sam thought it was improvement enough until the doctor could arrive. His crying faded to a soft whine instead of an intense wail.

"I'm going to try to get him to rest," Nina said as they looked down at his flushed cheeks and his damp little nose. "I really don't think it's his teeth this time."

Sam nodded before he went outside and searched for Jack. The man had a large coil of rope over his shoulder, as if preparing for a serious training session with one of the green horses. Sam immediately began to mime writing in a notebook. Jack dropped the rope and pulled the pad out of his pocket, handing it over.

The baby is sick. I need someone to get the doctor.

"Amos should be able to do it, he has to stop by the blacksmith for some horseshoes today."

It was the longest afternoon of Sam's life. He had tons of work to do. There were about a dozen horses to prepare for sale in addition to all the leather work that was on his mind. Some were green to wearing saddles and bridles, while others just needed a good grooming. There were also repairs; several of the stall doors started to rot in places. There were countless things he could have done to make the ranch bigger and better, but Sam just paced the old floorboards on his front porch.

I don't want anything to happen to Henry. Despite the child being abandoned on his doorstep, Sam could no longer imagine life without him. It would a large hole in his heart that would never heal.

He was cute and, without Henry, he never would have met Nina and their strange little family would never have formed. He didn't want to jump to conclusions, but if the illness was serious, it would cause grief and suffering that Sam didn't think he could endure again. The very thought made him want lie down and never arise.

Sam could feel his emotions starting to slip out of control. He had so much work to do and yet he was too tired to move. A crippling voice in the back of his mind told him that he could work hard and do all these improvements yet Donald Henderson would ruin it all anyway. *I'm only one person. How can I possibly stand up to them?* The thoughts made Sam feel so weak, like David facing Goliath for the first time.

A shiver suddenly coursed through Sam, as if someone dumped a large basin of ice water over him. Just recently, Nina read Henry the tale about the young King David and the Philistines. He couldn't believe he just made the connections now.

I'm David, Sam thought, *everyone else is too afraid to stand up and fight the Central Pacific. They're selling their farms, their running away. I can't do that. I must fight. As terrifying as it is, I must have faith in God that He is on my side.*

Sam felt his body lift like something divine imbued him with strength. He had to carry on. Taking action could occupy his worried mind and hopefully put Nina and Henry at ease until a better solution came to mind. He finally stepped off the porch and went to feed and groom a few of his horses. *I'll make my ranch so successful and well known they'll have to build the railroad around me,* Sam mused.

Sam became so absorbed in his work that he didn't notice when Amos eventually returned and stood in the doorway. Sam put down the brush he was using on one of his horses and strode to him quickly. Maybe the doctor was already on his way. When Sam got close enough to see Amos's face, he stopped cold. The ranch hand set his jaw in a hard, unyielding line, like he dreaded what he was about to say.

"I went to town, sir," Amos began. "The doctor was in, but he's overwhelmed with patients. Some kind of flu. Not serious, but every bed was full." He broke his gaze with Sam and looked down at the dirt. "He said it will be at least two days until he can get out here."

Sam nodded and waited until Amos was out of earshot before he kicked a bucket in frustration. He wasn't proud of how he managed setbacks as of late. He tried to have faith, but this was one more situation that tested his fortitude.

It was getting harder and harder to stay positive.

***

Nina and Sam were on their own. They resorted to giving Henry cold baths to keep his fever down and feeding him spoonfuls of broth. Sam had given up on trying to do ranch work, instead taking shifts rocking and holding Henry, desperate to get him to rest.

Sam had become so paranoid about the railroad and their intentions that he swore they had spies. He had a sneaking suspicion that someone watched the house and knew about Henry's illness, trying to make their situation even more dire in their vulnerability.

There were more blasts and explosions than ever before; the minute Henry would finally shut his eyes, a loud bang would rock the house and the boy would burst into sniffly tears. Sam's blood began to boil. It was as if they found things that would force him to give up.

On the second day of waiting for the doctor, a soft knock sounded at the door and Sam's chest filled with a desperate hope that all his prayers were answered. He and Nina stayed in the nursery for what had felt like ages trying to get Henry to nap.

"I can get it," Nina offered, trying to stand up.

Sam knew she was probably trying to help, especially if the doctor had questions that needed answering, but Henry looked so content and comfortable in her arms that Sam gently put a hand on her shoulder and shook his head.

I'll do it, Sam looked at her softly, wishing that she could read his mind. She knew everything she would ever need to know about his feelings—the railroad, Henry's sickness, and even how he felt about her. Since she couldn't, he rose quietly before whoever it was knocked again.

As he left the room and headed down the stairs, Sam hoped that the doctor would give Henry some medicine and he'd be back to his usual happy self in no time. He reached the front door, hoping to quickly usher the doctor inside.

When he opened the door, he quickly pulled his face into a hard, unyielding mask. It was not the doctor from Carson City, but Donald Henderson in his ominous black outfit, like a preacher come to deliver the family's last rites. The man looked delighted to see him, a smug sort of delight like a cat who spied a bird out of its cage.

Aggression filled his eyes as he took a weary, careworn Sam in. If looks could be fell a man, Sam would certainly be dead on the floor. He didn't want Henderson to know how nervous that cruel look in his eyes made him.

"Where's your little wife?" Donald asked looking behind the door. "How can take over your duties for you if she's not here?"

Sam felt his defenses go up. Nina wasn't his wife, but he still felt the need to defend her from this creep of a man. Nina always tried to help him; her intentions were pure, surely even Henderson could see that. He narrowed his eyes at Henderson, hoping his own expression conveyed his lack of amusement.

"I'm here to strike a deal with you again, boy," Donald continued, "I'm maybe a week or two away from reaching your property line. We can do this the easy way or the hard way," he snarled, raising an eyebrow like he was willing Sam to confront him. "Take my offer so you can buy a new piece of land for your wife and baby, or you'll find out if the rumors about what happens to people who cross the railroad are true." Donald Henderson almost seemed proud of his notoriety, his position at the heart of the town's gossip.

Sam gripped the doorknob with white knuckles, remembering all the things that Amos and the other ranch hands said. He recalled the sounds and smells of fire, the familiar scratch in his throat as the smoke tried to choke him. He could hear the piercing cries of his family, trapped in an inferno with no means of escape. There was no way that he could live through that again; there was no way that his heart could endure it.

"Hello?" Donald Henderson all but shouted through the screen door, "Are you some kind of imbecile that can't speak? Maybe I'd be doing everyone in this town a favor if I took care of you and your family. You seem like a bunch of simpletons."

Sam should have been disturbed by what Henderson meant about taking care of his family; the threat didn't sound as empty as it had the last time he paid a visit. Instead, the word *freak* brought him back to when he was a boy, the loss of his home and his family painfully fresh. Not everyone understood how he coped with the tragedy. His silence became the brunt of many jokes and mean comments.

"I thought real men didn't let things bother them."

"What, did your voice burn in the fire too"?

"Sam's a freak. Maybe Jenny should have lived instead of you. She wouldn't have been so weird."

Jenny had always been the more sociable one, but that didn't mean that the words didn't sting. People he once considered friends treated him like leper. Most were cruel or avoided him altogether. Shortly after, Sam left school and started looking for work. New people that didn't know his backstory were still confused by him, but they weren't rude about it.

At least until now.

Donald Henderson looked at him smugly, waiting for an answer, for his defeat. Sam supposed in the man's twisted mind, money or threats solved most problems.

Sam felt glad to let him down.

I will not let him win. I will not let him make me feel like those people made me feel.

The soft trill of Nina's voice singing the lullaby she used to get Henry to sleep drifted down from the floor above. It stirred something in his chest, something motivating. He had to fight for them as much as the younger version of himself.

Sam glared in Donald Henderson's eyes with a look of absolute hatred. He willed himself to say something, anything to make his point across, even if it was a guttural shriek.

"Leave."

It was gravelly, no louder than mutter, but Sam spoke for the first time in over ten years. As he moved to slam the door on Henderson once and for all, he could see the shock painted across the man's face.

Maybe Sam was a force to be reckoned with after all.

When he locked the door, he leaned his back against it, gently hitting his head against the wood. *I was able to say something out loud.*

Sam fought the urge to run up the stairs and try to tell Nina about it. Hell, maybe he'd be able to *tell* her about it. He listened carefully to the silence filling the floor above and hoped that Henry had finally fallen asleep. Sam vowed that he would tell Nina about it later somehow, even if he had to write it down for her.

I wonder if it was a heat-of-the-moment situation, Sam thought to himself as he eventually went to look out the windows in the living room to ensure that Henderson was really gone and not lurking about. *What if I'm not strong enough to say other words out loud yet?*

He supposed he would have to wait and find out.

Chapter Twenty-Six

Nina felt so sleep deprived that she wasn't sure how she could function anymore.

For nearly three straight days, Henry fought his fever, crying all the while. Nina thought the night when he'd been teething was difficult, but at least there was a cause to his pain and strategies she could employ to combat it. Henry needed medicine and the doctor should arrive soon, but Nina worried that she, Sam, and Henry will all lose their minds from lack of sleep first.

Something must change, Nina thought as paced the nursery with a squalling Henry in her arms. She was surprised that her boots didn't wear a trail in the floor from walking the same path over and over. *Sam hasn't done any work in days.*

Nina appreciated his help looking after Henry. He took over rocking and trying to soothe the babe so that Nina could cook or try to shut her eyes for a few minutes. Hearing Henry suffer was difficult. She tried to remain hopeful since his condition didn't seem to worsen, though his improvements were small.

The persistent work on the railway also contributed to their sleeplessness. She tried to push the encroaching railroad from her mind and ignore it, but she struggled. Even at night she could hear the constant tinkering of pickaxes and shouting men. It was a type of torture she never thought she must face.

Sam's gentle knock on the doorframe tore Nina from her melancholy thoughts. He carried a tray with a sandwich made with the crusty bread she enjoyed as well as a glass of water. He placed it down beside her before he reached out, showing her that he would take Henry for a spell.

"Thank you," Nina replied, gently handing the child over. "I've been trying everything, but he just won't sleep."

"No, no, no," Henry whined despite nestling against Sam's chest, "No, no, no." It was like his little mind wanted to sleep, but his body rebelled.

"Hopefully the doctor will be here tomorrow, Henry," Nina tried to soothe the boy as she offered Sam the rocking chair. She had no qualms about eating on the floor. "He'll give you medicine and you'll be all better." There was a part of Nina that feared that there would be nothing the doctor could do, that they must contend with this illness and the railroad for the rest of her days. She could feel the despair threatening to choke her.

Sam held Henry close, shushing him softly as they began to rock in the chair. As Nina ate, she noticed an inscrutable expression clouding Sam's features, a mix of pride and wonder with a little bit of worry. Nina had been so busy with keeping Henry's temperature down, she forgot to ask who had been at the door.

"How are you doing?" Nina asked as she ate her sandwich. "You've been so helpful. Thank you, I really appreciate it." She imagined she would have cracked and broken down by now if she had to manage Henry all alone.

Sam smiled before he shut his eyes, tipped his head back, and pretended to snore. He was exhausted, she could see the dark circles under his eyes that were purple like bruises. Henry looked up at him with a confused expression before he let out a despondent sigh.

"Yes, I'm tired myself," Nina replied, "If Henry would fall asleep, we'd all get some rest."

For a time, they fell into a silent sort of routine. One of them would rock or pace the floor with Henry. Nina sang songs, read stories from the Bible, and recited prayers; she tried everything she could to put the struggling baby at ease. Sam placed Henry in his cradle, on the floor, anywhere to see if he could get comfortable and fall asleep.

"No, no, no," Henry would reply every time, his rosy cheeks still visible in the low lamp light, but Nina noticed that his eyes started to droop.

When the moon rose high in the sky, Nina went to the window and threw it open. *Maybe a breeze would feel good,* she mused. The summer was starting to wind down. As the air caressed her face, Nina suddenly realized something.

"Sam," she whispered, "I think they stopped working."

The longer they listened, the more palpable the silence became; it was more beautiful than any hymn or songbird. Maybe now they would be able to get some rest even if the break wasn't for very long. Nina was so tired she plopped right down on the floor, pulling one of the blankets draped over Henry's cradle onto the floor so she'd have a little cushioning.

Sam must have had a similar idea because he carefully placed Henry on the floor before he also found a few blankets and lay on the floor as well. They weren't close enough to touch, but there was enough room to put Henry between them if he slid down from Sam's chest.

Henry grasped tightly onto Sam's shirt, but he rested his head on Sam's chest like it as the most comfortable place in the world. Nina felt her heart squeeze at the sight. She was happy that Henry seemed to enjoy Sam's company too.

"Goodnight, Henry," Nina whispered, reaching out the gently rub his back, "Goodnight Sam." As she smiled at Sam, she could feel her body giving into the exhaustion. Her eyes felt like they weighed a hundred pounds apiece.

As she shut her eyes and began to drift off to sleep, she swore she heard Sam whisper goodnight back to her. Nina smiled softly, convinced that she was so tired she began imagining things. She felt convinced that hearing Sam speak was something she'd only hear in her dreams.

***

The next day, the morning sun streamed in from the windows. Nina's back was stiff from sleeping on the floor, but that hadn't been what woke her. Unfortunately, she could hear booms in the distance and the din of voices coming in from the open window.

Had Henry finally fallen asleep, she wondered to herself. The last thing she could remember was looking into Sam's eyes before sleep had finally taken over. She carefully rolled over, and she was nearly overcome with emotion at the sight before her eyes.

Sam and Henry still slept, their breath in a steady, cohesive rhythm as they lay together. Henry's limbs were loose, arms draped across Sam's chest, and Nina felt elated to see that the normal color returned to his cheeks. When she crawled over and placed the back of her hand on Henry's forehead it no longer felt unbearably hot.

It seemed that his fever finally broke.

Thank God, Nina thought to herself, *maybe now we can finally have our lives go back to normal.* Yet Nina's brief moment of relief quickly curdled, like fresh milk left too long in the sun. *The railroad isn't stopping their project anytime soon*, Nina mused, *and normalcy as we know it no longer exists*. Her heart bled for Sam; he was going to have to make a decision about what do about the future of his ranch, and he was going to have to make it soon.

As he slept, Nina observed no worries or fear etched into his handsome face. He looked peaceful and youthful. Nina wondered if that was how he had looked when he was young, before he lost everything in the fire. He was still so young in the grand scheme of things, but he endured so much already. She decided to let them both sleep a little longer and got to her feet to search for something to make for breakfast.

She was about halfway down the stairs when there a soft knock sounded at the door. Nina felt her body lift even higher at the noise. Maybe the doctor finally arrived and could help Henry's health improve even more. She went to unlock the door and wondered for the briefest of seconds if perhaps Mr. Henderson had returned, and if she would have the gall to turn him away. Nina doubted he would listen to her anyway.

Here goes nothing, Nina thought as she opened the door, praying that things would be normal if for even a moment.

No doctor, no railroad project manager. Instead, there was a young man with a mail bag standing on the porch, with a letter in his hand.

"Nina Mason?" He asked, pushing the letter at her.

"That's me," Nina replied with a nod. She took the letter and gave him a wave before she shut the door behind her. In the several months she lived here, she never received any mail. When she looked down at the return address and her jaw dropped open. She certainly wasn't expecting to ever hear from the supposed person holding the pen.

Harper

13 Arlington Road

San Antonio Texas

She noticed that it was the address of the farm Nathaniel purchased before she discovered him in the woods with Jane. She felt her heart going to war with her mind. Nina wasn't sure why he would write to her or if she wanted to hear what he had to say. She was finally so far removed from that part of her life. Despite this, there was a part of her that yearned to know how he found out where she was staying, so she quickly tore open the letter.

"It's not like I have to write back," Nina told herself, "Maybe it will tell me what's going on around town since I left."

When Nina recognized the swirling looping handwriting, she suddenly realized that Nathaniel hadn't written her a letter, but Jane.

Chapter Twenty-Seven

Are you alright?

Nina sat at the kitchen table reading a letter. She was so engrossed that she didn't notice Sam or Henry enter, nor did she hear Sam scratch the question into his notebook. Even if he could speak, he wondered if Nina would have noticed.

Sam still tried to process things himself. He woke up on the nursery floor with Henry sitting on his chest, studying him. He felt pleased that Henry finally gotten some rest. When Sam touched his little hand, it no longer felt hot with fever, and he could have cried tears of joy that something finally seemed to be going right.

This deserves a celebration, Sam thought as he placed Henry on the floor so he could stand up. *We'll have to have a special meal.* It was then that he noticed Nina wasn't in the room and he went to investigate. When Sam didn't find her in her room or in the living room working on her sewing, his search brought him to the kitchen.

He gently touched her elbow, causing her to startle. Nina let out a yelp before she looked over her shoulder and saw Sam and Henry standing there.

"Oh, my goodness, you scared me." Nina put a hand to her chest and Sam felt a little guilty for not making a louder entrance. Both of their faces burned with embarrassment over the debacle. Sam looked at the letter on the table and wondered if it was from the Central Pacific Railroad; perhaps that was why she was too absorbed to notice him. He could feel his good mood slipping away as he tried to speculate what they were trying to convince them of this time.

Sam put Henry in his highchair before he gently cleared his throat and pushed the notebook closer to her. Nina finally looked away from the letter long enough to read what he wrote.

"Sorry for not noticing until just now," Nina apologized. "Honestly, I'm not sure how I feel." She bit her lip as she looked down at the paper, like she was deciding if she should share with him about what she was reading. "I suppose you have been so honest with me about your past that it's time that I came clean about mine."

Something compelled Sam to sit down across from her. He wanted to take in every frown or crestfallen look that crossed her face, as well as witness if she held her body rigidly or wistfully as she spoke. He needed to fully understand why she left San Antonio behind. He had been so worried about getting Henry what he needed and then all this railroad business that he hadn't thought to ask until now. Maybe he'd finally understand why she was nervous about his touch when they first started living together. Sam wondered if this would make him fall for Nina more or if it would make things between them more complicated.

"I think I mentioned that I also lost my family in a fire," Nina began, "I was only two years old when it happened, so I don't really remember much. Just vague things, like the smell of smoke and the sound of the flames destroying things. I was an orphan with no family, so I became the burden of a young couple in town that had a daughter close to my age."

The word *burden* and the way it furrowed Nina's brow as she said it moved Sam to pity. He hastily grabbed his charcoal pencil and wrote his reply.

What do you mean burden*? How could anyone feel like you were trouble, you were a child? Seeing how you are here; I have no doubts that you were a helpful daughter.*

Sam hoped she knew that his words were sincere. Even before his life had become tragic, he couldn't think of anyone more lovely or kind than Nina Mason.

"Thank you, Sam," Nina replied gratefully when she read what he wrote about her. "Unfortunately, they really didn't want me. They had my stepsister Jane and felt their family was complete. My whole life they treated me differently from her. Everything I did wasn't good enough. I was held to stricter standards when it came to chores and behavior. That being said, they didn't hit me or anything. They just had very heavy expectations of me that they didn't have for Jane. It didn't always seem fair."

Nina heaved a sigh and looked out the kitchen window like she was taking a minute to collect herself, so Sam took the moment to write his next questions.

Are your stepparents the reason you took the job here? Are they who wrote you the letter?

Eventually Nina looked back at the ledger and contemplated her reply before she answered him. All the while, Sam thought that she looked absolutely beautiful. Beyond her large doe like eyes and her defined cheekbones, there was a determination behind the sadness in her eyes, like she wanted to confront the future with honesty about her past. It was almost as endearing as when she was being gentle and kind.

"My stepparents are just a small reason why. I'm afraid I took the job offer for more dramatic reasons." Sam watched her face flush before she added. "I was engaged to be married before I came here."

This time it was Sam's turn to avert his gaze to the window, hoping that he kept his face neutral as the words hit him like a punch. *Engaged?* It didn't surprise him, Nina was beautiful, kind, and cared more about others than herself. *But why on earth did she walk away from a fiancé*, Sam pondered, incredulous. She would have most likely had financial security and home. Nina should have been home having her own babies and not being a governess.

Sam worried that he might have misunderstood something, that maybe Nina took the job to help save money for a home or a wedding. When he glanced back at the letter, he had an even more worrisome thought. Maybe the reason why Nina seemed so distracted by the letter was that it was from her fiancé, and he was begging her to come home.

Maybe they agreed that she would work for a while, and he couldn't stand being away from her anymore. Sam imagined Nina packing up and heading back to San Antonio leaving him and Henry behind. The idea made him want to get on his knees and beg her to reconsider. Yet another thought struck him; she spoke of her fiancé in the past tense, and the notion slowed Sam's plummeting spirits.

He hastily scratched the pencil against the rough paper of the ledger, his palms sweating against the charcoal, eager to learn more about this mysterious fiancé.

You were engaged? What happened?

Sam clung to the small hope that Nina's fiancé was in her past like a drowning man to a buoy. Was it selfish? Absolutely. Now that he had Nina in his life, he didn't want to know a world without her in it. The realization temporarily soothed his frantic thoughts.

"I found out that my stepsister and my betrothed, Nathaniel, were having an affair." Nina paused and Sam watched her chest shudder, her resolve failing, as she struggled to get out what she going to say next without crying. "When I confronted Jane about it, she told me that Nathaniel was only going to marry me because he pitied me. He felt bad that I had lost my real parents in the fire. Everyone in town, my stepparents included, thought Jane was a better match for him." Nina dabbed her eyes with her sleeve, and Sam wondered if it was the first time she spoke of the affair in a long while. "I was so hurt that I took the first opportunity that I could to leave. A friend at the post office showed me your ad and here I am."

Reaching for the notebook to write back, Sam never realized how well Nina hid all that she suffered. He assumed that Nina was homesick or turned off by his muteness. All this time, she grappled with betrayal and despair.

How could someone possibly betray Nina? Sam thought she was an angel, more perfect than he could ever be. If he had a different life, one where he wasn't damaged and broken, he would have scooped Nina up the first chance he got and never let her go. As he stared at her despondent face, Sam knew with every fiber of his soul that he needed to protect her. She needed a place where she would feel safe and loved. He would not let anyone make her hurt again.

Thank you for sharing. I'm so sorry that you had all of that happen to you. You don't deserve it. I know how kind you are. I'm sorry for pressing, but who wrote the letter?

Nina sniffled but smiled at him. "Sam you are so sweet. You are making me feel better, and I really appreciate it. I also find peace in knowing that we have something in common, even if it's tragic." she pushed the letter across the table to him. "The letter is from my stepsister. After our last meeting, I assumed I would never hear from her again. I'm surprised that I am wrong. You can read it if you'd like."

Sam raised an eyebrow as he picked up the letter. The handwriting curled with extravagance and he squinted to read it to the best of his ability.

Dear Nina,

I hope this letter finds you well. I all but begged Hamish to tell me where you are currently living. He is a loyal friend because he would not share it information at first. I wanted to write you a sincere apology, so he reluctantly agreed to give me the address of your employer.

Nathaniel and I married shortly after you left San Antonio. My hope had been that our relationship wouldn't have to be a secret anymore and it would continue to fill my heart with fire. I wanted that same thrill of loving someone I wasn't supposed to have to continue forever.

Nathaniel is a good man, and he provides me a comfortable life, but I must admit that I am not happy. There is no excitement now that we are husband and wife and I find him often staring into space lost in thought. I wonder if he is thinking about how he never got to say goodbye to you. I understand why you left without seeing him, but it's clear he longs for closure.

I know whatever I will say will never be good enough, but I'm so sorry for what I did to you. I see now that it was like you said, that everything I want and take is out of jealousy. We were constantly compared to one another our entire lives, and it upset me. I imagine it must have bother you as well.

I only pursued Nathaniel because I wanted to hurt you. You are such a gentle soul, so effortlessly charming, and pretty too. Even though mother and father claim to favor me, everyone else loves you. What I said about everyone thinking Nathaniel was a better match for me was a lie. The minute you ran away to Carson City it was like the whole town was mourning your loss.

I understand if you hate me and will never forgive me. I know things can't be the same as they were before you left, but we'd love to hear from you or even have you come home if you are open to it. We would welcome you with open arms.

Jane

Sam looked up to see Nina blinking away her tears, but he suspected that the letter was closure, in a way. Now she knew the truth about what she left behind, though Sam worried that Nina still might want to leave to talk with Nathaniel and find out how he really felt about her running away. Sam wondered if there was a part of Nathaniel that still loved Nina. He didn't imagine Nina's stepsister and former lover would divorce, but he didn't want to see Nina go through any more pain, especially with all the trouble they experienced with Henry and the railroad.

"She makes it sound so easy, to just love someone or not," Nina said wistfully. "As hard as it was, I'm so glad I came here. It would have been hard to watch them together every day and know they're miserable, to know that they both acted in haste when all I wanted was to be loved."

He handed her back the letter, expecting her to put it away and never think of it again. Sam was surprised when she took his hand into hers from across the table, holding it tightly while she gave him a soft smile. Any fear that she wanted to return to San Antonio disappeared as he stroked his thumb over her soft skin, as though they tried to soothe one another without saying a word.

I'm happy you're here, Sam thought to himself, savoring the moment instead of writing it down for her to read. *I hope you stay forever.*

Sam just had to find the right moment to tell her that so that she would.

Chapter Twenty-Eight

"The doctor said the medicine and a little cod-liver oil will make you good as new," Nina explained to Henry as she spooned out enough for one dose. The child's face soured into a pout, and he violently shook his head. "Please, Henry, it will make you feel better."

Henry improved so much, given the circumstances, and the doctor suspected that he got the nasty cold making its way through the town. Nina felt so thankful that he hadn't gotten sick enough where they would have had to take him into Carson City to stay overnight with the doctor. As Nina finally got him to open his mouth and take his medicine, she knew she should have felt better, but they were still so tired.

The workers for the Central Pacific continued their around the clock labor, working so hard that they finally arrived at the property line of the ranch. As Nina cleaned Henry's face with a damp rag and picked him up, she still couldn't believe it. She strode to the front door and went out onto the porch to take in the sight so that she could prove to herself that she wasn't trapped in a terrible dream.

Sam used to have to ride his horse to the furthest pasture to catch a glimpse of the newly-laid train tracks, but as Nina stood on the porch, she could actually see men standing by the gate at end of their long driveway. They crossed their arms over their chests, with daggers for eyes glaring at the driveway and farmhouse. Nina could tell that they weren't happy.

It was like they felt she was personally responsible for preventing them from going an inch further. Nina would have liked to protest that if they surveyed the land properly, they probably could have forged a route that didn't go through farms and homes, but it was too late for that.

Though the racket had grown quieter, they didn't sleep any better. The railroad company had gotten as far as they could go without crossing onto Sam's property and if they couldn't finish the job, they couldn't get paid. Nina feared that all that restlessness and resentfulness were going to build up and something terrible was going to happen.

Everyone seemed to assume that she was Sam's wife, so Nina supposed that made her public enemy number two after him. That was why they looked at her like she was lower than filth and probably blamed her for their hardship. The thought of what they could do if things went on for too long made her anxious, but as Nina stared across the property at them, she felt a twang of pity in chest. They were just victims or circumstance, it wasn't personal. Sam didn't seem like one to hold a grudge.

The Central Pacific worked the poor men like slaves. They looked exhausted; their clothes were dirty and tattered and their faces gaunt. Nina wondered when the last time they had taken a break or been allowed to eat anything. She also wondered if Donald Henderson told them lies, that Sam and Nina were horrible, nasty people who were unwilling to cooperate. The second half was true she supposed, but Nina didn't think she was either of those things.

Perhaps I could make them a peace offering, Nina thought, looking down at Henry and how he also seemed to watch the men with his curious blue eyes. She wondered what he thought about all the noise and people standing in the distance.

Who could resist Henry's adorable little face? Perhaps it's time to pay them a visit so they can see we aren't evil haters of the railroad.

Suddenly, she was full of purpose, and Nina returned to the kitchen. She gave Henry a few pots, pans, and spoons to play with on the floor as she set to work. Nina settled on making several loaves of sweet bread as well as batches of molasses cookies. They were her specialty back in San Antonio, and her step father requested them for any special occasion. When they were cool enough to touch, Nina put the baked goods into a basket, strapped Henry into his papoose she made for him, and said a silent prayer in the kitchen.

Please God, let them understand that Sam is trying to have a home and make a living. Have them have compassion for us. Keep us all safe. There was really nothing else to be done but go out and meet them.

She walked outside, trying to hide her shaking nerves as she made her way to the front gate. The sky was azure blue and the was a slight breeze that made stay hairs tickle her face. She tried to tell herself that she had no reason to be afraid, that she would find her way into their hearts through their stomachs. Still, she felt intimidated. There were so many of them and they looked so unhappy.

"Where go?" Henry asked, no doubt watching the house grown smaller and smaller as they walked away from it. "Where go?" He sounded apprehensive, the words turning up into a whine with each question.

"We're going to be friendly to the railroad people, Henry," Nina answered, "It's what God would want us to do." She hoped that the men would understand that more than the young child would.

The closer she approached the more railroad workers started congregating closer to the property line. They stood in groups, and she could tell they were talking about her. Their eyes drifted over her before they grumbled into each other's ears and laughed. She wasn't exactly sure what they found funny about the situation. Nina held her chin high, determined to not show her fear that made her heart smack against her chest.

When she was about fifty paces away, someone broke away from the group and walked right up to the gate, his hands grasping onto it tightly. If he could have broken it down and not gotten in trouble, it would have discarded on the side of the road.

Nina noticed that his clothes seemed to be nicer than the others and were the same dark shade that Donald Henderson wore when he paid a visit. Nina wondered if he was someone of importance in the Central Pacific Railroad, a way to distinguish himself from the regular workers.

"Okay Henry," Nina said with a shaky breath. "Time to be as charming as possible."

She was almost at the gate when she felt the atmosphere turn hostile. The man shook the gate, the noise making Nina jump in surprise. "What do you want?" The man barked. The lines on his forehead were deep as he glared at her. He bared his teeth at her like some sort of angry, hissing cat. Behind him several of the workers jeered and laughed. Again, Nina didn't understand how this was possibly funny.

Nina tried to ignore the harsh tone despite his intention to sting her with his words. She tried to tell herself that she was used to people being unkind to her, what were a few more? "Hello, I noticed that you've been waiting here for a while." She tried to step closer to hand him the basket. "I baked some bread and cookies for you and your men. I wanted you to know that we don't blame you for the decision the railroad is making."

Nina noticed that several of the men looked up at her with large eyes when she mentioned what was inside her basket. They reminded her of starving puppies begging for table scraps. Nina felt hopeful, like maybe they'd be swayed to at least hear her out. Maybe she could help Sam with his problems.

The man all but swatted the basket away. "Why would we take any handouts from you? Why would we believe anything you tell us? They're probably poisoned. Your husband wants us to stop building and you no doubt feel the same way. Why on earth should we trust you?" The man looked at her like he was she was a devil trying to tempt him to do the unthinkable.

Nina stepped back in shock. "Poisoned? How on earth would I know how to do that? I wanted to help you." She couldn't believe how tainted his view on her and Sam was. It made her more angry than sad.

"Get out of here and never come back!" The foreman yelled. "Go back to your house. That's where you belong."

She thought about arguing, she wanted to tell him that she had nothing but good intentions, but Nina knew it was a lost cause. She spent hours making treats for these men, and it was all for nothing. "Come along Henry," Nina sighed, defeated, "We'll give the cookies to the ranch hands instead. At least they won't go to waste that way."

Nina tried to not feel discouraged. She had no doubt now that Mr. Henderson probably convinced all the railroad workers to believe that they were awful, uncooperative people in hopes of widening the chasm between them. She felt foolish for thinking that bread and cookies would be enough to sway them. It seemed that nothing she or Sam did would ever be good enough. One thing was clear, though.

This was far from over.

***

I want to go into town. I feel terrible for using you as shield, but can you come with me? I think it might diffuse any situations should they come up.

Sam returned from one of the pastures when Nina made the walk back from the property line. Nina told him everything. She shuddered as she remembered the man's words and the way he glared at her.

"They were ravenous looking, Sam." Nina admitted sadly. "No wonder everyone is so hostile." It reminded Nina of when people purposely starved their dogs to make them more vicious. It was cruel.

Shortly after, Sam had retrieved his notebook and suggested that they go into town. They needed some flour and several other things, so Nina was happy to go with him. As soon as Jack, Amos, and Jim finished their work for the day, Sam hitched up the team and helped Henry and Nina up into the wagon.

Nina could feel her heart pounding against their ribs as they left the property. An irrational part of mind feared that the railroad workers would attack them or the house if they left, that she had somehow made the situation worse. Surprise overtook her when she saw that all the men from before were no longer there. Now that she no longer focused on trying to be kind, she could see just how close the worksite was to their home.

Piles of rail ties and steel littered the ground as they passed. Nina swore that she could see boxes of dynamite and areas designated as campsites. They were literally as close as they could be now without stepping onto Sam's private property.

This is going to come to a head soon, Nina thought with despair. She had no evidence to know exactly when, but it wasn't likely they would stop now after coming so far.

She watched Sam observe the scene, how his hands gripped the reins so tightly that his knuckles grew white. It was as if the reality and severity of the situation suddenly struck him as well.

"Oh, Sam," Nina wailed, "What are we going to do?"

Sam shrugged as he came out of his trance, snapping the reins so the horses would go faster. Nina reached out to keep Henry from falling over, and worry tugged at her heart. She feared Sam let his emotions drive him once again; she supposed she didn't blame him.

Carson City bathed in the amber glow of sunset as they pulled into town. Nina held Henry close and gingerly made her way onto the ground when Sam made her jump out of her skin. He moved so closely to her and she hadn't been expecting it; just a moment ago he had still been in his seat in the wagon. She wondered what caused him to move and act like that.

He pointed at her and Henry before he gestured in the direction of the general store. Nina got the feeling based on his serious face and how rigidly he pointed at the shop that he all but commanded her to go.

"What about you?" Nina asked. "I'm not sure if I can move the bag of flour myself." Then there was the whole matter of anything else they needed. If it wasn't light and required more than one hand, she wouldn't be able to do it.

Sam held his finger up, asking her to wait, before he gently nudged her in the direction of the general store. Nina didn't press further and went on her way.

I guess he will be joining me later and I should take my time. Nina thought to herself as she walked through the front door. *Maybe I can see what they have for fabric while I wait, Henry's growing more and more every day.*

Inside the general store, Nina perused wooden animals and tin trains on a shelf and soft fabric in an assortment of colors while she wore Henry swaddled against her body. All the while, she kept watching Sam through the window, wondering what went through his mind. After he stood by the wagon for several moments, she watched him take out his notebook and walk in the direction of the sheriff's office.

I wonder what he is planning on doing there, Nina thought as she watched him disappear through the doorway and it shut behind him. *Maybe he's letting them know about Donald Henderson.* Nina wasn't sure if getting the authorities involved would help or hurt things, but she knew Sam was desperate to do something. Hopefully it would go better than her attempt with the baked goods.

Henry began to fuss, and Nina wondered if he was getting too large for her papoose because he started struggling inside it when she wore it for long periods of time. He came closer to taking his first steps every day. Soon, he'd probably walk hand in hand with her as they did their shopping.

Nina moved away from the window, hoping that Sam would share the reason for his visit when they met up later.

Chapter Twenty-Nine

In the days that followed, Sam spent more time pacing his porch than he ate, slept, or did any work around the ranch. His eyes always squinted toward the property line and most of the day he waited for the mail.

Sam knew that he probably should busy his rattled mind with work, but the mail was all that he could obsess over. It was the only hope he had at the moment other than divine intervention, and God stepping in was probably a too much to ask. He was unable to save his family from perishing in the blaze all those years ago; maybe God wanted to teach him something or wasn't ready for him in heaven yet because he spared Sam and took everyone else. This situation was terrible, but it wasn't as dire. At least not yet.

I can work and sleep when I hear back from the sheriff. Then I can figure out if I'm truly alone in this fight. Sam tried to stay positive, but he felt desperate. The sinking feeling in his stomach was so intense and sometimes painful that he worried it was turning into an ulcer.

Maybe if I wait them out long enough, they'll just give up. Sam used his hand to shield his eyes so he could see slightly better. Since the railroad job came to a screeching halt once he'd told Donald Henderson to get lost, fewer and fewer men stood at the property line each day. They weren't getting paid while the operation was at a standstill, so Sam assumed that many of them left to find other work. He hoped they were too busy to come back if Henderson called for them.

Unfortunately, Sam knew that the railroad couldn't just end in his front yard. Most likely Henderson and his men regrouped and schemed a new strategy for dealing with him. The thought made him sweat a little and the porch was shielding him from the summer heat. There wasn't much more Sam could do beyond giving up and he wasn't ready to do that yet.

When a horse and rider trotted onto the property, Sam's pulse rocketed. Maybe he had become used to being on the defense, but he half expected it to be someone from the railroad, or even the young kid that delivered the mail. He shook his head and felt like a fool when he realized it was Jack, who had gone into town for horseshoe nails. He was so preoccupied that he forgot to pick them up when he weas in town with Nina earlier in the week.

I need to calm down or I'm going to accidentally hurt someone, Sam thought as a shudder coursed through his body. *I'm so adamant on protecting the ranch, Nina, and Henry that I'm becoming unhinged.* Sam worried what Nina would think if he shot or hurt someone in a fit of hysteria. All hope of her loving him would probably be lost, and Sam knew there would probably be no coming back from that.

Jack rode all the way up to the porch before he pulled his horse to a stop and slid from the saddle. He pulled the box of nails from his saddle bag before he stepped up to talk to Sam.

"The town is buzzing about your war with the railroad," Jack teased as handed him the nails. Despite the jovial tone, worry strained against his features.

Sam placed the nails on the porch and cocked an eyebrow at him as if to say, *what are you talking about?*

"Rumor has it you chased the project manager of the railroad off your property with a shovel and that you were speaking in tongues," Jack smirked for the briefest of moments, "I'm guessing that's not exactly what happened."

Speaking in tongues? Sam clutched onto his stomach as it shook with laughter. That was certainly not what he was expecting to hear, and it was the first time he found something funny in what felt like weeks. *Does that make me intimidating? Is that why they've stayed away?* If that was the case, Sam had no problem keeping up the act until they gave up for good.

Sam nudged Jack and gestured like he was writing something and waited for Jack to hand him his notebook.

I might have growled at him once.

Then Sam proudly added,

I might have also told him to leave. Nothing demonic. Hand to God.

"You spoke to him?" Jack asked, staring at Sam with impressed, wide eyes. "That's excellent news."

One word is hardly talking, but it's a start.

Sam tried every day since to say something else but didn't have much luck. He felt convinced that it was a fluke, or because he was mad. Still, he swelled with pride thinking about how he did it.

Jack looked like he wanted to find out more about what was motivating Sam to use his words when his face became gravely serious. "Look, I know we all said that we'd fight for this place, but wouldn't it be easier to negotiate? I would follow you wherever you decided to build next." Jack's face betrayed his fears of seeming cowardly; he barely looked Sam in the eye as he added, "You are rock solid in your beliefs, but I'm afraid it comes off as stubbornness."

Sam felt his pride at standing up to the Central Pacific Railroad quickly billow out of him like the sails of a frigate losing the wind. For so long it seemed like Jack and the ranch hands were on his side. He worried they were starting to have second thoughts and he supposed that he didn't blame them. Anyone in their right mind could see that this had no good solution. Sam feared he indeed lost his mind long ago.

"The people in Carson City were saying all the same things Amos was. There were stories about mysterious fires and people going missing," Jack continued, wiping his brow with the back of his hand as he swallowed roughly. "Every single time they were people who opposed the railroad."

It had seemed so long ago that they stood out in front of the barn when Amos shared what seemed ghost stories with them. Now, as he stared at the railroad creeping up on his doorstep, he wasn't so sure. He could feel the hair standing up on the back of his neck, wondering if the Central Pacific Railroad was capable of more than just threats. He wanted to believe they had limits and morals, but now he wasn't so sure. It made him shiver.

"I don't want you to get hurt," the concern softening Jack's voice brought Sam back to his senses. "Nina and Henry too. That's why I would rather see you on a new ranch someday than keep fighting this battle."

Sam nodded, and he reached for the notebook. He thought to soothe Jack's worries about the whole thing when a rider from the post office finally appeared on the horizon. Sam's body went rigid as he watched them approach, the feelings of anxiety and nausea from before even worse than before.

"Hello, Mr. Colt," the young man called as he reached into his bag and handed Sam a letter, "This is for you."

Nodding at him in thanks, he tore the envelope open while he and Jack both still stood there on the porch. He had to know; the anticipation of what he future held was too much to bear.

Dear Samuel Colt,

Thank you so much for your visit this week. The views and concerns of Carson City's citizens are taken very seriously and we encourage people to talk to us when problems arise.

Unfortunately, after hearing your account of what has been happening with the Central Pacific Railroad as well as what the project manager has corroborated about the incidents, I am afraid that I must remain neutral in regard to the situation. Technically, the Central Pacific is not building on your land without your consent and no threats or physical altercations have taken place at this time. I wish you luck as you decide if you will sell your property or stay.

Sam crumpled the paper in his hands in frustration, not bothering to read more. He was not surprised in the least that Donald Henderson would say that no threats were made. *Neutral?* Sam thought in disbelief. *Did he pay you to look the other way?*

That was exactly what happened, because all parties involved knew that this project couldn't be finished on its current timeline. The thought made Sam's stomach sink into his boots. What seemed desperate just moments ago transformed into something downright hopeless. If he didn't sell his ranch, what would happen to the railroad? An even more worrisome thought crossed Sam's mind.

What would happen to him, Nina, and Henry? His family?

"What does it say?" Jack asked. Sam wondered if his face betrayed his disquiet feelings. The corners of his mouth dragged down in a scowl, and it must have been obvious to Jack that the letter bore bad news.

Sam had a feeling that the situation would only get worse. It was only a matter of time.

Chapter Thirty

"You sell this farm *now!*"

Nina stood between Donald Henderson and Sam in the front yard. A sour green tinged the sky, as if a tornado were about to drop down from the heavens, making the world feel like it spun too quickly. Nina felt as though she might fall to the ground at any moment. She took in Mr. Henderson's balled up fists and how his face looked like an exaggerated caricature of itself. He looked absolutely villainous against the violent sky.

"I'd rather die than let you on this land!" Sam retorted back, and Nina suddenly knew that she was trapped in a nightmare. His voice wasn't the rich baritone that she imagined, inspired by his deep humming when tried to communicate with her. Nina's voice was the one to come out of his mouth. She felt relieved to know she wasn't witnessing something real as much as she was disappointed that she wasn't hearing his real voice. The situation was too terrifying, and she was ready to wake up; too bad her body wasn't listening to her mind.

"Oh, it can be arranged," Donald Henderson replied with a wicked grin, raising the sight of a long shot gun up to his eye.

The horrifying sound of the gun firing and Nina screaming finally woke her up with a start. Nina clutched onto her chest as she tried to take in the familiar sights of her room. *Henderson hadn't actually shot Sam*, she thought to herself, hoping to slow her racing pulse. Still, she let out heaving frantic breaths as she tried to calm down.

You were just dreaming again, Nina tried to soothe herself in the darkness of her bedroom, *It wasn't real.*

Ever since the sheriff wrote to Sam that he wasn't going to get involved, the dreams began. They were always slightly different, but in them Sam always came to some kind of mortal peril at the hands of the Central Pacific Railroad. She had a dream several nights ago where a locomotive barreled onto the property and ran Sam over, killing him instantly. It was absurd, but it still left Nina just as shaken as the dream with the gun left her tonight.

Nina didn't bother trying to lie back down once her pulse slowed to a reasonable level. The dream would pick right back up where it left off if she didn't walk around and try to clear her head a bit. She searched her dresser until she found a beige shawl and wrapped it around her shoulders. Nina plodded along the hallway and down the stairs. After stopping to light a candle and collect her sewing basket, she made her way onto the front porch.

Her body ached as she moved. The tension bunching between her shoulders spread to her entire body. She felt as though she fell down the stairs instead of walking down them. During the day, Nina did her best to put on a brave face so that Henry wouldn't see her fear. Despite being so young, she knew that he still understood what fear and sadness were.

She also did it to try to help Sam. He had so much on his shoulders that she didn't want to give him anymore stress. Unfortunately, she had a feeling that these dreams were a manifestation of her fear, she feared they wouldn't go away and would intensify if the situation continued.

The business with the railroad became more hostile by the day. Donald Henderson no longer came onto the property to threaten or make offers. Nina watched him stand with his foremen and gesture toward the house, as though they concocted a scheme. Nina worried that it would be dangerous or even deadly, and the thought left her wringing her hands with worry during her waking hours.

To make matters worse, what little men were left waiting for the project to continue threw their bottles of whiskey and used cigars over the fence onto the property, tainting Sam's land with their scorn. Nina could hear them cussing and yelling about Sam whenever she stepped off the porch to fetch water or bring in the laundry. The tension became so unbearable that Nina felt like there was a large stone on her chest, preventing her from doing more than taking in shallow breaths.

Nina focused on her quilting, determined that Henry would get to use it in this house. That they wouldn't be uprooted by this problem. When she stitched almost a third of the quilt and her eyes starting to feel heavy, she collected her things and brought them inside. She didn't feel much better, but it was getting too late. Hopefully the rest of her night would be dreamless so she could be ready for chores in the morning. After all, tomorrow was a new day.

As she made her way to her room, she made sure to stop in front of Sam's door and listen for a few minutes. She focused everything she could on hearing any noise coming from his room.

She would sleep better if she heard his sleeping breaths.

***

I noticed you were up late last night.

The following morning at breakfast, Sam wrote to her, worry swelling his eyes like rainwater in a river during a storm. Nina felt a twinge of guilt. She hoped that her nightmare didn't wake him; she knew that he struggled to sleep well as it was.

"I hope I didn't bother you," Nina answered. "I've been having disturbing dreams and they only thing that makes them go away is being up for a while. I worked on Henry's quilt for a while and then went back to bed."

Concern etched itself into his expression before his face fell as he picked up his pencil and wrote back.

Disturbing dreams? What do you mean?

Sam looked so upset that it made her feel guilty. He reached his hand across the table and gently placed it on top of her own, like he was trying to offer her comfort. Nina let out a shaky breath because she knew her confession would not help the situation. She also knew that Sam wouldn't let her go without talking about it. "Every night, Donald Henderson and the Central Pacific Railroad hurt you in some way and I wake up screaming."

Once she revealed her fear, it was as if a leak sprung in a dam. The worries grew and grew until tears blinded her vision.

"I've heard all the stories that everyone in town say happen to people who go against the railroad. I have no doubt that you've heard them too. I see them standing at property line looking like they are plotting something. I just can't shake this terrible feeling that something awful is going to happen. What if they use all that dynamite they have lying around against us?" Nina voice grew shriller with each word she spoke as she struggled to keep her emotions quelled. The tempo increased to the point where she wasn't sure if Sam could understand her anymore. "I'm so worried about something happening to you. I don't think I could bear it!"

Nina put her hands over her mouth and burst into tears. It was too much. Now wasn't the time to be telling Sam about her feelings. They had a desperate situation with the railroad that seemed to have become a matter of life and death.

Keeping Henry safe was more important than whatever unanswered questions lie between them. Nina felt angry at herself for having such a lack of judgement.

She expected him to write a reply in his notebook, perhaps he would agree that now wasn't the time for such concerns. Instead, he stood up and came around the table, the chair squeaking against the floor as it moved back. Sam pulled Nina to her feet and held her tightly against his chest.

He smoothed down her hair gently with his large hand as he shushed her softly, rocking them from side to side. She saw him do the same thing countless times with Henry when he was upset. Nina knew should have pulled back or told him that it was inappropriate, she had just been scolding herself for saying inappropriate things about her feelings.

She could smell the fresh scent of the soap she used to wash their clothes, but there was another smell, maybe it was his aftershave, that made her equally as entranced. It was the first time she'd been in his strong arms, and yet it felt so familiar. She finally felt at peace.

Maybe denying my feelings isn't what is needed, Nina reflected as she relaxed into his embrace. *People might make assumptions about us, but surely, they're already talking about us and all this railroad business.*

Henry, who had been quiet in his highchair all this time, giggled at Sam and Nina locked in their embrace. The noise brought Nina back to reality. Sam needed to get out to work and she needed to play with Henry and do a few things around the house.

"Thank you," Nina whispered, slipping out Sam's arms and over to the highchair. She saw Sam nod out of the corner of her eye before he excused himself from the room.

I should let Sam know how I feel someday, Nina thought as she let Henry down and placed him on the floor. *Maybe I can do it once everything the railroad is finally sorted out.*

It was unfortunately more important at the moment. Everything else would have to wait.

Chapter Thirty-One

Some nights Sam relived the fire.

He wasn't sure if it happened when he was very tired or when the real world became too overwhelming to bear, but in his dreams, he stood in his front yard, watching the world burn. He could hear the flames lapping greedily at the sky and his family screaming out to him for help. When he finally woke up, he swore that he could still smell the smoke despite the passage of time. Whispers of his tragedy would murmur through the dark room as he tried to separate dream, memory, and reality.

Nina's worries from the morning wrecked him, and he didn't think he could feel any lower. It never dawned on him that the sights and sounds of the dynamite would push her mind to get carried away. Hearing her cry and feeling her tremble in his arms—fragile and soft like a newborn fawn— was probably the second worse feeling he experienced in his life. He struggled with his next course of action as they sat together in the living room before bed.

Abandoning Bible stories, Nina read aloud the Book of Psalms as Henry sat on her lap. Sam could tell that she tried to read to find peace, but he could hear the tremor in her voice. Sam watched her leg bob nervously up and down as she sat in the chair, and he thought about interrupting their evening, loading up the wagon, and spending the night in the hotel in Carson City to give her peace of mind. He wanted to make sure that she never sounded like that ever again.

"'The Lord is my shepherd, I lack nothing. He makes me lie down in green pastures, he leads me beside quiet waters, he refreshes my soul.'" Nina read slowly, like she reflected on every single word. "'He guides me along the right paths for his name's sake. Even though I walk through the darkest valley, I will fear no evil, for you are with me; your rod and your staff, they comfort me. You prepare a table before me in the presence of my enemies. You anoint my head with oil; my cup overflows. Surely your goodness and love will follow me all the days of my life, and I will dwell in the house of the Lord forever.'"

Is Nina worried that she's going to die?

Sam tried to figure out why she read the Psalms instead doing the rosary, which seemed like a much more direct way to speak to God. She already read Psalm one through twenty-two and made it all the way to Psalm thirty before Henry fell asleep in her lap. Yet it was more so the subject matter of that particular Psalm that made Sam uneasy; a sense of foreboding seemed to stalk him like a predator lurking in the underbrush, ready to strike. He wanted to tell Nina that he would make sure that nothing would happen to her and the baby, but he no longer knew whether that was true or not. He hated the way it made him feel worthless.

Again, Sam entertained the idea to flee to the hotel, yet he could not shake the nagging feeling that doing so seemed like a surrender to Donald Henderson and his thugs. Perhaps Jack was right; maybe he was stubborn. He continued to listen to the Psalms in an uncomfortable, smothering silence before finally retiring for the night.

When Sam, exhausted, finally drifted into a fitful sleep, he had the strangest version of his reoccurring nightmare yet. Instead of hearing his family crying out for help, he heard the drone of male voices in the distance. The words were indistinguishable, but they sounded sharp and cruel. Suddenly, he felt as though he was blind—he could no longer see his childhood home, and everything seemed dark and distorted. The one thing that remained constant was acrid, choking stench of smoke. It pricked his nose until he finally opened his eyes in confusion.

At least I didn't wake up in a pool of my own sweat like I typically do, Sam thought to himself as he sat up and ran his hand through hair. He tried to make sense of what he felt and experienced in the dream. *That was odd, and I feel like I still smell smoke.*

Gooseflesh prickled at his skin as the hair on the back of his neck stood at attention. He definitely wasn't imagining it; he knew the scent of fire as intimately as he knew his own mind. The pungent musk that filled his nose was unmistakable and very real. Sam slid out of bed, muscles taut, and wondered if maybe Nina left the stove burning downstairs by mistake. His pulse quickened slightly. *The house should smell worse if Nina left burning after dinner. It must be coming from somewhere else.* He quickly made his way downstairs and along the hallway to find that the kitchen was in perfect order. It was all but sparkling from when Nina cleaned it after supper.

Confusion addled Sam's mind as the smoky scent lingered. As he stood rooted to the spot trying to identify the source, he thought he could hear the faint pop and crack of flames, which he couldn't hear upstairs.

Maybe there's a brush fire somewhere? That happens when it's dry sometimes.

Sam moved to the front door, wondering if a prairie fire burned somewhere in the distance. A few years ago, one roared through the east side of the property after a lightning strike. Luckily it didn't stray close to the house, but he felt thankful that his fields weren't ready for planting a great many crops that year. Yet there hadn't been a storm, and it wasn't hot enough for heat lightning. When he finally opened the door, the sight that greeted Sam made a brush fire look like child's play.

Flames engulfed the stables holding the horses he planned to sell. Embers popped and sparked out of every open window or stall door as smoked billowed toward the heavens. Sam could hear the horses trapped inside whinnying in terror while kicking at their stall doors.

Frozen in shock, he felt like he was fifteen years old again, reliving the burning nightmare of his past.

How can this be happening? Sam thought wildly. A sudden thought dawned on him. *Sadie is in there!*

Torn from his stupor, Sam bolted off the porch and toward the barn. Not only did he need to save the horses for the business deal, but his personal horse was in there, as well as countless others who would come to harm if he didn't act quickly.

The door to the barn hung open, revealing a scene of utter chaos inside. Horses reared and spun in their stalls, the violent cacophony of their frantic cries and the roar of the flames piercing his ears. Sam lunged to grab the nearest lead rope and halter when he noticed what looked like a flaming pile of hay laying in front of all the tack and gear. He couldn't stare at it for too long out of fear that the furious heat would blister his face.

How did that get there? Sam wondered, but there wasn't time to waste. He abandoned the lead rope and ran down the aisleway, unlocking stalls and slapping the horses' haunches so they would bolt to safety. Several did exactly as he hoped and started running toward the safety of the pastures.

Unfortunately, about half remained, too afraid to move through the smoke and flames. As Sam tried to shield his eyes from the smoke, he saw several more piles of hay throughout the barn, lying in places that he would never have left them. It was almost as if they were strategically placed there. Just hours ago, the aisleways had been clear.

Sam couldn't afford to lose any horses, so one by one, he tried to coax out the frightened ones, gently touching their withers as he guided them out of the barn and to freedom. Each time he returned to get the next horse, the smoke became more unbearable, choking and blinding him further. He couldn't help but feel as though it all seemed like a cruel prank of fate.

When he finally reached Sadie, he was step away from collapsing from the lack of oxygen. Sam vowed to not give up; he and Sadie had been on too many adventures to perish like this. She'd been his companion for nearly as long as he left home to strike out on his home; she helped him to forget his past. In the past when she became nervous, he would hum softly in her ear to calm her down.

It worked when the farrier came by or when they would encounter rattle snakes out by the southern property line. Sam could feel his throat scratching with effort as he tried to overpower the roaring fire. He swore he could taste blood, dredged from his ruined throat. Yet there wasn't time to dwell on that now.

Relief washed over him when he and Sadie finally escaped into the fresh air. He threw himself onto the ground, coughing and gasping as he tried to figure out how the fire started. All those years ago, he had been careless and left the lantern too close to a pile of hay when he should have extinguished it and put it away. Every night since he lost his parents, he vowed that it would never happen again. He always double checked his barn when he went in the house for the night.

What on earth caused this?

He thought again of the piles of hay lying in places that didn't make sense. *I didn't leave those there. Is someone trying to sabotage me?* If he couldn't get to the bridles he couldn't save the horses. If his business failed, then there would be no reason for him to stay on the ranch.

A terrible suspicion struck Sam in the stomach, yet a sickening noise interrupted his thoughts. A rumbling like a devastating earthquake forced Sam to scramble to his feet.

The roof of the stable caved in, collapsing dramatically to the earth. The force of the impact brought one of the walls to come down with it, and soon anything that could be salvaged inside was destroyed in heap of fire and rubble.

The rumors that Amos told him about months ago echoed in his mind; *they're just taking it and they don't care if you are on the property or not when they burn the house down.*

Sam suddenly did not care if all the barns burned down. He could rebuild them, they weren't important. He turned back to look at the house only to fall to his knees in shock and agony. The living room windows, now broken, revealed flames and smoke spewing out of them like the very image of hell.

Am I still in a nightmare? Sam thought, his mouth hanging open. He thought about pinching his skin to see if he felt pain or would wake up. *There is no way that this is happening to me twice in twenty-six years. That would be cruel.*

As much as it didn't seem real, Sam knew that the sight his eyes took in was not a dream. Looking over his shoulder at the property line confirmed everything he needed to know.

The railroad worksite was alive despite the midnight hour. Scores of men moved at a frenetic pace, hammering a new rail in place. Standing closest to Sam's gate, arms crossed in triumph over his chest, was Donald Henderson.

Through the smoky haze, Henderson's features distorted. Something sinister radiated from him as he glowered with pride. It was hard to see though the smoke, but Sam thought he could see his chest quaking with laughter.

Sam denied Henderson and the railroad manager did not try to negotiate. Instead, he chose violence. He intended to burn the ranch to the ground and force his way through. As Henderson once said, he gave Sam the easy choice, and he had refused. Now Sam faced the hardest outcome of all.

Henry and Nina are still upstairs!

The revelation made Sam feel as though he was slapped across the face. Sam didn't have time to figure out if the workers broke into his home or just set the house ablaze while he tried to save the horses. He didn't know if the stables had been a distraction, or whether Henderson planned to burn him in his bed as well. All Sam knew was that he had to move quickly to get to Nina and Henry; he had to save them. Life would be meaningless without them.

He couldn't past repeat his past.

Sprinting toward farmhouse, he knew he needed to find a way to wake Nina up. For all he knew, she might have already discovered what was going on and lay frozen in her bed with terror. He thought of Henry in his cradle, breathing in the acrid smoke and crying for them. The mere thought of their distress made Sam want to scream.

He reached the front door, and blistering heat met him as it poured through the screen. He choked as he threw the door open. With so much smoke, it was impossible to tell where the fire began or ended. It didn't matter—Sam would run through it all to save Henry and Nina. He would burn to get to them if he had to. He just had to let them know that he was there.

"NINA!"

Sam was so determined to find her and rescue her that he didn't realize that he screamed her name until he heard it echo off the house and what was left of the barns. It was so loud, Donald Henderson heard it by the property line.

Time was of the essence now.

Chapter Thirty-Two

When things were difficult growing up, Nina tried to remember what her parents had been like. When the details were too fuzzy to be useful, she switched her efforts to imagining who they were—their likes, dislikes, and quirks.

If Jane was cruel and her stepparents were cold, Jane imagined whose traits she inherited and what their voices may have sounded like. She would envision a dream world where they lived, and everything was picture perfect—a father who could play the fiddle and a mother who packed her school lunches with love. It made the sting of the real world hurt a little less.

Nina was in the middle of a deep sleep when a voice called out to her, rough and vaguely familiar. As she started to come back to her senses in the large bed, she felt temporarily disoriented. Her muscles still felt heavy as she tried to figure out where the voice might have come from. She wondered if this was her mind's way to soothe her, the stress of railroad looming in the distance becoming too much for her to bear.

Am I dreaming? Nina asked herself. The room seemed hazy and thick, and her eyes prickled as though she may cry. *Did I dream about my father again?*

She didn't feel upset, so she wasn't sure why her eyes teared up. There were countless other times where she wished she had her parents to turn to or ask for advice. Yet she fell asleep feeling somewhat at peace that Sam would figure out a solution to their problem. Something else must be the source of this reaction, of her eyes stinging eyes and heavy feeling in her chest. As she slowly became more conscious, her stomach filled with dread.

At the bottom of the door frame, smoke spilled into the room like water flooding the cabin of a ship. Nina gasped at the sight of it. The voice did not come from a dream, but perhaps it was some sort of otherworldly warning. Maybe someone spotted it and called to her somehow. All Nina knew was that there a fire burned in the house somewhere.

There is a fire in the house somewhere!

Nina jolted up with fright. If the smoke already billowed into her room, that probably meant it was too large to contain. She felt grateful that she was able to wake up at all and that the smoke hadn't kept her enveloped in an eternal sleep.

She threw back the coverlet and all but tumbled out of bed as panic reached out to choke her. From what she remembered from her first fire, she needed to move and get out. It wasn't often that the fire itself killed, but the smoke. The thought made a chill course down her spine despite the rising temperature of the room. She didn't want to find out if that was true.

With trembling hands, she reached for her boots. She attempted to put them on her feet and tie the laces, but her fingers fought against her, refusing to cooperate. Nina didn't realize how afraid she was until she saw them shaking uncontrollably. No matter how hard she tried, she couldn't grab hold of the laces.

"I am wasting time!" Nina scolded herself as she threw the boots across the room in frustration. *Barefoot it is, then,* she growled internally. In her mind, she attempted to make a plan. Despite her shaking fingers, her mind felt mostly intact. She would wake Sam and they would collect Henry before they escaped down the stairs. Once everyone had a moment to make sure they were okay, they would run to the next farm for help. Nina was certain everything would be if she could just get outside. There was no room for a lack of confidence when the other option was death.

The doorknob felt hot as Nina turned it and pulled it open, shaking her hand out when it burned her slightly. Her jaw dropped open in shock as flames licked the walls in the hallway between her bedroom and Sam's. The heat felt worse than any summer day she had ever lived through, even from what she remembered from her childhood. Nina worried that her skin might blister if she stood there too long.

"Dear God, what has happened here?" Nina asked as she tried to shield her eyes and mouth from the smoke. It billowed relentlessly in all directions, and it tried to choke and blind her as she thought about what to do next.

Nina attempted to keep her composure as she made her decision. Her escape could be easy enough. If her shaking muscles and taxed lungs would allow, all she would have to do was dash across the hall and snatch Henry from his cradle before she made her way downstairs and out the front door. She was agile enough. It wasn't that long ago that she raced Nathaniel in the school yard and won.

I hope Henry is sleeping through this, Nina thought as she willed herself to move and collect the child from his room. *A little burn won't kill me if it gets him to safety. For all I know, Sam might have already gotten him and left without me.*

She tried to remain positive and hopeful, but something about that idea didn't sit right with Nina. There was no way that Sam would leave without her. He always looked out for her, even when he'd just been her employer, before it seemed like he cared for her as more than just the baby's governess. They both experienced fires before. He would know how terrified she might feel and want to make sure that she was all right.

What if Sam doesn't know? What if he's asleep?

Terror seeped into every fiber of Nina's body. Losing his family caused Sam to lose his voice. What if he was in his room, frozen with fear and not able to call out to her because his voice wasn't strong enough? Nina didn't want him to be hurt or die, not after everything he'd done for her. Even if she only stayed Henry's governess, she would never forgive herself if she didn't check on him.

"Sam!" She screamed over the roaring, angry flames, trying to rouse him or least let him know she was there. "Sam, wake up!"

When he didn't come to his door and the fire continued to spread, Nina worried that he couldn't hear her or that he was too frightened to move. The roaring of the flames was so loud Nina could have covered her ears and still not been able to drown it out.

"Sam! Sam, please!" She cried even louder, her voice scratching as she tried to overpower the inferno. She felt like she fought a losing battle. "Sam, we need to get out!"

The longer she waited for a response the more desperate Nina became. She noticed there was a section by Sam's door where the flames were only about shin height and weren't as intense as the rest of the blaze. If Nina got a running start, she probably could jump over them without inflicting much pain upon herself. Nina's heart pounded, but she knew she had to try.

She couldn't leave Sam behind; she'd never forgive herself. The thought of trying to guide or even drag his body to safety made the hair on the back of her neck stand up with worry, but she'd do it if kept him alive. He deserved a better life than what had been given to him. It couldn't end like this.

Nina backed down the hallway closer to the staircase to get a running start. She figured the more speed she had, the easier it would be to jump over the flames. She willed her anxious body to cooperate. She took a deep breath as she stared at the flames standing in her way.

"Please God, protect me. I must get through."

She did the sign of the cross before she sprinted down the hallway, screaming as she leaped over the flames, her emotions heightened beyond what she had ever known. The heat was unbearable, and once Nina landed, she made sure that the hem of her nightgown hadn't caught on fire.

She swatted at the hem and her legs to makes sure that nothing would catch and burn her skin worse than the uncontrollable heat already had. When she was certain that she wasn't seriously harmed, she coughed as she strode to Sam's door and banged on it.

"Samuel Colt! We need to leave!" She exclaimed as she hit the wood as hard as she could, too worried to care about embarrassing herself. Maybe they would be able to laugh about her behavior when this was over, but now she was on a mission. When it seemed to be silent on the other side, she bit her lip and twisted his door handle open.

Don't panic. Maybe he's sleeping.

Nina pushed into his bedroom, expecting to see Sam sleeping deeply in his bed or cowered in a corner in fear. Instead, she was greeted by neither which made her stomach flip with terror. The room was empty.

The bed looked like it had been slept in. The sheets were crumpled and pushed back like someone left in a hurry. Just to be sure, Nina stopped and check under the bed, in the closet on the opposite wall, double checking that she really hadn't missed him. Knowing Sam, if he saw her enter the room, he would have done something to let her know that he was there. With every second that passed, Nina felt like she might be sick on Sam's bedroom floor from his absence. It was obvious that he hadn't been here for a while.

Where is he then?

Nina tried to keep her wits about her, but she began to fear the worst. Maybe he left without her after all, or he faced some sort of trouble somewhere else in the house. Maybe his focus had been on Henry after all, and when he finally tried to go back for her the fire grew too large and it was too late. Nina thought about the voice that woke her up and suddenly wondered why it seemed so familiar while she drifted in the strange place between sleeping and awake.

"Was Sam trying to warn me?" Nina asked before she succumbed to a coughing fit, her body doubling over with the effort it took to breathe. She wasn't sure what to think since he only just started to vocalize recently. Would he be able to yell for her? If it was Sam, she should have been thrilled to know that he was using his voice. The only problem was she in even worse danger now that she had jumped over the fire to get to his room. She was even further away from safety than she was before.

The thought of the farmhouse burning down made Nina's chest hurt as much as the smoke did. It had been so rough looking when she first arrived, but it had become her home. She loved curtains she sewed for the living room and the chairs between the oil lamp that she and Sam sat in every night. The kitchen was like a sanctuary to her, a place where she created things that brought Sam joy.

The sight of Henry sitting in his highchair while she did dishes was something that brought a warmth to her chest and would be seared into her memories forever. Nina knew it was all replaceable; in the end, it was just a house. Yet the fact that it would all be lost was a devastating blow. It was the first place where she truly felt herself. Sam worked so hard to make a place for himself after he lost everything as a boy.

Nina could feel her throat getting tight with despair at the thought of him facing that sense of homelessness, of having nothing, for a second time.

As more coughs wracked Nina's body, she knew it was time to go. She needed to jump to a backup plan. The longer she waited, the harder it would be to get to safety. The flames in the hallway were probably higher than before, but she'd risk another small burn if she could get past them once last time. Nina needed to move while her body still had some strength left.

She would check to make sure that Henry wasn't in his room just to be safe, but Nina was so sure that Sam must have already gotten him. It was a better alternative than him face down in the house somewhere while the child was still sleeping

Suddenly, a sickening crack shook the house. A heavy ceiling beam ell from above, embers cascading down in an angry rage, and Nina screamed as she collapsed to the floor. Wood splintered and sent hot coals shooting through the air, singing Nina's skin as she covered her face with her hands. She hissed, lying there for a moment before she gingerly brought her arms against her chest.

She panted to catch her breath and get her wits about her. She didn't think it was possible for the fire to roar louder than it already was, but the sound deafened her. It was as if the flames taunted her, desiring her destruction. Nina knew if she gave in it would be her end.

Nina scrambled to her feet when she realized that rafters from the ceiling in the hallway had come crashing down. When she got to the door frame, her blood went cold despite the heat rising violently from the flames.

She was trapped.

The fallen beams blocked her exit from Sam's room. They were to her waist, too tall to jump over, and touching the ignited wood would severely harm her. She had a better chance of jumping out of Sam's window and praying for broken bones.

"*SAM!*" Nina screamed as loudly as she could. The air was thick with smoke, and she endured another coughing fit as she realized it was futile. There was no way he would hear her if he was downstairs or outside. The fire was worse than a roaring wind, and she would be swept up into it if she didn't save her energy.

Nina was about to run to the window, to see if jumping was even remotely realistic, when she heard something else that made her feel even more hopeless. For the briefest of moments, she actually considered climbing through the rubble that had once been the attic and ceiling to get to other side. Burns would be worth it to stop what was shattering her heart.

Henry's desperate cry drifted in from the other side of the door. Even through the bellowing flames, she could hear the terror that gripped his voice. Nina wondered if there were flames in his room or if the noise of the rafters falling scared him. Nina dropped to her knees in anguish. She hadn't been much older than Henry when she suffered her first fire. It was something she wouldn't want anyone to live through, let alone someone as sweet and innocent as Henry.

Tears spilled down Nina's cheeks as she realized she couldn't get to him, the little boy that changed her life and whom she fell in love with. The thought of Henry coming to any harm in this fire made Nina feel like her heart was torn from her chest. She was trapped, helpless, no different than the poor babe. She was angry with herself for not checking on him first. If she had done that, they could be outside and safe.

"Henry!" Nina tried to call. Her voice began to feel scratchy, like it had been cut and slashed from the inside. "Henry, I'm here!" She had no idea if he could hear her through his door and the panic smothered.

Where on earth is Sam? Nina wondered once again she struggled over to the window and tried to throw it open. He wasn't in his room, and he wasn't with Henry. Nina knew in her heart of hearts that he did not run off and leave her alone to deal with this. It wasn't in his nature; she saw him stand up to Donald Henderson when he paid them a visit. No, she feared that he came to some kind of harm and was unconscious somewhere in the house. What if he'd hit his head or the smoke caused him to pass out? Then they would really all be doomed. All three of them would die here before anyone in town had any idea. Another devastating thought nearly caused Nina to swoon.

What if Sam was already dead?

As Nina tried to drink in the air that struggling to come in from the window, she crumpled to her knees once more. Perhaps the smoke finally fatigued her, or perhaps her legs gave out from fear; she wasn't sure. Nina took it as a sign of what she needed to do—the only thing she could do other than weep.

She began to pray.

Chapter Thirty-Three

The way the past came back to haunt him was like a slap to Sam's face.

He could hear Nina screaming and calling his name just like the night he lost his family. He felt crippled by the sound of her violent coughs and the fear in her voice. Her terror would drive him mad for the rest of his days, just as his parents and sister's anguish had. Sam was convinced that he was being punished for his stubbornness with the railroad. He wished he could repent so he could save them, or at least have Henry and Nina be without pain.

No, Sam chided himself, *I cannot let them endure the same fate as my family. I will not lose them.* He knew that if he was too late, he would never forgive himself. He would find a way to join them somehow. He could not live in a world that took Nina and Henry from him.

Yet this isn't even my fault, Sam thought with bitterness in his heart. *Henderson and his blasted railroad are behind this.* Sam felt his blood boiling as he turned back to look at the worksite on the edge of his property.

Just as he noticed before, many men were awake and moving, but most seemed to keep their eyes lowered as they passed. It was as if they thought that if they couldn't see the atrocity taking place, it wasn't really there. How could they just ignore it?

Donald Henderson continued to stare at the flames as they consumed what remained of the barn. Sam had no doubt that Henderson assumed his business was now ruined and he must give up his land. The triumphant look on his face wavered slightly as the fire quickly spread to the house. Sam felt the man's eyes on him and wondered if he was looking for Nina and Henry.

Did he not realize that Nina and Henry were still in the house? Sam thought in disbelief. *Is he so selfish and uncaring that he would just sacrifice them to his cause?* Sam didn't know if he should laugh at the man's foolishness or become even angrier.

All this time, Donald Henderson assumed that Nina was Sam's wife. Maybe Henderson thought they slept in the same room and that Nina knew what was going on. If that was the case, where would she be if not at his side? Sam bit his lip and shook his head, his teeth nearly breaking the skin as the guilt set in. He could have let Nina know where he was going. Just like the night he lost his family, he snuck out to see what the source of the noise was.

He never thought to let her know something was wrong. Never in his wildest dreams did he think he'd be dealing with this. Now she had no idea where he was. Sam pictured Nina worrying about him, and the image made him feel like he was drowning in his woes.

Sam watched Henderson remove his hat and start wringing it nervously in his hands as he continued to scan the property for Nina and the baby. Suddenly, something in Sam snapped. Instead of running into the house and up the stairs to save them, he turned on his heel and stalked across the yard to the property line. Donald Henderson would pay for all the suffering he caused.

Sam had been angry before. He was sometimes angry with God for taking his family away from him. He'd been upset when people teased him for muteness over the years. Even all the problems he had with the railroad got under his skin, but it had been nothing like rage that coursed through him now. Sam didn't consider himself a violent person, but he would beat Henderson into a bloody pulp if it made him remorseful for what he'd done.

As he approached, the railroad workers all suddenly began to scatter and take off for other parts of the worksite. Eventually, Henderson noticed him approaching. The railroad manager's face went pale and clammy as he took in Sam's wild eyes and rigid body as he closed the space between them.

"Mr. Colt," Henderson said after he nervously swallowed and licked his lips. "I can explain," he gestured to the fire with a shaking hand. "You see, I just wanted to send a message. I wanted you to comply and sell you land. I never meant for things to get out of hand. It was just supposed to be a warning."

He never meant for things to get out of hand. The words disgusted Sam. He closed the spaced between him and Henderson, drawing his hand back to punch the railroad tycoon in the jaw before he tackled him to the ground. Sam half expected any of the workers who were left to stop and defend their employer, but it caused anyone who remained to vacate the area in a hurry.

It seemed they at least had morals and weren't sticking around to see his house burn to the ground. That, or they were cowards and didn't want to be witnesses to a brutal crime. Sam no longer cared where anyone stood of the matter.

Sam knew he should have been upset that Henderson and the Central Pacific destroyed his farm and everything that he had worked so hard on the last few years. In a way he was. He put so much effort and time into the ranch; that was the reason why he didn't want to move and sell his land, after all. The house and his business no longer mattered. All he could see in his mind was Nina sitting in the living room with sweet blond Henry on her lap.

Sam could hear her singing a lullaby as he wrote his notes in his business ledger. They were more important than anything else—more important than the dishes that had once belonged to his parents, the cattle and horses that were currently scared out of their wits and roaming the property, and even Sadie, his prized horse that he owned long before Henry appeared on his doorstep.

Henderson never intended to inspire such an epiphany, but by targeting Sam's home, he taught Sam what really mattered in his life.

And now he stood to lose it all.

Donald Henderson let out a pitiful moan as his body smacked the ground, the wind completely knocked out of him. All the big talking and rudeness that he displayed when he came by the house vanished, as though it fled from his body when Sam struck him. Sam would have been lying if he didn't say that pleased him.

"Let me go! I'll pay you for your land," Henderson begged, "I'll find you a great place to live in the next town over. I'll do anything you need, just let me go!"

Is he serious? Sam questioned. *He's going to beg for forgiveness after everything he's done?* Sam didn't know he could feel angrier, and yet it threatened to come out of him steam from an overheating kettle. This man just didn't understand the severity of the situation.

"How dare you!" Sam bellowed into Henderson's face, once again shocked that his voice could be so loud after the years it spent hidden away inside himself. Sam wondered if he'd been faced with confrontation earlier he'd have found his voice sooner. "How can you beg me to stop when the woman I love and an innocent child are inside that house?"

Henderson's face crumpled when Sam seemed to confirm his fears. It was one thing to destroy property or threaten people off their land; it was another to knowingly be responsible for the lives of innocent people.

Donald Henderson now knew he had blood on his hands.

Were the stories Amos and the others heard exaggerated? Sam wondered as he watched Henderson writhe under him. *Had the railroad never killed anyone before?* Wasn't that how a ghost story or a legend went? The more time that passed and the more people who shared it, the more exaggerated and ridiculous it became. He no longer knew what to think.

Sam's chest went tight as he realized the time he wasted. Donald wasn't worthy enough for him to spit on, let alone reason with. He wasn't going to waste another minute when he could rescue Nina and Henry and get them to safety.

They would not have the same fate as his family. Even if they were dirty and homeless with nothing but the shirts on their backs after this, he would still be happier than he was before Henry and Nina entered his life. He would not be alone.

He picked Henderson up by his shirt before he slammed him in the dirt one last time. Then he clambered to his feet and began to sprint toward the house. He had to try to rescue his found family. He had to know that he tried.

"Wait!" Donald shouted behind him.

Sam refused to stop. As it was, he probably lost too much time already. He only hoped that when he could get to Nina, he could apologize for leaving without her the first time, and not with a notebook, but with his actual voice. She couldn't be angry with him if she saw what she help him achieve. That was what Sam hoped at least, and it was enough to drive him back toward danger when common sense told him to stay put.

He nearly reached the front porch when a loud rumble sounded, followed by a sickening crack from somewhere in the house. Sam's stomach twisted violently as realized that the fire consumed so much of the house that it threatened to cave in, just like the barn had done. If the house collapsed, he would never be able to save both Henry and Nina. There was a chance he wouldn't be able to find either of them or he'd witness the people he loved perish for the second time in his life.

"Colt!" Henderson bellowed behind him. "Now wait just one minute!"

Sam looked over his shoulder to see the railroad manager staggering in his direction. *What is he trying to do? Is he looking to keep fighting?*

Sam didn't know if Henderson didn't want a third potential death on his hands or if now that he saw the horrors he caused firsthand and decided to admit defeat. All he knew was that he had to do something before it was too late. Now wasn't the time for discussion, it was a time for action. He would deal with Henderson and the Central Pacific later.

Without another second to spare, he climbed onto the porch and opened the screen door. As smoke belched out of the house, Sam covered his mouth with his arm, squinted his eyes, and ran.

Chapter Thirty-Four

What does it feel like to suffocate and die?

Nina weakly pondered the question as she looked out Sam's bedroom window. There was nowhere to climb out safely and jump. Even if she wanted to, her body felt sluggish and heavy. She feared that she would tumble to the ground in a way that would make her land on her neck—death had come for her this night, regardless of the form it took.

To make matters worse, each coughing fit made her muscles sting, while the smoke made her dizzy, disorientated, and blind. She tried to breathe in the fresh air trickling in from the window, but it became harder to sit upright. Eventually, she slid from the sill and onto the floor. She couldn't even speak as she could hear Henry screaming for her down the hall.

All she wanted to do was to hold him and soothe him in what were probably his final moments as well. What had once been sobs slowed to silent rivers carving lines into her soot-stained cheeks.

Am I dying? Nina thought to herself. *Is this really the end?*

As she lay there, Nina couldn't help but think of her parents. She heard that her father saved her and died from complications with his burns, but now as she felt a heavy weight on her body and struggled to breath, she wondered if this was her mother's fate. She imagined that the smoke became too much, and her body became too heavy. Perhaps she just slipped away somewhere in the house and fallen asleep, choking to death slowly. Nina hoped that running out of air didn't hurt her body too much. She prayed that it would be far less painful than her skin blistering with burns.

Nina struggled as she turned her head toward the open doorway, her body already feeling so weak and tired. The flames continued to roar and surge around the bare, brittle rafters. She wept as she thought about Henry, too little to understand what was happening to him, dying like she was. It wasn't fair. The babe's life had been so short and filled with so much sadness—first he was abandoned, and now this.

Nina hoped that by being his governess, she was able to provide him with a bit of sunshine, even if it was temporary. She prayed that God had a good plan for the child up in heaven. He deserved to be loved. Nina would have made sure that he had everything he ever needed if she hadn't been given incredibly bad luck, if she hadn't been trapped in this middle of the night blaze.

Even if Nina remained just Henry's governess until he was old enough to no longer need her care, it would have been better than this.

Nina's heart broke as she thought about the fresh start she had been given being all but wasted. For the briefest of moments, she was able to see the kind of life she could have had; not a life where she had stepparents that never really wanted her or was constantly in her stepsister's shadow.

Here, she didn't have a lover who pitied her because her parents died tragically. In Carson City, she finally found her purpose. She discovered it in the little blond-haired, blue-eyed child that her stole her heart from the minute she set eyes on him.

He made her feel wanted for the first time that she could remember.

It had been more than that, though. What started out as a job tending to an infant transformed; she could no longer imagine her life without Sam sitting beside her in the living room each night. Her heart raced when she thought about what new meal she could make for him for supper.

For so long, she fought to maintain propriety, when all she yearned for was Sam to take care of her and let her become part of a proper family. It wounded her to realize that she took what were most likely her final breaths.

I love him, Nina realized. *I love Sam and now I'm never going to be able to tell him how I feel.*

The despair of that confession felt almost as heavy as the smoke. Suddenly, Nina's mind flooded with all the situations that could have been, the life they could have lived and future they could have shared if she lived. Henry could have grown up with parents who cared for him, and they could have filled the farmhouse with more children after they finished fixing it up and making it shine.

Even if the railroad had gotten their way and Nina and Sam were forced to move, at least they could have done it together. The adventure in navigating that together would have been worth it.

I wonder if Sam would have learned to speak if we had more time. Once more, regret overcame Nina as she pictured his handsome face and his kind eyes, deep pools that always reflected his true feelings. *What could we have talked about if we had just had more time?*

Nina imagined he would have told her he loved her. Even if it wasn't the truth, the notion could still off her solace in her final moments.

Just as Nina hoped that her death wouldn't be too painful, she also hoped that Sam, if he was still alive, wouldn't blame himself for what happened. Deep in Nina's soul, she knew that he had no cause in this; it was nothing more than unfortunate luck. A small part of her wondered if perhaps the railroad stepped over the line and caused this, but she would never know. It was a shame.

Sam still had so much to offer the world if he survived this. Nina hoped that she could look down on him and watch him achieve success somewhere else in Carson City. She hoped that he could find love again. Once more, she wept silent tears at the thought of it being anyone but her.

The room grew dark, the black smoke closing in on almost every shaft of light, like the lid of a tomb slowly shutting. Nina knew the cause was more than just the fire; she began to suffer from tunnel vision, and she may have just mere minutes before she left this world forever.

I would have liked to a have been more to Sam than a governess. If I had a second chance, I'd tell him to his face, Nina thought as she closed her eyes.

What happened next was difficult to ever imagine. Nina imagined that an angel arrived to guide her to heaven. She saw their blurry face in the doorway, a stark contrast to the smoke and flames. They swooped in over the rafters and flames, scooping her up in a bridal carry. They were strong, not straining at all to whisk her out of the house.

Nina let out a long sigh as she nestled into their arms. She waited for the angel to rise above the roof and take her up to heaven, but they took her down the stairs instead. Nina squinted her eyes in confusion as she could swear that they dashed out the front door and onto the front lawn. Either this angel wasn't very good at flying, or something strange was afoot.

What is happening? Aren't I dead?

The angel tumbled to the ground and Nina landed roughly on the dirt. The sensation caused her body to ache, and suddenly she realized that she was still alive. If she had died, she would no longer feel any pain. Someone coughed as they clapped her roughly on the back, and she also began hacking and seeing stars as she tried to catch her breath.

When she realized that she struggled to breath, she confirmed that she remained among the living. Relief temporarily washed over her before she tried to get her bearings.

Nina suddenly realized that her angel wasn't otherworldly at all. Sam knelt over her, rubbing large circles over her back, and she could feel his hand trembling wildly against her as he met her eye. He looked like he'd seen a ghost, his skin was pale, and his eyes were wide as he took her in. Nina swore he looked like he had been crying because not only were his eyes wide, but red and glassy as well.

I'm alive. Nina not only felt her chest burning from the smoke that still lingered behind in her lungs, but suddenly she was overcome with emotion. *I thought for sure I was doomed, and Sam saved me.* All the fears that she had about never getting to tell him how she felt washed away.

She had been given a second chance. Nina knew he would never leave her behind.

Suddenly, Nina's heart seized with a fresh wave of terror. *Henry! He was still in the house!* She was so preoccupied by Sam's rescue that she completely forgot about the child trapped in his room.

If Henry died, Nina wasn't sure if she could live without him.

"I'm fine!" Nina croaked. Her throat felt like she swallowed hundreds of sharp stones. The pain was intense, but she needed to let Sam know how desperate the situation was. For all she knew, they were already too late, but they had to try.

She clutched Sam's shirt collar and tried to get him to listen. "The baby, Sam! The baby is still upstairs."

Nina's stomach flipped when Sam's face crumpled. He looked as though the realization caused him physical pain, like someone stabbed him with knife. There wasn't time for him to react; Nina would go back in herself if she wasn't feeling so weak.

"Forget about me!" Nina sobbed, "Save Henry!"

Sam climbed quickly to his feet and turned back toward the house. Nina stared in horror as flames violently erupted from every window on the second floor. Her heart shattered into a million pieces knowing that Henry lay trapped in his room. She choked down sobs, wondering if he was even aware of what was happening or he was desperately searching for her, waiting for help. Nina wondered if he felt betrayed and alone, and she wished more than anything that she could trade places with the innocent boy.

How could God be so cruel? Nina despaired, picturing the tiny boy smiling at her when she went to wake him in his nursery each morning, and how he would rest his head on her shoulder when he became drowsy at night. *How am I ever going to trust myself taking care of a child after what happened tonight? How will I ever recover from losing him?*

Nina knew that the fire wasn't her fault. It could have been caused by plenty of things, but the idea that she searched for Sam first when she was Henry's governess made her heart feel as if it were made of lead. How could she ever forgive herself for abandoning him?

She dropped her eyes to the ground, tears coursing like a river onto the dirt. Nina wondered if she cried long enough if she could make mud beneath her. She wondered how long it would take for the fire to burn to ash so they could search for Henry's body.

As despair threatened to make Nina swoon, something miraculous happened.

The front door to the house swung open, smoke and flames pouring out like demons trying to escape. Nina put her hands over her mouth in shock as someone stumbled onto the porch.

When on earth did he arrive?

Donald Henderson, the railroad manager, emerged from the house clutching something in his arms, the flames silhouetting his form as he staggered closer. Nina gasped when she recognized the pale blond hair poking out of his jacket. Henderson did not hold some material thing in his arms; he held Henry.

Just when she thought that fate had taken Henry forever, it would seem it wanted to be kind.

Chapter Thirty-Five

Donald Henderson

How can you beg me to stop when the woman I love and an innocent child are inside that house!?

The words rang through Donald's mind as he watched Sam Colt race toward his burning home without a second thought. He thought Colt was insane—the house had burned to the point that it was a walking death trap. He'd be lucky if he could make it up the stairs without something falling on him and crushing him. If that wasn't the reason why he died a gruesome death, surely the smoke and flames would consume him instead.

Yet, Donald had no doubts that the man was willing to give up his life so that his family could live. There was something heroic and admirable about the way Colt would sacrifice himself for the ones he loved.

I don't understand, Henderson thought to himself in confusion. *Why risk your life when they were clearly not smart enough to get out themselves?* He didn't have many relationships, even with his coworkers. *The Central Pacific Railroad is more of a spouse to me than any woman has ever been or ever will ever be.*

The railroad was to be his legacy, like it had been for his father before him. *That's why I work at all hours and try to crush anyone that stands his way.* While he didn't pressure others to the brink of death, but he preferred to deliver a serious message—to make the average man understand that there was no hope if they crossed him.

The people who owned land that lay on the railroad's path might own farms, priceless heirlooms, and have future generations to create, but what Donald would have when all was said and done would be much bigger than any of them. Their material possessions would have no value next to the future of the country. *The world will see my completed railroad and know that I was the one to create it. I don't need a woman and children to complete me if I have glory.*

Or, at least that was what he told himself at the time. Even when he terrorized people in the past and ran them off their property, he assured himself that it would all be worth it someday. Their sorrow would be temporary, and one day when they could travel to places on the railroad, take journeys that once spanned days or even weeks.

The people would thank the Central Pacific for the sacrifices that were made. Donald hoped that perhaps they would understand his motivations and maybe even regret their reluctance to sell and move.

Now, he wasn't so sure.

As he watched Sam Colt sprint back toward his burning building, he wondered if he should have cared more about the relationships he made with others. Ever since Donald first paid the family a house call, he took note of the way Colt protected them. It reminded him of the alpha in a wolf pack.

He'd come across many fathers and heads of households during his time on the railroad, but no one had threatened him quite like Sam Colt. Either Colt loved his wife and child so fiercely that he would let nothing harm them, or his body was incapable of experiencing fear. Both notions gave Henderson pause and made him wonder what it was like to feel that way.

When he was old and alone, who would come to visit him, who would care? Was it possible for him to care as strongly for someone as Colt did?

"Wait!"

The word slipped from his lips as he thought of the gentle young woman who met him at the door when he tried to convince Colt to sell his land. If he shut his eyes, he could picture her large eyes and how they had stared at him nervously. It was obvious how much she cared for the man that ran frantically to her aid; she tried to intercede on his behalf more than once. Donald thought of the young child he saw the woman carry on her back when he spied on the property. The little boy couldn't have been more than a year old.

He was ruthless in the past. He and his men would stand on the lawn while a family would frantically load a wagon with their belongings, the wife sobbing hysterically. Once, there was one piece of property that he particularly wanted, so he went and opened all of the paddocks and pens.

Come morning, whatever animal didn't run would have been eaten by coyotes. Donald suspected that the Colt property, would be no different. Yet, as more time passed, the more he worried that some terrible fate befell them amidst the raging fire.

Did I go too far this time?

Donald didn't want innocent blood on his hands. He didn't care if Colt lived or died; he was the stubborn one that refused to sell his land and listen despite Donald's multiple attempts to sway him. In his heart, he knew the woman and the child didn't do anything wrong. In fact, he heard that she tried to deliver baked goods to his men, and one of his employees chased her back into the house.

I am a monster. I will be doomed to hell if they perish.

He was shrewd and vicious, but Donald couldn't let the stories that people whispered about him and railroad become true. He was not a murderer. His mother would never forgive him for turning into an even more sinister version of his father. Donald's father had been cold and removed from everyone, even his mother, before he took his final breaths.

He could still picture his father's final days clearly in his mind's eye. When Donald was a teenager, he traveled with his father while they laid new track. His younger self was simultaneously eager to watch the laborers blow up mountains to change the landscape and in awe of the wild prairie and endless plains.

Despite these wonders, young Donald could see how dangerous conditions were for these men and how hard his father worked them; he was nothing short of a slave driver. Donald vowed that when he reached his maturity, he would inspire his workers with notions of glory and provide them with a decent wage.

When he was about fourteen, he overheard his father and one of his business partners arguing about sending immigrants deeper into a tunnel to blast a path to the other side.

"There was nearly a cave in there the other day, surely, we must find another way," the man pressed.

Donald remembered the biting, scathing tone of his father's retort. "Who cares? We have so many we can send another group in the next day to blow the rock away again."

"Sir, you can't be serious, they're men just like the rest of us."

"Well, if that's how you feel, you can be join them on the job." Donald could hear the gravity in his father's tone. It wasn't a suggestion; it was an order.

The next day, that business partner went into the tunnel. The dynamite caused the project to cave in, and Donald wondered if the man had any regrets. That day, he realized that his father believed that all human life was dispensable. It stayed with him even now.

Now, he had to make up for this terrible mistake with Sam Colt.

Donald sprang to his feet and ran toward the house. Despite calling for Colt to stop, yelling at him so he could tell him what to do, the man was on a mission and would not slow down.

He already entered the house and reached the top of the staircase when Donald hit the threshold. The smoke was so strong and moving so fast it nearly stopped him from taking another step.

Even over the tumultuous flames, he could hear cries coming from the second floor. Donald slunk low to the ground, attempting to crawl under the smoke on his hands and knees. He took the stairs one at time, finding it easier to breathe and see as he made his way to the second story of the house.

He felt like he swallowed something heavy as he took in the handy work of several of his lackeys. This was not the first time they started a fire to encourage property owners to leave their land, but this was the first time he'd been inside a home after the fire began. He watched as they dipped rags in kerosine tied them around rocks.

They placed them all over the barn with bales of hay after they broke the lock. Then, they threw the rest through the windows of the house. One of his men had a good arm and was able to reach the second floor. It was effective and the fire spread quickly. Too quickly, because the celling already began to sag like it would collapse completely. Any means of escape would quickly become nonexistent.

When Donald finally got to the next floor, the heat felt blistering. Colt was far ahead of him, sailing over some rubble and into a bedroom at the far end of the hallway. Even if he tried, Donald wouldn't be able to yell loud enough to be heard. The child sounded like its room was nearer to him. There was a bedroom a few paces away, and the shrieks were so frightened and desperate that Donald feared the child was being burned alive. When his mind vividly painted a picture of what that might look like, his stomach rolled, and he thought about running right back out the front door again so that he didn't have to see if his imagination was more vivid and twisted than real life.

Coward! Donald scolded. *You must save him. You have to at least try.*

He bit his lip before he tried the door handle. Donald initially drew his hand away when it felt like he touched a blacksmiths hot iron rod. The child's bedroom must be engulfed in flames if the knob was hot enough to nearly brand him. He hissed as he shook his hand, trying to ignore the pain that jumped through his wrist and into his elbow.

This would be harder than he thought.

Knowing that precious minutes or even seconds separated life from death for this child, Donald tried the doorknob once more, grimacing through the pain as the metal seared his hand a second time.

The nursery was large, and Donald swallowed hard as he discovered a wall of flames between him and the cradle on the other side of the room. The baby sat there, chest heaving frantically as he sobbed and coughed. The look of horror on his face was enough to even make Donald's heart clench with grief. Other than his traumatized expression, Donald couldn't see any harm done to the child.

"Help!" The child screeched when he saw Donald standing there. "No, no, no!"

Its old enough to speak? He was surprised. Other than observing the child from a distance, the few times he dealt with Colt and his companion, the child slept or was not in the room. *Why, this little lad has his whole future in front of him, and I was going to just snuff his life out like it was meaningless.* The thought was more sobering than any slap or punch could ever be.

He quickly thought back to his cold, cruel father. Who would have continued his legacy with the railroad if something like this happened when Donald was young? Perhaps this child was destined to create or do something great in his adulthood. Who was he to prevent whatever it was that fate intended for him?

Donald needed to make sure that the babe lived to see another day.

Maybe your legacy can be more than a railroad, he thought as he appraised the angry wall of flames that stood between him and the child. *Maybe people won't just tell the stories where you were cruel. Maybe they'll call you a hero.* Donald seemed satisfied with that idea. It didn't mean he was we weak; even he had morals.

When it was clear that he made his choice, Donald let out a long, deep breath before he ran through the flames. He screamed in anguish as they licked at his skin and burned his clothes. He rolled on the ground in front the cradle and swatted himself to make sure hadn't caught on fire before he snatched the child from his bed and held him close.

"It's all right," Donald whispered, struggling to quell his pain for the child's sake. He could already feel welts forming from where the flames bit into him. His skin stung, and he tried to fight the urge to shake. "I'm going to get you out of here and back to your mama and papa as quickly as I can."

As his body throbbed, Donald felt the child nestle into him, desperate for anyone to rescue him from this hell. The boy was surprisingly light as he took him into his arms. The poor thing trembled like the room was frigidly cold instead of on fire.

Guilt wracked Donald as he clutched the child tightly. Perhaps he should have planned better and burned the house down when no one would have been inside. He could have studied the family's patterns and done it when they were in town or at church or anywhere but here.

It was too late think about alternatives now.

Donald now faced a writhing wall of flames. He would have to run through them again to get to safety and potentially face more before reaching the front door. Donald wondered if Colt was able to get to the woman further down the hallway or if they, too, were trapped amidst the endless flames. Unfortunately, there wasn't time to check. He needed to move.

Donald used one hand to hastily unbutton his black jacket. He would have taken it off and covered the child with it if he didn't think the seconds would be better spent elsewhere. Instead, he wrapped the babe in the jacket he still wore it, protecting most of the boy's skin and body from the fire. Donald made sure to use his arms to shield the boy's face before he decided there was nothing left to do but run.

"Hold on, little one," he urged, and he swore he felt tiny hands grip onto his dress shirt as tightly as they could. Donald was certain they would rip the shirt before he would let go. "We'll be free of this fire soon."

After letting out a shaky breath, Donald ran toward the blockade of flames and the door beyond. Once more, he felt the fire singe him cruelly. He bit his tongue to stifle a scream until he tasted the copper tang of blood in his mouth.

Donald wasn't sure if he was on fire or not as he leaped through the flames and clutched the boy tightly as he used his free hand to open the door. His back throbbed, reminding him of the time he picked up a hot skillet when he was young. All he wanted to do was focus on the pain and how hot his suit jacket felt, but he willed himself to keep his composure for the baby. It was as if the devil himself tried one last time to claim the child and prevent Donald from fleeing.

The more Donald thought about it, maybe hell came for him now, demanding repentance for every misdeed. The demons were going to have to wait until he got the child to safety before he satisfied them.

When he reached the hallway, a raging inferno greeted him. Hardly any space was not filled with flames and smoke. He coughed and tried to continue to shield the baby from the terror and fumes that threatened to consume them. Donald even tried to sing over the roar of the blaze so the child would feel less afraid.

Donald had no idea if Colt made it out alive with his wife. Despite their differences, he sincerely hoped they did. The pain radiating through his body and the labored breaths heaving in his chest proved to him that a fire was not a dignified or easy way for a man to die. He tried to subdue the thoughts that he might not make it out himself when he was so close to freedom.

Donald pushed on, walking through the fire, feeling it blaze through his shoes and pants like he was being cooked in an oven, and he tried to remember where the staircase was. He was certain he would have collapsed by now if it weren't for the fact that he had the child in his arms. The boy drove him to continue.

The devil could take him for all he cared; it was probably what he deserved for being such a selfish monster, but he would not let the baby die. The child needed to live and become someone important. His future glory would make this all worthwhile.

A thunderous crack sounded behind him, and Donald was grateful that the smoke nearly made him blind as part of the structure collapsed behind him. Startled, he and the child tumbled down the last few stairs that separated them from the ground floor. Luckily, Donald had a tight grip on the child, and he remained in his arms, but the poor boy cried even harder. The sounds heart wrenching wails compelled Donald try to move again despite the excruciating pain from his burns.

"We're so close to fresh air," Donald croaked. "Please, hold on just a bit longer."

Feeling weak, but knowing he needed to press on, Donald finally staggered to his feet. He groped blindly through the smoke toward the front door—the same door that just a few days ago had been slammed in his face and angered him to the point that he vowed to burn the place to the ground. Would things be different now if he hadn't been so vain and prideful? Would this poor child not have to endure such trauma? Donald was so motivated to expand his railroad, he couldn't say for certain. The only thing he knew now was that what he thought was humiliation should have been a warning that building here wasn't meant to be. Perhaps, if he lived through this, he wouldn't act so hastily next time.

As he finally found the doorknob and realized that the heat of it no longer made him jump back in pain, he wondered if there would be a next time. Donald wasn't sure if it the adrenaline coursing through him dulled his pain, or whether his body simply went into shock.

When he finally threw the door open, he couldn't see much. His eyes still watered from the smoke, and he was disoriented, but he could hear despite the ringing in his ears. He could make out voices over his thundering pulse and the fire that still raged behind him.

"Forget about me! Save Henry!"

Donald almost fell to his knees on the porch at the sound of the woman's voice. Relief flooded him as he realized that she survived. Now he wouldn't be a murderer. He wouldn't have blood on his hands. It filled him with renewed vigor.

Slowly, the world came back into focus. The fire raged at his back—he could feel the heat and smell the smoke as it belched behind him. The midnight blue sky contrasted starkly against the orange glow of the flames when he was trapped inside the ruined farmhouse. The air felt cool, simultaneously soothing and stinging as he tried to inhale it as quickly as he could.

Down in the yard, Colt and the woman that Donald assumed was his wife were covered in soot and looked as though they were crying. The woman lay on the grass, staring at Donald in awe.

I know, he thought as he took in her reaction, *I didn't think I was capable of doing something this kind either.*

Colt looked like he was poised to race back into the house for a second time when Donald finally emerged. When it seemed that he finally understood what he saw, he closed the space between them and reached out for Henry, eyes glassy at the sight of the boy safe and sound inside Donald's coat. The child still sobbed, no doubt confused and terrified, but he wriggled out of Henderson's grasp and into his father's arms. He all but melted at the touch, still sniffling against Colt's chest.

"I protected him from the flames," Donald explained as he stepped off the porch and onto the lawn. "Call a doctor, but I pray the only harm done is from crying."

Donald watched Colt's brows knit together as if he was preparing to start yelling at him again. He didn't blame Colt for being angry. If Donald hadn't pushed his men to start the fire, none of them would have been forced to endure this situation. He deserved every curse for what he did. Yet Colt didn't get the chance. A strange, melting sensation overtook Donald's every nerve ending, his body slowly shutting down as he stumbled down the yard.

"I had to run through the fire," he continued to recount the tale despite his failing body. *It feels like someone poked my burns with countless needles*, Donald mused to himself, confusion enveloping his mind. Each burn throbbed in time with his heartbeat. "It hurt, but it was worth it. I saved the little boy." Donald tried to crawl on his hands and knees, and it suddenly felt as if he'd aged fifty years. Every bit of his body ached as he admitted defeat and rolled onto his back, facing the stars. They twinkled so beautifully despite the fire stilling burning yards away.

"Should we call one of your men?" It was the woman, who sounded like she too had done a fair bit of screaming while she was still trapped in the house. Her once sweet, soft voice was nearly hoarse. "Perhaps they can ride into town and wake the doctor?"

Donald's eyes grew heavy, and he wasn't sure if he could lift his limbs to inspect the damage. Everything felt like when he spent too long in the sun on a hot summer's day, yet magnified beyond comprehension. As the adrenaline ebbed away, he could tell that what he did to save the baby had been too much for his body to bear.

Now that he was on the other side of it, he regretted nothing. He'd do it a hundred more times if he had to. At least he knew the child didn't have a mark on his body thanks to his sacrifice.

"You can call him for you and the boy," Donald finally managed to reply. "Make sure you are both all right. I...I think it might be too late for me."

There was a long, grueling pause; the only sound the soft whimpering of the child and the crackling of the flames as they consumed what little remained of the farmhouse. He wondered if they could see the extent of the damage wreaked on him and didn't want to alarm him. Donald decided that it was probably for the best as he felt himself starting to slip away.

"Thank you for saving him," the woman murmured.

Donald tried to nod, but his body felt thick and fluid, almost like it didn't belong to him anymore. "Take good care of him. Have him grow up to be someone that does great things." He almost felt remorseful that he would never learn what the child became.

There was another lull in the conversation, and he wondered at Colt's reaction to all of this. He was typically so short on words, so Donald longed to know what his facial expression was; anything to give him an indication of how he really felt.

Finally, Sam Colt answered, voice soft and deep, "We will." Donald almost smiled when he heard the woman gasp in surprise.

What, did he never talk to her either? He wondered. It seemed there would be more secrets that would never reveal themselves to him.

Donald could feel that time had run out. If he was about to face judgement, he supposed he needed to make amends now.

"I'm sorry for what I did. I was so determined to make the railroad my legacy that I refused to see any other option." As Donald let out a raspy breath, he tried to shake his head. "Look at where that got me."

No one spoke after that. In fact, he had no idea if they walked away from him or stayed by his side as he stared up the stars. It didn't matter—Donald Henderson felt absolved for everything he had ever done. Even if he went to hell, he hoped his punishment would only be slightly painful.

I did what I thought was best at the time.

At last, he shut his eyes, let out one final shaky breath, and slipped away.

Chapter Thirty-Six

It all seemed like long, bad dream.

Sam still couldn't believe that it had been real, that he lived through another fire. The difference this time was that while he lost his home and everything in it, he hadn't lost his entire family. In a strange way, it was almost like this incident canceled out the one from his childhood. One took away his voice while the other returned it to him.

What once caused him to doubt his faith in God brought it back to him. As Sam watched what remained of his house smolder, he knew that he would never be angry with God again. The fire raged through his farmhouse and nearly claimed Nina and Henry, but they had been spared and barely harmed.

Sam would thank God every day for letting them live, as well as for ensuring that Donald Henderson absolve his sins. Sam still tried to make sense of what motivated the railroad manager to help.

Once Sam knew no one had been seriously hurt, his mind churned over the fire's repercussions. He tried to be grateful that he was alive to deal with them at all, but the aftermath still left him feeling tense and numb and like he was adrift on a ship in the midst of a terrible storm.

All his horses, what made his livelihood and his business, were displaced. He had no doubt that he and the ranch hands would be able to collect all the animals that wandered off his property, but he now had nowhere to house them. He was nearly positive that all the animals survived, but they were most likely agitated and anxious, and Sam knew he would have to do something to remedy that soon or he would end up losing them.

He loved the animals like they were members of the family, but if they died, his business would be that much harder to get off the ground. The thought made Sam sweat despite being away from what was left of the fire.

The house was unsalvageable; even the frame had caved in. Sam tried not to think about how much time and money he put into fixing it up over the years, but it he struggled to quell the lump in his throat as he watched it fall apart and smolder in the rising sun.

He had no idea what the day would bring, or if he could afford to stay at an inn long term. Part of him wanted to believe that people were kind in situations like this, but he wasn't sure what to think. Sam just stood there, staring at what had once been his home in stunned disbelief.

"I have so many things to say, they are all fighting to get out," Nina said plopping down onto the ground beside him, her night dress a dull grey after the events of the fire. Henry was in her arms, eyes open, but his head rested on her shoulder, as if touching Nina brought him comfort. His little face looked uncertain of what was happening, but Sam was just happy that he'd stopped crying. His fear had been almost as painful as watching the house burn.

Sam felt the opposite, like his mind was blank and his body was numb, but he still nodded as he continued to gape at the ashes. If she wanted to talk through what she'd been through, he'd listen until every last word was out.

"I heard a voice," Nina's said evenly, soothing despite the trauma they endured. "It made me wake up. I don't know where I would be if it hadn't been there."

"It was me," Sam whispered, and he saw Nina noticeably jump at the sound. He would smile if his whole world wasn't crashing down around him. In all the horror, he nearly forgot that he hadn't told her about finding his voice.

"Sam, you're talking!" She replied with fervor. "When? How? You must tell me everything." Nina's smoke-stained face light up in the dawn, like his voice was the only thing that mattered to her. "I'm so happy for you." Sam swore that tears of joy shone in her eyes.

"It wasn't the first time," Sam attempted to explain, finally breaking his gaze with the smoldering ashes and looking into Nina's exhausted, but hopeful, eyes. "The night you had been reading Psalm twenty-three, when you were worried about what Henderson would do, I had wanted to tell you. He'd come to try to talk to me one least time and I told him to leave."

Nina looked crestfallen that he didn't interrupt her at the time. "Why didn't you tell me?"

Sam shrugged; he did feel a bit guilty for not sharing, especially after what transpired tonight. "At the time, I didn't want you to worry that he'd been here. I figured I would have time to tell you another day. I had wanted to make it a happy surprise." He heaved a disappointed sigh, wondering if they would have been more prepared if he had been more forthcoming. "Unfortunately, Henderson and the railroad had other plans."

Nina balanced Henry's weight so that she held him with one arm. With the other, she reached across the space that separated them and placed her small hand on top of Sam's larger one. Her skin still felt soft and velvety despite enduring the inferno's extreme heat. "I'm so happy that you were finally able to find your voice."

He turned their hands over so he could properly lace his fingers with hers. "Me too."

They lapsed into silence for a few minutes before Nina's gaze shifted to Donald Henderson's body lying several yards away. They closed his eyes after he took his last breath, but they didn't have anything to cover him with. Everything was lost, but it still felt disrespectful to just leave him like that.

"What are we going to do?" Nina asked, exhaustion trickling back into her voice.

As much as Sam enjoyed the reassuring comfort of holding her hand, he knew he needed to let go. "I should probably find Sadie and ride into town." He looked over his shoulder at the railroad worksite. It seemed when the fire had grown to out of control proportions, the workers had cut and run. Sam had no doubt they worried about being accessories to the crime; even worse, if they knew Henderson was dead, they feared not getting paid. Desperation would lead even the sanest man to make an irrational decision. "The sheriff and doctor will need to be notified. Henry should be looked at," he rose to his feet, "You too."

Nina nodded, giving the child an encouraging squeeze while she still stared at Sam. "We'll be waiting for you."

After everything that happened, the fact that she was alive and able to make that promise was music to Sam's ears.

***

When the doctor arrived some time later, what was once the house still smoked and smoldered. The sheriff wasn't far behind. At that point, Henry finally succumbed to sleep, lying heavily in Nina's arms. Sam hoped the child wouldn't be plagued with nightmares like the kind he often had after the fire from his childhood.

They stood over the body of Donald Henderson and confirmed that the burns had been too much for his body. The shock of having so much of his body burned while saving

Henry claimed his life. Nina looked devastated at the news. Initially, it confused Sam because Henderson nearly killed her, and he had no idea how she could feel so much pity for him, even if he was the reason that Henry was still alive.

"It's a painful death," Nina clarified when she saw his bewildered face. "They say that was what killed my father back when I was a child. Like Henderson, he'd been the one to get me out of the house that fateful night."

Sam always assumed that his parents and sister had been choked to death by smoke, and he was very glad that he'd never know the truth. It made the memory less gruesome.

When the doctor assessed Henry and Nina, he quickly reassured them that they were going to be okay, much to Sam's relief. Both would have a lingering cough and some weakness for a while from breathing in so much smoke, but things could have been far worse. Once again, Sam was indebted to God for looking after them.

"I have plenty of open beds at my office in town," the doctor offered, "You are welcome to stay there to rest for as long as you need."

"Thank you for offering," Nina answered as she looked over at Sam, "but my place is here helping Sam. If Henry doesn't improve in the next day or so, we will pay you another visit. I want him to be as healthy as he was before this."

"Very well," the doctor replied before he collected his horse and rode back toward town.

Once everyone was confirmed in good health, the sheriff stepped up to begin his investigation. He was curious to know what had happened. Sam couldn't help but feel irritated, knowing that he asked for the man's protection and the sheriff wanted to remain neutral. Would his house be a pile of rubble if someone else also stood up to Henderson?

Unfortunately, it was too late to find out.

"Now, why don't you tell me your side of the story." The sheriff had a notebook and paper and looked like he was going to pass it over to Sam so that he could write his side of the story, just as he did in the past.

Sam pushed the notebook away, no longer needing it. It felt strange to be able to simply state what was on his mind. It was going to take some getting used to. "I was woken by the sounds of my livestock in distress," he said aloud, and he had to try his best to keep from smirking when the sheriff's eyebrows raised so high that they were practically at his hairline. If this was the reaction people would have each time he spoke, it would also take some time to adjust to. At least things would be amusing for a while. It was the only thing about this situation that was able to keep him from sinking into despair. "I first discovered the fire in the barn. There were bales of hay in places that didn't make sense, almost like they had been put there and then lit with some sort of accelerant. I thought I could make out a rag or something on top, but the fire was already well established by the time I got there."

The sheriff took a note of it, pausing several times to eyeball the railroad worksite behind them. It was as if he just noticed how barren it looked for a weekday. "When did you notice the fire in the house?"

"After I rescued my animals. I have no idea if they broke into the house or if the wind helped it spread somehow. I don't remember any broken windows, but they may have thrown things through the glass. By the time I saved my last horse it was out of control."

"When you say 'they,' who do you mean?" The sheriff asked, looking up from his notebook.

Really? Sam thought. *Isn't it obvious?* Perhaps he had to be the one to say it out loud to make a formal accusation, allowing the sheriff to investigate. "The Central Pacific Railroad," Sam replied without hesitation. "You'd never know it now, but they were looking on and working as the whole thing began to burn."

The sheriff swallowed uncomfortably. "And how did Mr. Henderson end up..." He looked down at his body which the doctor had been kind enough to cover with a sheet that he'd brought from his office. "The doctor said he died from his burns." It was just as before. He waited for Sam to explain what happened, and did not accuse Sam or Nina of foul play.

Sam nodded. "I don't think he realized that Nina and the child were still in the house when he or his men decided to start the fire." Sam still found the whole thing ridiculous, because where else would they have been at that time of night? He shook his head, knowing now wasn't the appropriate time to be bitter. "He helped me rescue them and unfortunately he was gravely injured."

"I see," the sheriff replied as he jotted more notes down. Sam studied his face and wondered whether the sheriff's neutrality inadvertently allowed the entire tragedy to unfold; he wondered whether he felt remorse. If Henderson and his men had been successful, he too would have been responsible for Nina and Henry's deaths. The man's brow furrowed, and he chewed on his lip as he shut his notebook and pocketed it.

"I'm doing to see if I can find someone from the railroad and see if they can corroborate your story," the sheriff stated, already striding toward his horse before he added, "I'll be in touch."

***

The minute Jack rode to the property line expecting to work and saw a billowing smokestack instead, Sam's foreman rushed to his side, desperate to do anything he could to help. As soon as the others arrived, they helped Nina, Henry, and Sam into a wagon and brought them off the property to a temporary space.

There was no reason for them to stay when there was nothing to save in the house. Jack was unmarried and had his parents living with him, but before sundown, they were guests in his house. He had them fed, cleaned, and clothed while the town organized donations of food, money, and anything else they might need. Sam was in awe of how well his friend orchestrated it all, but it was nice to sit back and rest after the trials of the day and let someone else take the lead.

Sam had no idea how someone from the Central Pacific railroad found him so quickly, but the following morning, someone dressed eerily similar to Donald Henderson showed up at Jack's house. Sam nearly did a double take when he thought Henderson inexplicably came back from the dead, poised to haunt him.

If he hadn't been there to hear Henderson take his final breath, he would have thought it was some kind of cruel joke. The man on Jack's porch was older, but had softer looks, and Sam tried to hear him out despite wanting to strike anyone that was even remotely responsible for burning his house down. The man looked remorseful, which Sam didn't think was possible.

"I want to be the first to apologize for what happened to your home. My supervisor, may his soul rest in peace, was obsessive about the railroad being his glory and legacy."

Are they expecting me to accept an apology? Sam thought as he listened to the man's excuse. He didn't know what to say, so he said nothing, waiting to see what would happen next. All the while he felt leery; if the company was truly sorry for what transpired, why weren't they just leaving him alone? He needed that more than he needed condolences and excuses.

The railroad representative looked slightly anxious as he continued the conversation. "That being said, Mr. Henderson laid the route months, if not years ago, and we do still need to build on that land." The man dropped his eyes to his boots and porch floorboards. It was as if he recognized the callousness of his words, but there was no other way to get around the difficult topic.

After everything that happened, they're still going to bother me about my land? Sam didn't even feel angry anymore, only defeated. His house was ruined, his business faced a dire setback. Didn't they have any decency or respect? The idea that the Central Pacific had ultimately gotten what they wanted all along would have made Sam feel enraged if hopelessness hadn't consumed every last inch of his body.

Sam thought of the letter he ripped up in the post office that day when the whole situation seemed barely real. *Why didn't I just sell when I had the chance? Why did I have to be so stubborn?* Sam imagined that he'd probably be asking himself many questions that he didn't have the answer to in the coming weeks and months. There probably wouldn't be an easy answer to any of them.

"I understand your reservations, but we're going to pay you handsomely for the plot," the man asserted. "We know you are basically starting from scratch and there were emotional damages as well. The sheriff told me about the woman and child being trapped inside. We really did think you'd all gotten out at the same time." The foreman reached into his pocket and produced a cheque. He outstretched his hand in offering, still not meeting Sam's eyes.

Sam attempted to ignore yet another shallow excuse. He knew there was no use in fighting anymore. If he complied, they would finally leave him alone once and for all. Ever so tentatively, Sam took the cheque. As he scanned the numbers, he felt his heart skip a beat as he realized it was three times as much as Henderson was willing to give him before the fire. It would be more than enough to buy new land and build a new home.

There was a part of him that felt his sense of pride eroding at the thought of accepting the money. *I don't need their handouts*, he mused bitterly. It would be a betrayal to take something from the people who ruined his life and nearly killed the people he loved. Surely, he could find a way to make the money elsewhere and do it without their help.

After all, he did it once before. For a moment, he stopped and listened to what was happening in the house behind him. Nina spoke with Jack's mother, commenting on how charming the house was, while Henry sat on the floor singing a little tune in his own unique baby language. It almost sounded like one of the songs that Nina sang to him, and Sam found himself moving toward an epiphany. This was no longer about just him anymore—he needed to provide for his found family.

They were the most important thing he had now.

"I'll take it," Sam finally agreed, taking the cheque and placing it in his pocket. "And I never want to deal with you or the Central Pacific Railroad again."

The representative nodded, looking relieved that there would finally be closure over this ugly situation. "Glad to hear it." He reached out his hand and they both shook in agreement. "I hope you have a good life, Mr. Colt."

As Sam watched him walk away, he vowed that it would be—for Nina and Henry's sake, if nothing more.

Chapter Thirty-Seven

"Sam, there's a plot of land not far from here. It's smaller than what you had before, but I think it could suit your needs," Jack explained out by his shed one afternoon, a few weeks after the fire.

Sam felt mildly uncomfortable staying with Jack and his family. For years, Jack had been the one to come to Sam's property and help him with the horses and upkeep of the ranch. Now, the roles were reversed. It was an odd sensation, finding his voice only to lose his independence.

Typically, he was the one giving people jobs to do, but now that his ranch was gone, Jack assured him he could relax and rest. As well-meaning as Jack's intentions were, it just wasn't in Sam's nature to do nothing. Sam was so desperate for something to do that each day, he helped muck the stalls of the few horses Jack owned.

He organized a heap of firewood into a tidy stack and polished every tool he could find. It was a good distraction from wondering what he was to do about his future. He spent plenty of time worrying about that as he tried to sleep at night.

Amos, Jim, Jack, and Sam worked tirelessly to relocate all the livestock displaced by the fire to a neighbor's pasture for safekeeping. Unfortunately, it couldn't be a long-term solution. Sam knew that money was no object now that the Central Pacific paid him for his land, but he still found himself afraid to commit to buying a new property.

The chances of a fire burning down my home for a third time are very slim, Sam tried to assure himself. *It is just the work ahead of me that seems so daunting.*

266

"I don't know Jack," Sam replied, chewing on his lip as he thought there must have been some flaw or problem with it. With how quickly people were moving west, it should have been snatched up by now.

"Take a look, you'll never know if you don't," Jack pressed, exasperation coloring his expression. Even when they spoke through his notebook, the ranch hand had a way of making him do things that initially made him uncomfortable. Usually, he was better for it in the end, but it took a lot of convincing to get him to make a decision.

I can't live with Jack and his parents forever, Sam admitted to himself, though he was certain the family would at least be sad to see Nina and Henry leave. Nina had quickly taken over her role as homemaker here, cooking everyone their meals and helping with the wash and out in the garden. Sam smiled as he pictured Henry sitting beside her as she weeded, picking up carrots she pulled out of the ground by their tops and waving them around happily.

Once again, Sam realized that the land, the future, was more than just about him now.

"All right, I'll do it," Sam finally replied.

Jack stopped their conversation and immediately went to hitch up the wagons. It made Sam wonder if he and his little family had outstayed their welcome, or if Jack knew something about this property that made it extra special. He hoped it was the latter as he followed his friend into the barn to help get the horses ready.

***

As they rode toward the piece of land that was for sale, Sam reflected on how Jack had been a reliable and steadfast friend. When they met, he wasn't perturbed by Sam's inability to speak. When he raced to the ranch the morning after the fire to see it in ruins, and Sam spoke to him instead of writing things down, he didn't say a word.

His eyes crinkled with joy at the corners, and they sparkled brightly like he felt fit to burst with pride, but they carried on as if Sam had always been able to communicate this way. They were able to focus on their next steps, which was more important.

Sam appreciated how they spoke so freely now. He didn't realize how much he had missed it, talking with a friend.

"I think it was two larger pieces of land, but the owner passed away and left it to his sons," Jack explained with his hands on the reins. "One son moved in next door and built a small farm. The other is far more interested in property in town and is motivated to sell. His loss will be your gain."

"If I decide to buy," Sam reminded him. He hadn't even seen the property yet.

Jack adjusted the reins so that they were in one hand and pointed toward the right side of the road. "It's coming up over here."

He steered the wagon onto a small dirt path off the side of the road. Sam stepped off the wagon carefully before he took in the view. They were closer to the mountains here than they were at the old ranch. The range loomed, strong and impressive, in the distance, but there was something almost secure about them. When Sam realized what it was, he found himself laughing.

"They can't build the railroad through here," he said aloud.

Jack stood beside him, smirking as he too looked up at the peaks, some of the tallest ones snowcapped. "It would certainly cost them a lot of money, what with blowing a tunnel through the mountains and all."

Sam heaved a sigh of relief as he began to walk amongst the prairie grass. It wasn't as much as he had in his favorite pasture, nor was it filled with wildflowers like his old property, but it would be great place for a yard. He crouched down and ran his hand along it. It was soft, perfect for Henry to play in when he could run and jump on his own.

The closer the property crept toward the mountains, the more the sagebrush dotted the land, and a cluster of dogwood trees off in a corner piqued his interest. Sam walked across the property, trying to imagine where exactly he'd build a house and raise a barn when he heard water.

A sizeable creek coursed beneath the dogwood trees. The water reflected the sun and the sound of it babbling over rocks was so soothing that Sam heaved a contented sigh. He could see Henry playing there too, and perhaps another child or two—maybe one that looked a little bit like him, and another that had Nina's looks. Sam gasped at his revelation.

My old ranch was my first house. It wasn't complete because I was alone. Now that I have who I need in my life, this can be where I can make myself a home.

"Do you know the seller of this land personally?" Sam asked when Jack finally joined him on the banks of the creek.

Jack raised an eyebrow at Sam, as if he could see that his friend was being swayed. "I would consider him an acquaintance. His brother is probably working somewhere on his farm today if you really wanted to make an offer." When Sam continued to stare at the water like all the answers were in its cool depths, Jack pressed, "Are you thinking of making an offer?"

Sam nodded, finally breaking his gaze to meet Jack's eye. "I am."

He could see himself growing old here, and he wouldn't be alone.

Chapter Thirty-Eight

"I spent most of my youth by a creek," Nina said about a month later.

The warmth started to leave Carson City as autumn snuck up on them. Despite this, Nina, Sam, and little Henry had a picnic on the banks of their creek, trying to enjoy the last few warm days before it got too cold to stick their feet in the water and they had to spend more time indoors.

Nina made friend chicken, apple pie, and packed some berries that she picked in the garden at Jack's house. They sat on a large tartan plaid blanket that someone gave them for a housewarming gift. Sam wished he was a painter, because the scene set in front of the dogwoods was something he wanted to remember forever.

"The creek was the reason I decided to buy the land," Sam admitted in between bites of his delicious lunch. "The whole place seemed like a good place to grow up. I wanted that for Henry."

Nina nodded with bright, ecstatic eyes and a soft smile. "I think it will be a grand place for Henry. I'm so happy that he'll never know the struggles we had. I hope that he is too young to remember the fire at the old house." Sam noticed that a shudder coursed through her as she remembered.

Sam took a glance in the opposite direction, toward their new farmhouse. It was smaller than his former one, but it already had more character than the old house ever did. The place had bright white, freshly painted clapboard siding and new windows that opened and closed with ease.

Sometimes living on the new plot of land felt like a dream. Sam worried if he shut his eyes and reopened them that he'd be back at the ruins of the old place. He feared that if he pinched himself, he'd find himself in a time before Henry and Nina came into his life.

It was real, though. It felt like the whole lot of Carson City came together to help build the house and barns. Jack and the ranch hands, his old neighbors, the sheriff, and even a handful of Central Pacific employees came every day for several weeks to make it come to life. Even on Sundays after church they sawed, nailed, and painted until the project was complete.

Just as the community came to his aid when Henry had been left on his doorstep, families from the church and surrounding farms helped with the inside of the house too. The fire destroyed everything at the old place—even Sam's parents' dishes and the curtains Nina sewed when she first arrived were nothing but ash. The kind townspeople donated kitchen items, old furniture, and tools for the barns that they no longer needed.

They also took up a collection of money. When all was said and done, Sam added it to what he had left over from the Central Pacific Railroad. He felt pleased to see they were finally in decent shape, and he could sleep a little easier at night. Sam nearly wept the first time he walked into the house once everything was in place.

Not only was it beautiful, but he could see a piece of each member of the community when he saw a quilt on the back of a chair or a pitcher stored in a kitchen cabinet. They wouldn't be here if it hadn't been for the kindness of others.

"It still seems surreal, doesn't it?"

Nina's peace-filled voice brought him back to the banks of the creek. She watched him stare at the farmhouse, eyes still full of wonder. "How often do people get a second fresh start?"

"Not very often at all," Sam replied, reaching across the blanket so he could take her hand in his. "I plan on making the most of it this time."

Since finding his voice on that fateful day and nearly losing the people he cared for most, Sam felt like he needed to live each day like it could be his last. He found himself growing bolder in his interactions with Nina. There was a time when he was afraid of what she thought of him. He worried that he would be impossible to love.

Yet, she never wavered in her care of him or Henry. If anything, she seemed to have more resolve than ever that Carson City was where she wanted to be. Sam feared she might want to go back to San Antonio after the perils she experienced.

"*We'll weather this storm together,*" Sam remembered her telling his shortly after they moved in with Jack and his folks. "*If we can tough this out, we can do anything.*"

Sam felt elated to know that she wouldn't be going anywhere, but something still felt incomplete about the whole thing.

He wanted her stay forever, but he didn't want her to be just Henry's governess anymore. As he looked down at their intertwined hands, he knew that things were going to get complicated if he didn't state his intentions soon. After he heard Jack's mother ask his father if Nina was Sam's wife, and the more time they together in public, he began to worry that people were going to get the wrong idea about her.

Nina didn't deserve to be talked about in such a way.

"I'm happy for you," Nina smiled so wide that her eyes nearly closed. "I feel like I've gotten to know the real you, even before you were able to speak to me." She squeezed his hand tightly. "Now everyone will be able to hear how wonderful you are."

Sam's heart pounded as he took in her full lips as they spread in a grin at him, the way her cheekbones were so defined as she glowed with joy. She seemed like sunshine incarnate. There was no way that he could ever let things go back to the way they were before. Now that he had his voice, he needed to use it without resolve.

There was no way that he could ever let her go.

Just as Sam was about to reply, little Henry stood up, his fingers and face sticky with berry juice. "Water, water!" He said excitedly as he began to step off the blanket and toward the riverbank. Nina gave Sam's hand one last squeeze before she let go, rising to her feet and following the toddler as he took wobbly, tentative steps toward the creek. Henry took his first steps in Jack's house, and Sam was so grateful that Donald Henderson saved the boy from a different, more gruesome fate.

Sam was glad he didn't have to mourn, nor even think about what could have been.

For a few minutes, Sam watched as Nina used one hand to hold onto Henry's arm. She used the other to roll up the hem of her skirt so it wouldn't get wet as they both splashed and played in the water. All the while, Nina watched the child with pure love in her eyes. If Sam didn't know better, he would assume that she really was the boy's mother. The scene once again motivated him to want to act.

"Henry, you must be careful," Nina reminded in a sweet but serious tone. "I don't want to have to go in after you if you wander too deep."

Sam reached into his pocket, feeling the small box that resided there every moment for the last few weeks. He didn't have the courage to take it out before today, but as he stood there watching Nina be more of mother to Henry than he ever could have been, he knew it was the right time.

"Henry, come here," Sam called.

The child looked over his shoulder at Sam in wonder, his face lighting up at the sound of Sam's voice. He let go of Nina's hand and tried to walk over, making it about three steps before he fell on his bottom on the sandy bank.

"Help," he called out with his hands raised. "Help 'Ry!" The child started trying to say his name over the last week or so as well. Sam was proud of Henry's progress as much as he was proud of his own.

When Sam picked up Henry, Nina still stood in the water, looking at him curiously. "Do you have work to do?" She tried to keep a happy face, but Sam could see how disappointed she was that their lunch was ending already. It was as if she thought he called Henry over to say goodbye so he could move on to something else.

"Not yet," Sam said, shaking his head. There was plenty to do—he already had clients looking to purchase horses and make breeding agreements, but for what he was about to do, he was willing to wait as long as necessary. "I actually wanted to talk to you about something."

Nina returned to her usual cheery disposition. "Of course. I'm here to listen and to help."

Sam stole a look down at Henry, who placed his tiny hand against Sam's chest as he collected his thoughts. "I wanted to talk to you about Henry."

"He's adjusting so well, isn't he?" Nina stepped out of the water and closed the space between them, running the back of her hand gently along Henry's soft cheek. She looked absolutely smitten, and once again, Sam knew in his heart of hearts that he was making the right choice.

"Yes, I thank God every day for that," Sam answered honestly. "I wanted to see how you would feel about adopting him. You take care of him so well. It seems only right to make him officially your child."

Nina's eyes flashed to Sam's. Emotion made them glassy, as though at the very notion, her heart overflowed with love and spilled out of the hazel pools. "I would love nothing more. He's been more to me than just a child I look after for so long. I love him so much." Her smile faded away as she must have realized something. "I'm a young, unwed woman. Would such a thing be allowed?"

Henry wiggled in Sam's arms, reaching out so that Nina would take him. It was the perfect reason for Sam to finally reach into his pocket for what he hid there and intended to share with her.

"What if you didn't have to be an unwed woman anymore? What if you didn't have to worry about what people thought about us?" Sam asked with an edge of nervousness in his voice, dropping to one knee on the sandy bank of the creek. He played this scene over and over in his mind for weeks, hoping that Nina would want to marry him—that she loved him as much as he loved her. "What if you married me?"

Nina's mouth hung open in shock as she watched Sam take out a small wooden box. She covered her mouth with her free hand as Sam opened it and a fine gold ring lay inside, sparkling in the sun.

"Pretty," Henry cooed as he looked down at it. "For 'Ry?"

"No Henry, it's for Nina," Sam replied, staring up at her hopefully. "You changed my life, Nina. You accepted me for who I was when you arrived. I was able to be myself around you. Every day I see how you take care of Henry and myself, and I want that every day for the rest of my life." Sam was surprised to hear his voice shaking with emotion as he held the ring up higher. "I want you to be Henry's mother. I don't want to know what a life without you is like. Don't go back to San Antonio, Nina. Marry Me."

Nina's eyes welled with tears and eventually overflowed, silent rivers cascading down her cheeks. She placed Henry back down on the ground so that she could wipe the wetness away.

"Whatever gave you the impression that I was going back to San Antonio?" She asked through her tears.

Sam shrugged, his pulse booming in his ears as he waited for her answer to his proposal. "I don't know. Eventually Henry's going to get older. Maybe someone else will want you to be their governess. Maybe you want to mend things with your stepsister."

Nina stepped closer to Sam, gently placing her hands on his shoulders as he still knelt before her. "I'm not going anywhere, Sam."

"Nina Mason, will you marry me?" Sam proposed. He needed her to say the words. Sam needed her to tell him that she would never leave because she wanted to be his wife, the mother of Henry and any future children they had. He wouldn't be able to relax until she said it out loud.

Once more Nina cried, nodding her reply because she couldn't speak. "Yes," she finally managed to answer. "I can't think of anything that would make me happier."

Sam stood up, took the ring out of the box, and placed it on her slender finger. Then he took her into his arms, kissing her like he often imagined when he lay awake at night, and like he often day-dreamed when he stared at her sweet, red, and full lips. Now that no proprieties stood between them, he didn't hold back. Her lips were as soft as he hoped.

Nina melted under his touch, a soft sigh escaping her. Sam thought about continuing, about kissing her to make up for all the times he wanted to and couldn't, when he felt Henry pulling on his pant leg. The child giggled.

Sure enough, when Sam and Nina finally separated, Henry was at their feet looking up at them with his big grin. He was starting to get more teeth, but it was still just as endearing as the first time Sam had seen it all those months ago.

"Silly, silly," Henry said with a shake of his head. "Now water."

"Okay, Henry," Nina said, still in Sam's arms. "We can go back down to the water."

The child plodded over to the creek and Sam and Nina watched him splash until his trousers soaked through. All the while, they stood hip to hip, Sam with his arm around her waist.

All the suffering he endured had been worth it in the end. He finally had a family. He finally had something to live for. In a way, it was freeing. All the worries that plagued him as he tried to sleep would hopefully slip away for good. Maybe all he needed was someone by his side.

Sam finally knew he was needed as much as had been searching for someone to fill the hole in his heart. The feeling made him think that he could do anything.

Epilogue

Three Years Later

"Mama! Mama, watch me!"

Henry ran across the yard with his stick horse made of yarn and fabric, throwing an imaginary lasso over his head. His little feet traveled as fast as they could carry him, as though he imagined that he rode across the plains astride a real horse.

"Look at you, Henry," Nina called from the porch, watching him with a soft smile. "Wait for your brother! He wants to play too."

A younger child, just over two years old, scurried along behind Henry. Since he was a toddler, he wasn't as sure-footed as his older brother, but he made up for it with pure determination. He a familiar sparkle lit his eyes as he tried to keep up with his older brother. Nina saw it in her own reflection sometimes.

"Mama, do I have to? He's slow." Henry protested as he circled back with his stick horse so that he could fall into step with the younger child.

"Matthew, tell your brother 'thank you' for waiting," Nina called.

"Tank you," Matthew said, not quite getting word out right, reaching up for Henry's hand.

Nina watched him erupt into giggles as they skipped together across the yard, Henry slowing his pace just enough so that he wouldn't make his younger brother topple face first into the dirt.

"Come on," Henry urged Matthew as he pretended to be a cowboy or a ranch hand, Nina wasn't sure which. "These horses need to be trained by Friday."

Nina stifled her laughter when she realized that Henry emulated his father. It was something he started doing recently. At night, when Sam would make note of his business expenses, Henry would pretend to write his in a book of his own. The child was always observant and filled with wonder. She knew Sam's heart would swell when she told him about it later.

It was almost amusing to think about how Sam had initially been terrified at the thought of raising Henry. He called for a governess because he didn't think he could manage it. They'd come a long way since then.

A family of four.

Nina didn't think her life could feel more complete once she accepted Sam's proposal. Shortly after they married, she found out she carried Sam's child, and she discovered her heart had even more room for love.

Named for Sam's father, Matthew Colt was the final piece of their family. Where Henry was blond with pale blue eyes, Matthew had Nina's shock of brown hair and hazel eyes. The child really was an ode to the family they both lost to fire. Nina recalled how Hamish said she looked like her mother. Now, her looks would live on in Matthew as well.

Life felt sweet; the new ranch flourished, and Sam really did have horses to breed and train by certain deadlines because people came from near and far to do business with him. He became a bit of legend, fighting the Central Pacific Railroad and nearly winning.

Jack, Amos, and Jim came back to work as they promised. With a ranch in better condition than the old one, they were able to focus on new ventures instead of constantly maintaining old ones. It was the second year they were able to grow crops and a thriving garden.

Now that Henry and Matthew were a little bigger, Nina could help tend the vegetables without worrying about them running off or getting into trouble. Henry even used the watering can to help; anything to please his father and emulate Sam at the same time. It made Nina's heart sing as much as it made her laugh.

There was always something to do. Nina was just about to call the boys in so she could make lunch for everyone when she noticed someone walking down the path from the main road. She had to squint and put her hands over her eyes to attempt to make out who they were. When they got closer and she didn't recognize the person's face, Nina felt perplexed.

"We're not expecting any visitors," Nina said aloud.

The visitor was a woman dressed in a pale pink calico dress, her hair covered in a maroon-colored sunbonnet. As she approached, Nina saw that she held a scrap of paper in her hands. Nina watched her glance over at Henry and Matthew as she made her way toward the house. Nina furrowed her brow as she took in the visitor. Now that she lived in Carson City for three years, she knew many of the woman in town, but she still couldn't place the one approaching her.

"Hello," Nina finally called when she was close enough to be heard. When the woman waved in reply, Nina asked, "Can I help you with something, Miss?"

"Does Samuel Colt live here?" the woman asked when she reached the porch. "He once lived on a different farm, but the railroad cuts through it now."

More perplexed than ever, Nina gazed at the woman. She really wasn't much of a woman at all; she was so young, maybe eighteen years old at the most. Her blue eyes were as piercing as the blue sky above them and her hair a pale blonde that seemed familiar, though Nina struggled to place it.

"He does. Are you looking for a horse?" Nina asked. "I can go fetch him for you." Nina thought it odd that if she was here on business, she traveled alone. Perhaps the horse was to be a gift for her father or husband.

The girl suddenly looked apprehensive and dropped her eyes to the ground. "I'm not here on business. I wanted to thank Mr. Colt, and I suppose you as well." She bit her lip before she continued. "I wanted to thank you both for looking after my son."

Suddenly, Nina realized where she recognized the shade of bright blonde hair. It was the same color as Henry's.

Nina's heart spasmed with worry. Had Henry's mother finally come back to take him home?

"Let me get Mr. Colt," Nina said at last, her eyes bouncing between the girl and Henry, who still played ranch hands with Matthew, totally unaware what was happening over on the porch.

Nina wanted to prepare her husband for their impromptu guest as quickly and graciously as possible.

***

A short while later, Sam was washed up from working outside, and sat on the porch in a rocking chair he brought out from the living room. Nina made lemonade and offered the girl a plate of biscuits and jam.

"I'm sorry I don't have anything fancier prepared," Nina apologized. "I do most of my baking on Saturdays for church."

The girl shook her head. "Oh, it's no problem. And please, I can tell from your faces that you are worried that I'm here to reclaim the boy. That is not my intention."

Nina hadn't realized the tension tightening her chest until she finally let out the large exhale she held in. Her whole body slumped with relief and when she looked over at Sam, she saw him visibly relax in his chair as well.

"Oh, I'm so happy to hear that," Nina said, placing a hand over her heart. "We've raised him as our own this whole time. It would be so hard to let him go."

"Honestly," Sam added, "you leaving him with me is what joined us all together. We should be the ones thanking you."

The young woman smiled. "I haven't come through this way in a while. I just wanted to make sure he was all right. When I went to your old property, I was shocked to see that the house was gone."

Nina shared a glance with Sam. They didn't often talk about the night they almost lost Henry. That night she had been so close to dying as well, but just like Henry being left on Sam's doorstep, they wouldn't be where they were today if Donald Henderson's greed hadn't escalated to uncontrollable levels.

"It was a shock for us as well," Nina finally answered. "But we are all stronger for it."

The woman seemed satisfied with that answer. "What did you end up naming him? I'll be honest, I was so unprepared for motherhood, I didn't give him one."

"We named him Henry, after my father," Nina replied. "Each of our boys are named after someone we lost when we were young."

"What a lovely tribute," she replied. "What is Henry like?"

"He's inquisitive," Sam answered this time. "Strong willed and energetic."

"His father is his world," Nina added, thinking of how just a bit earlier he pretended to be a ranch hand training horses for a client.

The lull in the conversation caused the trio of adults to stop and watch the young boys playing together for a moment. Henry abandoned his stick pony and instead tried to lasso the closet rock while Matthew looked on with interest.

"I'm going to get that bronco back where he belongs," Henry announced before he asked Matthew, "You going to help me a saddle him up?"

"My, he has quite the imagination," the woman observed. "I'm so glad to see him thriving."

"If I might ask, what happened to make you not ready to be a mother?" Nina asked as she refilled everyone's glasses with lemonade. Nina felt ready for children the minute Nathaniel stated his intentions all those years ago, before she knew about his secret affair with Jane. Perhaps it was her own sad upbringing, but she wanted nothing more than a family to shower with love and affection.

"I was fifteen when I found out I was expecting him," the young woman confessed. "A sweetheart of mine at the time and I got into a bit of trouble. His father was the sheriff in town, and it was going to look bad if he had a grandchild born out of wedlock. I worried what my parents would think so too, so I ran away."

Nina's heart broke at the thought of feeling so alone that running away to have the baby seemed to be the best option. She looked at the young woman sympathetically as she continued with her tale.

"I can sew quite well, so I was able to find work in various towns. I covered my stomach with aprons and larger dresses. I told everyone I had a sick relative and that was why I was working instead of going to school. Eventually, I had to stay holed up at a boarding house because I showed too much. As soon as I gave birth, I knew I had to keep moving. No one could find out how young I was, or that I wasn't married. I was in Carson City when I heard people talking about a man that didn't speak on a ranch off the beaten track." She looked up at Sam with apologetic eyes. "I figured you wouldn't be able to snitch on me if you caught me. I'm so sorry."

Sam nodded as if he understood. "I wouldn't be able to speak today if you hadn't brought Henry into my life. I hired Nina to care for him. I fell in love with them both. It gave me something to live for."

The young woman looked so moved that bright tears brimmed in her eyes. "My child is the reason you fell in love? I'm so happy."

"What are your plans now?" Nina asked. "I feel terrible, we don't even know your name."

"I'm Florence," the young lady answered. "I'm so glad that I finally get to meet you both. As for my plans. I want to go as far west as I can. I've heard there are growing communities out in California. Maybe someone needs a seamstress there."

"Does your family know you're okay?" As Nina asked the question, she knew that she herself was overdue to write back to Jane in San Antonio. It was simply too easy to get swept in the day to day of taking care of the farm and raising a family.

Florence nodded. "Yes, shortly after I left Henry with you, Mr. Colt, I wrote to them and came clean about what I did. They told me that I could always come home, that we could make up an excuse for why I had been away, but I think I've grown accustomed to wandering."

Nina knew all too well that sometimes it was easier to move on. It made her reflect on where she was today. Perhaps there was an even bigger and brighter future for Florence in California. She and Sam would happily continue to raise Henry as their own child as she discovered what awaited her.

"Would you like to stay the night?" Sam offered. "I could take you into town first thing in the morning."

Once more Florence looked grateful, but she politely shook her head. "Oh, you are far too kind. It's quite all right, I plan on taking the last train out of Carson City tonight." She smiled brightly. "Checking up on the child—*Henry*—was the last thing I wanted to do before I headed on. My things are still at the boarding house."

"At least let one of my ranch hands give you a ride back into town to save you some time," Sam offered.

"That won't be necessary," Florence assured. "That's the great thing about the Central Pacific Railroad. The trains run nearly at all hours now that it's completed. What a time to be alive with all these wonderful advancements."

Sam and Nina locked eyes across the porch. The Central Pacific seemed like such a curse when they first met, like something evil looming to breathe down Sam's neck. Yet Florence had a point. Now that the railroad was complete, more and more people moved west, bringing more people to do business in Carson City. And, as a result, their farm thrived. It seemed like it was less of a burden and more of a blessing every day.

Sam gave Nina a little smirk before he got up and offered Florence his hand to shake.

"Well Florence, I will be indebted to you for the rest of my life. You gave me Henry and Nina; you gave me my family. Thank you."

Florence shook his hand firmly before she refastened her bonnet over her hair. "Thank you, Mr. and Mrs. Colt, for taking care of my son. May he have a good life."

Sam and Nina stood on the porch, arms across each other's backs as they watched Florence walk through the yard and in the direction of the road at the end of the property. Henry and Matthew ran over to see where she was going; they hadn't gotten to say hello yet.

"Leaving already?" Henry asked. "We didn't even get to show you our rooms inside the house."

Florence stopped, stooping down to be on Henry's level. "That's okay." She smiled at the child warmly. "You be good to your mother and father, okay?"

Henry nodded before he nudged Matthew with his shoe, like he was instructing him to do the same. "We will. Don't worry."

"Good," Florence rose and mussed Henry's blond hair. "Goodbye."

Florence continued on her way and the Colt family watched her until she reached the road and eventually turned out of sight, never to be seen again.

"Mama, who was that?" Henry asked still watching the road where she had been.

"Someone very special," Nina replied as she reflected on her fate.

It would seem when a person was at their darkest moment, the light was just around the corner, waiting to be found.

Nina had never felt so lucky or thankful that she went for walk in the woods on that fateful day.

THE END

Also by Ava Winters

Thank you for reading "**A Western Love Forged in Silence**"!

I hope you enjoyed it! If you did, here are some of my other books!

My latest Best-Selling Books

#1 An Uninvited Bride on his Doorstep

#2 Once upon an Unlikely Marriage of Convenience

#3 Their Unlikely Marriage of Convenience

#4 An Orphaned Bride to Love Him Unconditionally

#5 An Unexpected Bride for the Lonely Cowboy

Also, if you liked this book, you can also check out **my full Amazon Book Catalogue at:**
https://go.avawinters.com/bc-authorpage

Thank you for allowing me to keep doing what I love! ❤

Made in United States
North Haven, CT
11 August 2022

22575853R00159